"I loved you with all my heart...."

Silvia swallowed against the sudden tightness in her throat. "I...I loved you, too, Rick," she whispered.

"But you left?"

"I had to...I just had to."

Cupping her face, he lifted her head. "We could have worked something out."

"I...I don't think so."

His breath was warm and sensual against her cheek. "We had everything going for us, baby." His voice deepened. "Everything. It was perfect."

She blinked. "I think your memory may be rewriting the past. Nothing's ever perfect."

He shook his head and leaned even closer. "It was...and I can prove it."

Dear Reader,

Once again, Intimate Moments offers you top-notch romantic reading, with six more great books from six more great authors. First up is *Gage Butler's Reckoning,* the latest in Justine Davis's TRINITY STREET WEST miniseries. It seems Gage has a past, a past that includes a girl—now a woman—with reason to both hate him and love him. And his past is just about to become his present.

Maria Ferrarella's *A Husband Waiting To Happen* is a story of second chances that will make you smile, while Maura Seger's *Possession* is a tale of revenge and matrimony that will have you longing for a cooling breeze—even if it *is* only March! You'll notice our new Conveniently Wed flash on Kayla Daniels' *Her First Mother.* We'll be putting this flash on more marriage of convenience books in the future, but this is a wonderful and emotional way to begin. Another flash, The Loving Arms of the Law, has been chosen to signify novels featuring sheriffs, those perfect Western heroes. And Kay David's *Lone-Star Lawman* is an equally perfect introduction. Finally, enjoy *Montoya's Heart,* Bonnie Gardner's second novel, following her successful debut, *Stranger In Her Bed.*

And, of course, don't forget to come back next month, when we'll have six more Intimate Moments novels guaranteed to sweep you away into a world of excitement and passion.

Enjoy!

Leslie J. Wainger

Leslie J. Wainger
Senior Editor and Editorial Coordinator

Please address questions and book requests to:
Silhouette Reader Service
U.S.: 3010 Walden Ave., P.O. Box 1325, Buffalo, NY 14269
Canadian: P.O. Box 609, Fort Erie, Ont. L2A 5X3

LONE-STAR LAWMAN

KAY DAVID

Published by Silhouette Books

America's Publisher of Contemporary Romance

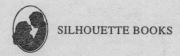

SILHOUETTE BOOKS

ISBN 0-373-07845-5

LONE-STAR LAWMAN

Books by Kay David

Silhouette Intimate Moments

Desperate #624
Baby of the Bride #706
Hero in Hiding #725
And Daddy Makes Three #784
Lone-Star Lawman #845

KAY DAVID

resides in her native state of Texas for the moment, but in the past she's lived from one corner of the globe, the United Arab Emirates, to the other, Argentina. Her background is just as varied. Holding two separate undergraduate degrees in English literature and computer science, she also has a master's degree in behavioral psychology. Reading and writing are her two favorite activities, but she also enjoys beachcombing in Florida and traveling with Pieter, her husband of twenty-three years, and their globe-trotting cat, Leroy. She is hard at work on her next novel.

For my brother, Jody, a fantastic musician, and my sister, Dana, an outstanding teacher. Your talents have made the world a better place.
Also, a big thanks to Dr. Patricia Luan-Miller for her special assistance. I'll be calling you again!

Prologue

He was late. Almost two hours late.

Silvia Hernandez glanced for the hundredth time at the slim, gold watch on her wrist. *"Oro puro,"* her mother had said proudly when she'd given the present to her last week. "Nothing but the best for my *chica*—Miss Valedictorian, eh?"

The watch was beautiful and expensive, but when Gloria Hernandez had presented the graduation present to her daughter, Silvia had felt a clutch of emotion tug at her heart that went beyond the gift's worth. How long had it been since anything had passed between them but anger?

Looking back toward the street and sighing, Silvia knew the answer. One year, two months and three days. Since the minute she had walked inside the tiny house on San Luis Street and told her mother she was dating Rick Hunter. Nothing had been the same at home since. With a dark expression, her mother had launched into Spanish so rapid that even Silvia had caught only snatches.

"This boy—why does he date you, Silvia? He could have any girl in town. He takes the football, he runs so fast—everyone loves him. Why would he pick someone like you? Someone from San Luis Street, eh?"

"He likes me, Mama." Silvia's dark eyes had met her mother's in the mirror as she'd slipped so carefully into her pressed skirt that first night. "And I like him."

"Well, you shouldn't. He's not our kind. You aren't *his* kind." She shook her head. "I tell you this—it will not end good. These things never work." Her mother had shaken her head ominously and stalked away.

A tremor of guilt rippled down Silvia's back now. God, if her mother only knew…

Forcing herself not to think about that, Silvia peered around the corner of the house once more, dropping her wrist to her side, the gold glints disappearing into the folds of her skirt. Where was Rick? They'd planned this evening weeks ago. Their first date after graduation. Their first date as adults. They were going to talk about their plans, about what they were going to do now that they didn't have school anymore. Part of her had been praying he would say those magic words—*Let's get married, Sil, right now*—but the other part of her was praying just as hard that he wouldn't.

She loved Rick Hunter like she'd never loved anyone in her eighteen years, but marriage? She wasn't ready for a little shotgun house like her mother's on a dead-end street where there was never enough grocery money and a car that didn't run half the time. She didn't want a figure like her sister Yolanda's stretched out at twenty from too many babies and not enough time in between them. She wanted to travel, to see the world, to have a career. Rick had college plans, too.

She looked down at her still flat stomach then spread her fingers over it. What would he say? What would he do? She loved him with all her heart, but she wasn't ready to settle down and she didn't think Rick was, either.

She strained to listen for the rumble of his pickup, but the only sound breaking the hot summer night was a chorus of crickets and, one street over, the low strains of some *Tejano* music. For a few more minutes, she stood uncertainly near the edge of the house, then finally, reluctance dogging her steps, she returned to the front door and gently eased it open.

Stepping into the now darkened living room, she crossed the tiny space as quietly as possible. Carlos had gone to his room hours ago and she didn't want to wake him. Her brother disapproved of Rick even more than her mother. *You're betraying La Raza,* he'd admonished. *Where's your pride?* His animosity was really more personal, though. Rick had everything Carlos had always wanted…a perfect family, a football scholarship, plenty of money. There was more than just race between them—there was envy.

She tiptoed past Carlos's closed door and darkened room and eased into her own bedroom, softly swinging shut the door behind her. Glancing at the twin bed on the other side of the room, she could see the outline of Consuelo, her ten-year-old sister. She was sleeping like a rag doll, her arms and legs thrown over the covers with limp abandonment.

Unzipping her skirt, Silvia quietly got undressed, her

thoughts returning to Rick. Where was he? Had something happened to him?

Her white batiste nightgown settling on her shoulders, she picked up her hairbrush and pulled it through her long, dark hair. She couldn't stand the thought that he might be lying in a ditch somewhere, thrown out of his truck or hit by another car....

A tapping sound suddenly broke into the silence, and Silvia jerked her head toward her door, her eyes flying open, her heart pounding at the unexpected noise. Had Carlos heard her after all? She took two steps toward the hallway then realized the sound was coming from behind her. Swirling around, her gaze shot to the window.

Rick's face was framed in the glass...and something was wrong. His expression was unlike any she'd ever seen on his face before. If she hadn't known him better, she might have thought he was scared. That wasn't possible, though. Rick didn't get scared.

Flying to the window, Silvia eased it open and prayed her brother hadn't heard the sound as well. "What's wrong? Where have you been?" Her eyes searched his face. "I waited for hours then I gave up and came inside—"

"I need to talk to you. Right now." He reached through the open window and grabbed her hand.

"It's past midnight. If Carlos hears—"

"Would you forget him for once? He's just your brother, for God's sake, not the ruler of the universe."

"He rules *this* universe," she retorted unhappily. "And if he hears you, I'm in deep trouble."

Rick's expression instantly softened. "Ah, damn, I'm sorry, Silvie...I don't want to get you in trouble. I— I've got to talk to you, though." He tightened his hold on her hand as his voice crackled with urgency. "Can't you come outside? Please? For just a little while?"

Glancing over her shoulder at her still sleeping sister, Silvia hesitated, then finally gave in, just as she'd known all along she would. Turning back to Rick, she opened the window as far as she could and gathered her nightgown in her hands. A moment later she was stepping over the windowsill and into his waiting arms.

Her body slid down his until her toes were barely touching the ground. He didn't remove his arms and for just a few minutes, she let the forbidden feeling wash over her, let the desire bring with it the old, familiar sense of weak surrender. Slowly though, a dim, uncomfortable sensation penetrated her consciousness. Taking a deep breath, she opened her eyes and pulled back slightly.

"You've been drinking!" Silvia put her hands against his chest, the smell of alcohol almost overwhelming her now that she had recognized it.

"No." He shook his head emphatically. "I haven't been drinking—"

"I can smell it." She was more amazed than angry. Rick never drank. Not even an occasional beer. She'd heard the other jocks make fun of him for it, but he'd simply ignored them and given her another reason to admire him.

He put his hands over hers and squeezed her fingers. "I have *not* been drinking, Silvia."

Even as he spoke, she realized another layer existed to the smells surrounding them. A cloying fragrance she couldn't quite identify. Her hands tightened against his chest, and then as her eyes finally adjusted to the darkness, she noticed his shirt. It was torn, a long, jagged rip that edged from one side of the collar to his shoulder. Two buttons were missing as well. Along the side of his face, a dark red line of blood had welled up. He'd been cut or maybe scratched. With a gasp, she reached up to touch him, and he pulled back abruptly, the collar of his shirt falling to one side. There was no sign of the gold Saint Christopher medal she'd given him for graduation the week before. He'd promised to never remove the chain and medal after she'd closed the clasp at the back of his neck. Now it was missing.

"What happened to you?" she said slowly, her eyes not believing what they were seeing. "Where have you been?"

He ignored her questions. "Do you know how much I love you?" His blue eyes locked on hers. "I mean *really* love you?"

Mystified, she nodded. "Yes, but—"

He interrupted her before she could say more. "It's really important you know how I feel about you, Silvia." He took a deep breath and let it out, almost shuddering in the process. "Because I—I've done something horrible. Something…oh, God, I can't believe it happened!" He covered his eyes with one hand and bent his head so she couldn't see his face.

Shocked and disbelieving, Silvia felt her mouth drop open. Was he crying? It couldn't be possible. She stared at him for just a moment, then automatically reached out to comfort him. "It's okay, sweetheart…please… just tell me. It's okay. Really—"

He looked up, his eyes red rimmed and desperate. "It's not okay. It's never going to be okay." He shook his head. "It just got out of hand. I didn't plan it, I swear—" His stare jerked to a point behind her, his expression suddenly turning even more wretched.

Swirling around, Silvia watched in alarm as the flashing blue lights of a patrol car filled the yard with an eerie blue light. Her mouth went dry with instant unease. "What's going on? Rick?"

Without saying a word, he stepped in front of her as the men opened their doors and came out of the patrol car. Silvia couldn't see, but she could hear and that was all she needed to identify the sheriff's deputy crossing the yard. Robert Tully picked on Rick continually, stopping him for the slightest infraction—a broken taillight, not using a turn signal, driving too slow. The overweight deputy envied Rick, just like Carlos did. But Tully's reasons were different, of course. He wanted Rick's youth, his prowess, and his abilities on the field and off.

The deputy's voice cut across the night air like a rusty knife. "Is that you, Hunter? Who's that hiding behind you?"

Silvia peeked around Rick's shoulder. Now standing at the edge of the house, Tully was cracking the knuckles of his left hand with his right, his wide fingers gleaming in the moonlight. Just like him, they were ugly, misshaped and rough, evidence of the short pro football career he'd had and botched.

He didn't wait for Rick's answer. "Where you been tonight, Hunter? Whatcha been doing since ten o'clock?"

She glanced toward Rick as he answered. "What do you mean?" His expression was guarded.

"What the hell do you think I mean?" The deputy spit off to one side, his eyes narrowing. "Do I have to ask you in Spanish?" He cut his gaze to Silvia's hovering figure, his greedy eyes taking in what he could see. "That all you understand these days?"

Silvia could actually feel the tension coming from

Rick's body. It rose off him with an almost electric disquiet. Her own unease went up another notch.

"Keep her out of this, Tully. If you've got a problem, pick on me, not her."

"I wouldn't be handing out advice, if I wuz you, Hunter." Tully took another step forward. "You're in enough trouble right now to sink a ship."

"Tr-trouble? Wh-what kind of trouble?" Rick's voice sounded suddenly hesitant. "What are you talking about?"

"I'm talking about pretty damned serious trouble, kid." He hitched up his pants and glared across the porch. "Were you with Linda Willington tonight?"

"Linda Willington?" Repeating the name, Silvia spoke, her puzzled gaze going back to Rick's face. What did she have to do with all this? The petite blonde, who sat three rows over from Silvia in English lit, had been after Rick since junior high. She'd made no bones about her interest in him, either. She'd actually had the nerve to call Silvia earlier that week and ask her if she and Rick were still serious. Rick had laughed about it when Silvia had told him.

"Were you with Linda Willington tonight?" Tully repeated the question almost patiently. "Out on Cemetery Road?"

Rick stood perfectly still, frozen with an intensity that was almost painful to witness. Silvia watched him and felt herself go cold as well. He didn't have to say a word to answer Tully's question. His expression did it for him. From fear and uncertainty, it had shifted into one of complete and utter guilt.

And she suddenly understood why he hadn't shown up for their date.

Tully understood as well, his words cutting into Silvia's mind with a brutal ugliness. "Yeah...I thought so. You're in big trouble, kid." The deputy paused for effect. "Big trouble—that's what murder is."

Silvia heard someone gasp, then she realized it was her.

Rick's voice cracked with obvious disbelief, shocked astonishment coming over his face. "Murder! Wh-what in the hell are you are saying, Tully?"

"I'm saying Linda Willington got herself raped and shot tonight out on Cemetery Road. I'm saying she's dead as a run-over skunk, and I'm saying some bright-eyed good citizen saw your red truck leaving the area about thirty minutes ago and called us." He tucked his thumbs into his belt. "Thirty minutes ago...just about the time she probably ate it."

Numbing shock washed over Silvia. Her legs turned to water and her stomach flipped over in a sour roil of confusion.

Rick reached for the post that held up the porch, his expression pale and dazed with bewilderment. His fingers curled around the wooden support, the nails digging into the soft wood with painful intensity. "Linda Willington's dead? I—I don't understand."

Silvia closed her eyes and swayed.

"What part don't you understand?" Tully's voice forced Silvia's eyes open. "Her heart ain't beating anymore and I'm looking at the guilty party unless you can convince me you weren't near her tonight."

"Guilty party! That's crazy. I didn't kill her! I—I was—" Rick stopped abruptly, his eyes cutting desperately to Silvia's.

She understood instantly. He wanted her to lie for him. All she had to do was say three little words. *He was here.* His expression begged her to speak while beside them, breathing heavily, Tully waited.

"I've done something horrible...it got out of hand...I never meant it to happen...." Rick's words of only a second before reverberated in her head like a death knell. Her fingers moved to cover her mouth, a subconscious effort to stem the rising tide of nausea inside her as she realized something else. The floral scent clinging to him earlier—she knew now what it was.

Jungle Gardenia. The only perfume Linda Willington ever wore.

Silvia opened her mouth to speak. But nothing came out.

Rick's gaze burned as it locked onto her eyes. The moment seemed to stretch on forever. Finally, after a long painful heartbeat, comprehension came into his expression. She doubted him. She wasn't sure. She couldn't lie for him.

His eyes flared with a moment's anger, then they turned into stones, dead and dull. Silvia started to speak, but it was too late. The damage had been done. As if he couldn't bear the sight of her a moment longer, he turned his head and stared out into the night.

"Silvia? What's going on here?"

Carlos's voice broke the thick silence. Silvia felt ill as she turned to look at her brother. He stood in the doorway, his pants perfectly pressed, his white shirt gleaming in the dim light. Even his hair looked freshly washed and combed. Peeking around him, her younger sister, Consuelo, stood, her brown eyes enormous and confused. Behind her, Silvia's mother trembled, one hand on her chest. The whole house was now awake.

"I asked you a question, Silvia." Carlos's words were measured, precise, like they always were, but he was chillingly furious, she could tell. "Where are your clothes? Why aren't you dressed?" He shot a glance in Rick's direction. "And what is *he* doing here?"

"Linda Willington's been shot," she answered numbly. The words tasted like ashes in her mouth. "She—she's dead."

His onyx eyes flickered for just a moment with what Silvia knew had to be shock, but like always, he regained control of himself within seconds. He turned around and spoke rapidly in Spanish. With a stricken expression, Silvia's mother glanced toward Silvia. A second later, she bowed her head in acquiescence at Carlos's words, turning and disappearing into the house, taking Consuelo with her. Carlos spoke again. "And what does this have to do with us?" he asked, arching one eyebrow.

"Your sister's boyfriend was seen leaving the area," Tully replied.

"I'm not surprised." Carlos spoke coldly, sending a burning look toward Rick before turning to Silvia. "I always told you this *idiota* was no good. Now he's killed someone—"

Rick jerked around to glare at Carlos, anger deepening his voice. "That's a damned lie, Hernandez. I can explain everything, believe me—"

"You ain't explaining nothing, Hunter, cause I'm hauling you in, right now." Tully stepped forward, his hand on his handcuffs. "Turn around."

Rick spoke with desperation now. "But I didn't kill her."

Tully completely ignored him. "Turn around."

Rick stayed motionless, and moving unexpectedly fast, the overweight deputy shot forward and slapped the handcuffs roughly around his wrists. Pulling Rick off the porch, Tully pushed him toward the patrol car. A moment later, he threw open the back door and booted him inside.

At Tully's movement, the enormity of the situation hit Silvia. Rick was actually going to jail. For killing Linda Willington. Crying out, she ran forward and began to pound on the window of the rear seat. Within the narrow confines of the car, Rick struggled upright, his eyes finally meeting hers as he sat up. *Why?* She heard the question as clearly as if he'd spoken. *Why couldn't you stand up for me? Why couldn't you trust me?*

Her heart shattered as she realized what she'd done. She cried his name, but the car's engine roared to life and a moment later the vehicle wheeled away from her. Watching it disappear, all she could do was stumble after it and sob. Oh, God! What had she done?

Instantly Carlos was by her side. He grabbed her arm with his right hand, his fingers as biting as his voice. "I told you weeks ago you were not to see Rick Hunter anymore. How could you do this?"

She couldn't stop crying. "I love him," she wailed. A light came on at the neighbor's house and a puzzled face was framed in the window. She forgot about her earlier reservations. "We were going to get married!"

"Get married?" He spit out the words. "You actually think Rick Hunter would marry someone like you? How could you be so stupid?"

"He loves me," she sobbed.

"He loves what he's been getting from you…along with what he was getting from Linda Willington, too. Didn't you hear Tully? You're a stupid, stupid girl, Silvia." His expression was cold, ruthless. "Stupid and dishonorable. I won't have it. Not in this house. Not a second longer."

Wiping her eyes with the back of her hand, she blinked and stared at him. "Wh-what do you mean?"

"I want you out of here," he stormed. "Tonight. I won't have you under the same roof as the rest of us. I've had enough of you and your slimy boyfriend."

Stunned into silence, Silvia lifted her gaze to meet her brother's black eyes. A glimmer of cold triumph hovered in their dark depths. He was thrilled to be kicking her out, thrilled to be sacrificing her to feed his hatred of Rick. She swallowed hard. What in heaven's name would he do if he found out she was pregnant? She didn't even want to consider the answer. She spoke between tears, almost as if to herself. "But where will I go?"

"I don't really care." Leaning closer, he spoke again. "You've dishonored this family by going with him and you've brought shame to us by sleeping with him. Go get your stuff then leave. You aren't welcome here anymore."

An hour later, the door slammed shut behind her.

She stood outside the jail for another hour, weeping.

And then, she left town.

Chapter 1

The Present

The heat was suffocating.

Silvia pulled at the collar of her blouse and told herself to ignore the temperature, but she couldn't. Years of living in Washington had dulled her ability to handle the dry, white-hot sun now baking the San Laredo street she was crossing. Washington's heat was softer, more gentle, easy on the skin. It felt like a comforting sauna.

This felt like hell.

Opening the door to the city building, she stood for a second and let the frigid air-conditioning wash over her. It chilled her, but offered no other comfort. Her stomach was in knots, she hadn't slept since Friday, and she wanted nothing as much as she wanted to turn around and get back on the plane to D.C.

Don hadn't given her a choice, though. Go to San

Laredo and help solve this case, or forget about field-work forever. If it had been up to her, the choice would have been easy. Fieldwork no longer held the same allure it once had.

"You're too good to stand in front of a blackboard, and just talk about profiling criminals, Silvia. You need to be out there. In the field again. The longer you wait, the harder it gets."

He was right, of course. Don Rogers had been her boss at the Department of Criminal Affairs for the past ten years, and he was always right. But he didn't understand completely. He didn't understand the night sweats and the panic attacks and the horrible lost feeling that came over her whenever she thought about returning to the field. In the office, she couldn't make fatal mistakes. She felt safer in front of the blackboard.

And coming back to San Laredo made those kinds of feelings seem like nothing because coming back to San Laredo meant even more, went even deeper than that.

It was personal and private.

It was secret.

Taking a deep breath, Silvia pushed open the door to the reception area of Rick Hunter's office and stepped inside. He wasn't there, his secretary said. Tilting her head to indicate his interior office, the woman told Silvia she could wait inside, if she liked. Sheriff Hunter was expecting her, and he would be back any moment.

Feeling relieved at the momentary reprieve, as temporary as it was, Silvia walked into the other room and put her leather case down on one of the two chairs that faced his desk. Slowly, she turned around to survey his office, to look for clues, indications of any kind that might tell her about the man Rick Hunter had become. Eighteen years had passed since she'd seen him, and she really had no idea who or what he was now. For someone who gathered information about people as a profession, her ignorance in this was more than maddening.

Her eyes went over the room slowly. It was small, with a huge, wooden desk taking up much of the area. The top of it was scarred, the soft wood dented and marked from years of use. He looked organized, with most of the papers covering the area in folders or in stacks, their edges neatly lined to match. There were no photos anywhere.

Against one wall, bookcases stood like sentinels, packed with every size of book imaginable. Her gaze brushed the titles—they covered a wide range of topics, and there seemed to be no rhyme or reason to their arrangement.

A block of windows covered the other wall. Dusty blinds were rolled to the top in a haphazard fashion, and as she stared outside, she wondered why he didn't just drop them. His view consisted of the parking lot where the heat she'd just escaped shimmered in undulating waves. She was standing directly under an air-conditioning vent, but just looking at the melting blacktop, she felt more uncomfortable than ever.

Pulling at her collar, she turned back to the room.

What did he think when he sat in that chair? Stared at these walls? Did he ever think of her? Remember their moments together? Wonder what had happened? She closed her eyes for just a moment, a gesture of denial that failed. In the last eighteen years those questions had filled her head on too many occasions to count, but every time she thought about calling him, her stomach would start to churn and her emotions would go on a rampage. Time had proven exactly how wrong she'd been that last night. She'd let him down dreadfully—even more than he really knew. If he ever found out the whole story, all the details, he'd never forgive her.

She knew—because she'd never forgiven herself.

Restlessly, she returned to stare out the window and tried to put these thoughts behind her. The history between her and Rick Hunter meant nothing now. She was here to do a job, to be a professional. Any entanglements they'd had in the past were just that—in the past.

Behind her, the door squeaked suddenly, and with her heart leaping into her throat, she swirled. A man was standing in the doorway. It was Rick, but she had absolutely no idea how she'd recognized him.

There was nothing of the boy she'd once known in the weary-eyed man filling the space before her.

He was tall, tall and muscular with a powerful presence that had little to do with the gun strapped low on his hips. Dark hair, with only hints of the blond it had once been, fell over his forehead. The suggestion of a beard shadowed his cheeks even though it was obvious he'd shaved earlier that morning. His uniform was pressed and neat, but something about him seemed slightly off. For just a moment, she couldn't figure out what was wrong, and then it struck her. He didn't look like a lawman at all.

He looked dangerous. Dangerous and deadly.

Leaning against the doorway, he met her eyes and stared back. Stared hard. Just when Silvia knew she couldn't handle the silence—or his gaze—another minute, he spoke, his voice a deep rumble that reached out and touched her with an almost physical awareness.

"I didn't think you'd actually come."

She was a psychologist. She understood exactly why

her pulse was pounding in her ears, and her hands felt as though she were clutching a tray of ice cubes. *Anxiety, fear, nervousness*—she had a million words for the sensations, some a lot more technical than these, but there was nothing she could do about the feelings, no matter what she called them.

Controlling her voice to make it sound calmer than she felt was the only action she could take. "And you thought this because...?"

"Lots of reasons," he answered cryptically. "But mainly because I heard you've been out of the field. I didn't think you took assignments outside the office anymore."

She spoke without thinking. "You've been keeping track?"

He blinked, but his expression didn't change. "Let's just say, I've got my sources, and leave it at that."

Part of her felt a twinge of something strange that he knew this detail of her life. Another part of her understood exactly. She'd known he was the sheriff since the moment he'd been elected. Yolanda, her oldest sister and the only member of her family she ever talked with, had told her.

Silvia had read about the election, too.

His first race had been one of the few times she'd allowed herself to find a San Laredo paper. Her curiosity about his career had been something she'd been unable to control, and when she'd realized that, the paper trembling in her hands, it had scared her enough to squash her interest instantly. Control was her middle name. It was how she survived. After he'd won, she'd never returned to the library to scan the paper, and months had passed before she had spoken to Yolanda again.

He straightened up and moved into the room, his presence sweeping ahead of him like a powerful wave as he took his seat behind his desk. "We don't really need your help, you know. Everything is under control."

"If that's the case, then why am I here?"

"The mayor doesn't share my assessment of the situation. He managed to convince one of your bosses that the entire economy of the Texas Valley depends on finding this killer. He thinks a murderer might scare off the snowbirds. Having a brother-in-law at the DCA helped his argument as well." He picked up a battered pencil from the top of his desk and twirled it slowly in his fingers. "But I really don't need your help. I'll be happy to drive you back to the airport."

She felt her throat turn even more dry. If he was going to be blunt, then she could, too. "There's no need to let our personal history get in the way here. Eighteen years have passed. Clearly things are different."

His eyes—those sapphire blue eyes that had gazed so long and hard into hers when they were eighteen and in love—glared at her now. Their depths were chilly and distant. "You're right about that. Things are *very* different."

When she was younger and less experienced, he'd been able to turn her on with just a single word. His voice had been liquid, deep and breathtaking.

Some things might be different now—but that wasn't one of them.

Before she could answer, a quick knock sounded on Rick's door. It opened without his response. A short, tubby man wearing a dark brown suit stood in the opening. He was a bureaucrat, a politician. Silvia recognized the look about him before he even opened his mouth.

"Aha, you *are* here." He bustled into the tension-filled room and extended his hand in Silvia's direction. "I *thought* you had arrived. I'm Edward Alvarez, the mayor of San Laredo. And you're Dr. Hernandez. How do you do?"

She stood and shook his hand. It was clammy and cold and she wondered instantly, her psychologist's skills on high alert, why he was so nervous. "It's nice to meet you."

"Have you been giving her the details, Hunter?" The mayor glanced officiously from Silvia to Rick. "We haven't got all day, you know. We've got to catch this son of a—"

"We haven't started to discuss the case yet," Silvia interrupted. "The sheriff here isn't sure I'm the right person for the job."

The mayor shot a glance toward Rick. "I thought we'd discussed this already, Hunter. I don't want—"

"I know what you want and what you don't want, Edward. Repeating it isn't going to change my mind."

"Then maybe this will." He flung a rolled-up newspaper onto Rick's desk. It fluttered open noisily in the tense silence. Silvia could read the upside-down headline from across the room.

Social Worker Murdered—Killer Loose?

Rick's cold gaze met the mayor's. "And how did *this* happen? I thought we were going to try to keep the publicity down."

"I have no idea how they got the story." He straightened his tie with a jerky motion, his eyes darting away from Rick's.

Rick's mouth went into a single line of disapproval. Undisguised anger radiated from the strained set of his shoulders. "No idea, huh? Well, how about this little scenario, then? I think you decided it would benefit you more to tell the story than to keep it quiet.''

The little man started to bluster. ''Th-that's ridiculous. Why would I do that?''

Rick gave him a withering look. ''You're the one who called in the cavalry. I would suspect you want to look like the hero—the hero who needs to be re-elected.''

Sputtering, the mayor tried for an honest look of wounded defensiveness...and failed. It was more than obvious he'd called the newspaper. ''I don't know what in the hell you're talking about, Hunter. Why I would never—''

Rick stood abruptly and pushed his chair away from his desk. ''Forget it, Alvarez,'' he said in a disgusted voice. ''None of that matters anyway. The woman's still dead, whether you're an idiot or not.'' He took two steps closer to Silvia and glared down at her. ''Can you really help us or is what you do just a bunch of mumbo jumbo?''

He was standing so close to her, she could see the tiny white line that bisected his left eyebrow. They'd been fishing when she'd accidently hit him with her hook, throwing her line over her shoulder. She'd cried so hard at County General she'd almost thrown up.

Shifting her gaze away from the scar and back to his eyes, she stared at him, her nervousness almost too big to contain. ''I can help you find your killer. The question is—do you really want me to?''

Chapter 2

Her words hung in the strained silence just a second too long. The mayor jumped in to speak, but not before Rick read exactly what Silvia Hernandez was telling him in the dark depths of her eyes.

She hadn't trusted him eighteen years ago and nothing had changed.

"Of—of course we want your help," Alvarez sputtered. "That's why we called. You're staying, and that's all there is to it. Bring her up to speed, Hunter. I want this thing resolved." He shot Rick an aggravated glance, then rushed out of the office, muttering something about hardheaded law enforcement.

Rick turned away before Silvia could see what was in his eyes. He didn't need her getting the upper hand. He didn't need her seeing his real feelings.

He didn't need her knowing he still cared. Had never *stopped* caring.

He cursed silently. God, this was just what he had

been afraid would happen! When he'd walked in and seen her standing there in his office, her prim black suit so professional, her attitude so cool, he should have turned around right there and then and left. But he hadn't. And he knew beforehand he wouldn't have. Since the moment he knew she was coming, he knew it would happen this way. He wanted to see her, wanted to look into her eyes, wanted to get close enough to her to see if she still wore the same perfume.

And she did.

God help him, she did.

The heady aroma of Chanel No.5 perfume curled in the corners of his office like smoke from a fire. He'd bought her her very first bottle when she'd turned sixteen. His mother had almost had a stroke when she'd found out. Why spend so much money on a girl *like that,* she'd said, her patrician nose lifting into the air.

Silvia rose, ignorant of his turmoil. ''I'll need all your files on the case. Reports, photos, whatever you've gotten so far. I like to start with the victimology, then study what you've got on the crime scene itself.''

He hesitated, then accepted reality. There was nothing else he could do. ''I'll see that you get everything we've got. Do you want an office here, too?''

''Yes, please, but a small one will do just fine. I like to work at home as much as I can.''

''Where will you be staying?''

''With Yolanda on San Luis Street. She lives in Mama's old place.''

''Why not with Carlos? I hear he has a fancy trophy house out on the north side…you'd probably be more comfortable there.''

She stared at him then, the slightly bitter tone in his voice bringing her eyes toward his in an effort to read him better. He turned his gaze to the window, making sure her effort was useless.

Carlos Hernandez. Alvarez always referred to him as a two-bit Mexican attorney, but Silvia's brother was more than that...a helluva lot more. To the locals, he was a hero. Whenever they needed donations, he was the first one to give. Whenever they needed volunteers, he was the first one to offer. He'd developed a lucrative practice from fighting for the rights of the poor and downtrodden.

Or so he'd have people think. Rick knew differently, and had suspicions about a lot more. Pretty soon, he'd know for sure.

"The house on San Luis is fine by me," she said finally. "I don't need anything fancy."

With that, she moved toward the door where she hesitated, one graceful hand on the doorknob, her scarlet fingernails glimmering in the late afternoon light. "I'd like to get started as soon as possible. When do you think you can get those files to me?"

He turned to stare at her. She'd become a beautiful woman—polished with an air of authority. Everything about her, from her clothes to her attitude, told him she knew exactly what she was doing. Beneath the polish, though, he still saw the girl. The gorgeous teenage girl he thought had loved him...the girl he thought he'd loved. Part of him wanted to wrap his arms around her and carry her away...and the other part of him wanted to lash out and demand the answers he'd been wanting for eighteen years.

Why in the hell did you leave? Where did you go? What's your life been like? Did you ever really love me or was it just a game for you?

Instead he asked something else. "Why are you in

such a hurry?'' His stare met hers. ''Planning on leaving in the middle of the night again?''

She blushed darkly, just as he'd known she would. For a second, he thought she would come back at him, but she said nothing. Instead, she turned around, opened the door, and left.

He smelled Chanel No.5 the rest of the day.

Silvia caught only the barest details of town as she drove her rental car through the streets. Boarded-up buildings, neglected yards, playgrounds without equipment. The economy of the Valley wasn't doing too great, but then it never had. San Laredo had always been a way station of sorts and nothing more. People passed through on their way to somewhere else. No one who could afford to leave ever stayed.

Except Rick.

Ignoring the scorching heat, Silvia tightened her hands on the steering wheel. Seeing him again had been just as painful as she'd thought it would be. His voice brought back memories she'd fought for years and his eyes—God, those eyes!—they had made her remember things, places, touches, she'd long ago forced herself to put aside.

On the other hand, he wasn't at all what she'd expected. He was a far cry from the spit-and-polish lawmen she'd been familiar with throughout her career. Not, of course, because he looked disheveled in his uniform, God no. He looked wonderful in it. No, he was different because of something inside him. In the few short minutes they'd been together, she'd sensed a deep, underlying emotion that was hard to define. He was like a pot simmering on the stove, calm on top, hot and roiling just beneath the surface. The turmoil could have been anger, or just a certain level of intensity. Even with all her skills, she couldn't define it.

Whatever it was, she could think of no other word to describe him except the one that had popped into her mind when she'd first seen him. He was dangerous. Dangerous in ways she didn't even want to think about. Dangerous in ways she was afraid she already understood. Not dangerous in a physical sense but dangerous to her emotions, something even more threatening to her than physical harm.

Dangerous.

Before she could think about him any longer, Silvia realized she'd reached the house on San Luis Street. She pulled the car up next to the curb and cut off the engine. A television blared from someone's living room down the street, and two children, skipping rope on the sidewalk, stared at her curiously. Back when she'd lived on San Luis Street, not too many shiny, new cars had parked on their street. Apparently that was still the case. When Silvia opened the car door and stepped outside, the two little girls began to whisper and giggle. Obviously, not too many women in expensive black suits came this way, either. A second later, the children ran off down the broken strip of concrete, dragging their rope behind them.

Shifting her gaze to the tiny house set back from the street, Silvia took in her childhood home. Until she'd started dating Rick she had adored the little house, had always felt protected and loved inside it, unlike Carlos who'd lied to his friends about where he lived.

It still looked wonderful; Yolanda obviously took great care of it and had kept it in perfect condition. The white clapboard gleamed in the hot Texas sun, the light glinting off the windows that sparkled now as they always had when Silvia had been at home, and it had been her duty to keep them clean. The porch was well swept, too. On the right-hand side, under the deep eaves in the shadows, a swing moved somnolently in an almost nonexistent breeze. Her throat closed against itself in a spasm of remembrance—this was the same swing where she and Rick had huddled after dark, kissing and holding hands and whispering quietly to avoid her brother, Carlos.

Carlos. She started up the sidewalk to the house, nervousness sweeping over her. Yolanda had said he'd be pleased to see her, but Silvia wasn't sure about that. They'd spoken so rarely in the past eighteen years he was more of a stranger to her than a brother. Did he still hate her? Did he still hate Rick? Years ago, she'd begun to accept that he'd done what he'd thought was best when he'd kicked her out. He'd only thought he was protecting their mother from scandal, keeping the family intact, and Silvia could almost understand his motivations. But his method... It had been a harsh one, and she was still struggling to understand and totally forgive him for the way he'd handled it all.

She stepped onto the porch, the boards creaking under her heels. With her heart tripping against her chest, she raised her hand to knock. Instantly, the front door swung open. Behind the screen, in the shadows, a man stood. A man dressed in the expensive suit of a businessman. A man who had to be her older brother. Behind him were at least ten other people of all ages and sizes.

"Carlito?" The childhood name came unbidden to her lips. "Is—is that you?"

"No one's called me that in a thousand years." From behind the screen, he stared at her, his voice almost amused as it rose above the rabble of noise coming from behind him. "But yes—it's me, Silvie. Carlito." He pushed open the door, and his dark eyes met hers as he spoke smoothly. "Welcome home."

Carlos hugged her. She'd lived the moment a thousand times in her dreams, but the reality felt strange. He smelled of expensive cologne and cigars. When he pulled back and their eyes met, his expression was a mixture of guarded politeness and open curiosity. Looking at him, a flood of memories washed over Silvia— good ones where she could recall their childhood together, happy ones where she could remember how much she'd adored him, looked up to him. The immediate urge to pull him closer and finally put the past behind them swept over Silvia, but before she could do anything, he stepped away, surprising her.

Had he read her intention? Did he not want to forget? Not want to forgive? Before she could analyze it more, his place was taken by a well-padded woman in a shapeless housedress.

The woman was dabbing at her eyes with a tissue. For a moment, Silvia's heart stopped, then she realized who she was really seeing. It wasn't her mother, as she first thought, but her older sister, Yolanda.

The years had carved lines of worry on her face in the same places it had touched their mother's. Yolanda smiled sweetly as if she knew what Silvia was thinking, and Silvia realized with a start that her sister always had been able to read her. And why not? She was the only person in the world who knew Silvia's secret.

Unexpectedly, tears came into Silvia's eyes, burning and stinging. "Yolanda—" was all she could manage to say.

"*Bienvenida, chica,*" the older woman whispered as

she hugged her. "Welcome home…it's so wonderful to finally see you again." She pulled back and stared at Silvia. "So *linda!* So gorgeous! I can't believe it."

"Come on, Yolanda—share!"

Yolanda laughed but refused to move. With her arm still wrapped around Silvia's shoulder, she spoke. "Okay, okay…"

Silvia watched as a younger version of her older sister came forward. "You remember little Consuelo," Yolanda said. "Well, she's not so little anymore!"

A very visibly pregnant Consuelo waddled toward Silvia. "I'd hug you," she said apologetically, "but I don't think I can get close enough!"

Silvia reached out and squeezed her younger sister's hands, a funny catch coming into her voice. "You're pregnant!"

Everyone laughed, but Silvia's eyes involuntarily went to Yolanda's. Their gaze connected with a jolt, then Silvia looked the other way, grateful when Carlos began to speak again.

"Lydia couldn't be here just yet. A catastrophe at her office." His voice held a note of tension as he said his wife's name, but he shrugged his shoulders elegantly, making Silvia wonder where the polish had come from. "You'd think she was running the county instead of merely keeping the books." He laughed lightly.

The flock of children milling around Carlos's legs came forward, and Silvia was introduced to them as well. It was obvious Carlos knew each of them as if they were his own, but their names flew in and out of Silvia's head even though Yolanda had sent her photos through the years. She'd have to sit down later and sort them all out. She pushed away the tug at her heart as she took in the huge, brown eyes, the smooth, little arms, the clean smells of sunshine and dirt as the children all hugged her in turns. She was good at pushing the sensations away—she'd done it for years.

"Enough—enough!" Carlos clapped his hands finally and the children dispersed like a flock of reluctant swallows. The screen door banged behind them as they ran outside. In the silence that followed, he stared at Silvia.

"You look very good," he said, nodding almost as if to himself. "Very successful."

She wondered if he was surprised by that state of affairs, but Yolanda spoke before Silvia could ask.

"Of course, she looks good," the older woman said. "She's beautiful, smart—a Ph.D. for goodness' sake." She smiled warmly at Silvia. "She's gone a long way, our little Silvie has."

"And all by herself. Without benefit of husband or family." He moved toward the couch and sat down, indicating Silvia should take a seat as well. His look seemed to challenge her, to dare her to bring up the past, but part of her knew this was simply her own paranoia coming out. "A big important job, lots of prestige. How have you managed, Silvia? Has it been hard without—"

"Oh, stop it, Carlos!" Yolanda's voice held a hint of indignation, a touch of resentment. "She's just gotten here, give her a chance to settle in before you start with your cross-examinations." Patting Silvia on the shoulder, she smiled warmly. "Just ignore him, Silvie. He thinks like an attorney—all of the time."

"It's all right, Yolanda. I'm used to dealing with lawyers. One way or another I cross swords with them in court all the time." She looked at Carlos straight on, trying to decide if he was being antagonistic or not.

Surely he wasn't still mad at her after all these years. She couldn't make up her mind as to how he really felt, so smiling at him, she spoke, her voice light and teasing. "I can hold my own against them."

He dipped his head, an acknowledgment of her words, then Consuelo spoke. "So tell us all about your job, Silvia." She eased into a nearby recliner. "Yolanda said you analyze bad guys? Tell us about it."

Silvia launched into her standard explanation of her job, the one she gave at cocktail parties and to people on planes. For some reason, under Carlos's steady stare, she didn't feel like saying more about her work. A built-in defense mechanism, she wondered briefly, or the sense that he might still be as competitive as he always was and not appreciate having another professional in the family?

When Silvia finished, Yolanda elaborated for her. "She knows all about why people commit crimes...and what makes them crazy, too. She's here to figure out who killed Bonnie Kelman."

Yolanda barely got out the victim's name before Carlos jumped in. "You make her sound like a psychic!" he scoffed. "What do you think she does? Read minds?"

Silvia turned back to her brother. "Actually Yolanda's partly right," she said with a smile. "I do have to read minds sometimes. I'm pretty good at it, too. You'd better watch out."

The women all laughed, but Carlos's mouth went into a thin, narrow line, and he gripped the arms of the chair where he sat, his knuckles going white with the effort. He clearly wasn't accustomed to anyone—especially a woman—generating laughter at his expense, regardless of how trivial the conversation.

"Thank you for the warning," he said tightly. "I will guard my thoughts."

After that, the women moved into the kitchen and started lunch. Feeling awkward and out of place, Silvia stood to the side and watched until Yolanda, a practiced housewife, grabbed her arm and handed her an onion and a knife. "Chop this up, really fine," she instructed. "We need it for the tacos. When you finish with that one, do at least five more!"

Silvia did as she was told, and by the time the meal was on the table, she understood why. The crowd had grown even bigger. Yolanda's husband, Carl, arrived from his job at the nearby gas plant, and with him was Johnny, Consuelo's husband. They had friends with them, and the little house swelled at the seams.

Silvia's eyes followed Johnny, as he went straight to Consuelo and talked to her softly, an expression of caring and concern on his weathered face, his hand placed protectively over her stomach. Silvia's throat tightened, and she couldn't help but wonder how it would feel to have a man care that much. As always, though, she shook off the question.

A moment after the men arrived, Carlos's wife, Lydia, came into the kitchen. She greeted him briefly, said a shy hello to Silvia, then turned to the sink and began washing dishes. The contrast was immediate. There were no sweet words or kisses between her and Carlos, and Silvia got the distinct impression that any affection between them had stopped years before—if it had ever existed at all.

But she forgot about Carlos and his wife as the kitchen filled with children. All different sizes, ages and types. There must have been at least a dozen milling around in the tiny house. It was impossible to ignore them all, and part of her didn't want to anyway, even though it was how she'd survived emotionally for years. She finally gave in and let the feeling of family sweep over her.

It was a bittersweet feeling, tinged with regret, love and strangely enough...envy.

By eight that evening, Silvia was reeling. She'd eaten too much, been hugged too often, and held too many small hands. Everyone had been so nice, but they'd all wanted her attention, her love, her emotions. The reception had been overwhelming to a woman who'd made it her life's work to distance herself from exactly such entanglements. Knowing she needed a break, she walked outside to the tiny porch that stretched across the front of the house. A few minutes later, Yolanda joined her.

Her eyes were full of understanding. "It's *loco*, no? So many of us at once. I should have known better than to have this big crowd here on your first day back— even though it's not all of us! Are you all right?"

Silvia pushed her hair away from her face. "It's okay—really. I—I'm just tired, that's all. The flight and everything, you know..."

Yolanda put her hand on Silvia's arm. "You don't have to put on a face for me, *chiquita*. I understand."

Silvia let her eyes go to her sister's, but once again, she couldn't hold the stare. There was too much between them, too many secrets, too much emotion.

If it hadn't been for Yolanda, Silvia had no idea what would have happened to her the night Carlos had thrown her out. For a week afterward, Yolanda had hidden Silvia, then after their plans had been finalized, she'd given Silvia every dime she had and made her promise to call the minute she reached Houston and the home of their twice-removed cousins who'd agreed to help. And later—when it had gotten even worse—Yolanda had come through for her.

A jangle of keys sounded in the still night air. "Here," Yolanda said, "take my car for a drive. Cool off. You need to be alone, I think."

It was *exactly* what she needed, Silvia realized with a start. She reached for the keys, then stopped. "Won't everyone miss—"

"I'll tell them I sent you to the store for more *masa*." She lifted her hand and made a shooing motion with it. "Go—go—before someone comes out here and decides you need company."

Silvia stared at her sister, then they hugged each other tightly, a world of communication going between them. A second later, Silvia was walking down the steps and heading toward the vehicle Yolanda had pointed out. The car started easily and before she knew it, she was pulling out of the driveway and going down San Luis Street.

Ten minutes later, she was on Cemetery Road.

The deserted stretch of blacktop was still as scary as it had been when she was a teenager and all the kids would dare each other to walk the one-mile length without a flashlight at midnight. It had been dark, lonely and quiet—and that situation hadn't changed one bit. The giant elm trees loomed and met each other in the middle above the faded yellow stripe. The green tunnel they formed overhead was a little more dark and endless, but the feeling was just the same. The moonless night didn't help, either. Silvia found herself remembering things she'd rather not...like how Linda Willington's body had been found on the side of this very road that fateful summer.

And now…another woman had died *right here*. While they'd cooked, Yolanda had talked about Bonnie Kelman's murder. The local newspaper had apparently reported the event and all the details they could, including where the body had been discovered. Silvia had been shocked by this information. She couldn't help but wonder why Rick hadn't mentioned the fact that Linda Willington and Bonnie Kelman had both been murdered in the same place. Obviously there was no substantial evidence linking the two murders, other than the location, or Rick would have told her. He must have simply felt it was a coincidence.

But was it?

She cut off the engine to the car and let the nighttime silence envelope her. The quiet was so deep, so dark, so complete it almost felt claustrophobic. She found herself opening the car door just to reassure herself that she could. Stepping outside to the lonely pavement, she breathed deeply.

Whenever she was involved in a case, she was always drawn to the scene of the crime, and there was something definitely spooky about this spot. The empty fields on either side of the road, the gleaming white trunks of the elm trees in the distance—so bonelike in their paleness—the mournful cry of the night birds resting in the trees overhead. Rick's face shot into her mind, and Silvia wrapped her arms around her chest protectively while moving to the front of the car to lean against the grill.

What had really happened the night Linda had died? After Silvia had left, Rick had never even been charged with the murder and had been completely exonerated.

Silvia's moment of doubt had been just that—a moment only. She'd been a teenager and had thought like one, jumping to conclusions, thinking the worst. Any kid would have done the same, seeing Rick as she had.

Through the years, as she'd become older and more analytical, she'd come to realize Rick Hunter was totally incapable of murder. Something had happened out here, though—something between Linda and Rick—but it hadn't been murder. Silvia had had eighteen years to think about it, and she knew that for sure.

But what *had* happened?

The sudden crunch of a footstep drove the question from her mind. Her eyes flew open, and with her heart in her throat, she scanned the lonely road.

There was no one around. She was completely alone. She let her breath out and chastised herself for acting nutty. *Just because you're paranoid it doesn't mean they're not after you.* It had been a joke in graduate school. It didn't sound so funny right now.

She heard the sound again. Distinctly.

Twirling around she stared into the darkness behind the car. Inky blackness filled the void. "Hello? Who—who's there?"

The only sound that came to her was the sound of her pounding heart. She swallowed hard and told herself again she was being silly. What kind of criminal psychologist was afraid of the dark?

"Is—is anyone there?"

Slowly—so slowly she thought she was at first imagining it—a darker shadow began to detach itself from the gloom at the side of the road. Without a sound, it moved closer to her. Silvia's mouth went completely dry. She wasn't able to manage a scream even though her life could depend on it. It took only thirty seconds for her to realize what was really going on, but once she had, she wasn't so sure she felt relieved.

"Rick!" she exclaimed, her hand at her throat. "I—I wasn't expecting to see anyone here."

He loomed out of the darkness as his gaze slowly traveled over the jeans and T-shirt she'd slipped into during the middle of the party. "I didn't recognize you either, or I would have said something," he said. "You're driving a different car, and you changed clothes since you left the office."

She looked at the Toyota, her hand fluttering toward it in a gesture of explanation. "It—it's Yolanda's. Mine was blocked." Glancing down at herself next, she spoke again, hating the flustered way she was acting and feeling. "And I—I wanted to get comfortable. We were having dinner back at the house but I decided to take a drive and—"

"What's the matter? Couldn't you handle being part of Carlos's little kingdom again?"

She didn't respond to his bitterness. He'd never liked Carlos, and the feeling had apparently gotten stronger through the years instead of diminishing. Part of her didn't blame him for it. She could understand. "It wasn't like that at all," she answered quietly, turning more calm. "I just needed some air—the house was getting crowded. I thought a quick drive might help."

"And you ended up out here?"

"I like to see the scene before I read the files. It helps me put things into perspective, maybe even see things before the evidence prejudices me." She lifted her hand to push her hair from her face. "Why are *you* here?"

He came closer to where she stood. Close enough for her to finally see his face. The emotions she'd sensed earlier in his office seemed even nearer to the surface.

"I wanted to check out some tire tracks. One of my investigators said something about there being some out here, but the only ones I could locate were old. Too old to mean anything."

She nodded, and in the silence that followed, a mourning dove called out, his call lonely and hollow sounding in the distance. She shivered unexpectedly. When she spoke, her voice came out unexpectedly loud. "Why didn't you tell me the victim had been found here? Right where Linda had been?"

He stared at her through the darkness, his eyes cutting through the gloom. "I wasn't sure it mattered."

Something in the way he said *wasn't* made her stop. "And now? Has something changed your mind?"

He shook his head. "I'm just not sure."

The silence built between them, thick and heavy. He turned away from her and looked out into the field. Finally, he spoke again, his voice husky. "So?" He looked back at her. "Who did it? Who killed them?" He raised a hand and waved it toward the lonely, empty field beside them. "Who came out here and ended the lives of two beautiful women—eighteen years apart?"

Her startled eyes jerked to his. "You *do* think the two murders are related? That it's possible Linda's murder had something to do with Bonnie Kelman's death?"

"At this point, I think it would be extremely premature to speculate on that fact." He paused. "Don't you?"

"But you just linked them."

"I was just stating the facts. Both bodies were found here. *You* linked them." His dark eyes raked her face. "And *you're* the expert.... So you tell me."

Under his penetrating stare, she spoke stiffly. "Well, it's obviously not something I can determine yet. I'll need more data, more evidence.'' She heard the correctness in her voice, the formality in her speech. It was a defense mechanism, a way of keeping him at bay, and she needed the distance it provided. Desperately needed it.

"Data? Evidence? I didn't think you shrinks operated on data and evidence. I thought you *perceived* the killer's intentions, then explained it all by telling us about their hard childhoods. Then you try to get them easy time even though they've slashed and burned their way through life.''

His attitude didn't surprise her. Local cops always resented the Feds' help, especially when they were being forced from a higher authority to accept it.

"You don't know anything about me,'' she said quietly. "You don't have the slightest clue about how I feel regarding criminals.''

He crossed his arms over his chest and stared at her in the darkness. "I can make a pretty good guess.''

Bitterness tinged her reply. "Guesses aren't good enough in this business. You have to be sure.'' She stopped herself from saying more. He obviously knew of her troubles at the DCA but she wasn't about to inform him of the details. "As soon as I know more, though, I'm sure I'll be able to help.''

"And that's why you came out here.''

"I find it very helpful to view the scene.''

"This late at night?''

"Yolanda said the paper reported the victim was killed this late at night. Was that correct?''

He nodded slowly. "It's all in the file I'll be bringing you, but yes, it's right. The examiner said she'd been hit around 1:00 a.m.''

Silvia looked out into the darkness and imagined how

lonely the woman must have felt, how scared. Even if she'd known her attacker, there came a moment when his intentions must have crystalized, became apparent to her. At that instant, how had she felt?

Silvia turned her head and looked up at Rick. He was standing close to her. He'd always been tall, but he seemed bigger now, more powerful. He was easily capable of overcoming a good-size man, much less a more helpless woman...especially if she might think his purpose was something other than killing her. Without thinking about what it meant, she put herself in the victim's place and Rick in the role of the killer. A shivering fright started deep inside her, and she had to fight to bring herself back into the present.

"Did you know the victim?" she asked.

"Yes." His voice was flat, without inflection. "She worked at city hall in the social services department. She was..."

Silvia waited for him to say more and when he didn't, she prompted him gently. "She was..."

"A good woman. Attractive. Smart. She had her stuff together."

"Married?"

He nodded. "With two children, a boy and a girl."

He said nothing else then, and Silvia couldn't help but wonder. How well *had* he known the victim? Did Silvia even want to really know that answer? Was it her imagination, or was he holding something back? Not telling her the whole truth right off the bat?

"And was she killed here? Or brought here afterward?"

His eyes studied her face as if he were memorizing how she looked. She held back a shiver.

"She was killed here." He paused. "Just like Linda.

Out in the open with a large-caliber gun, shot at very close range. There were signs of a struggle, but it was brief at best.'' He stared at her, his eyes gleaming in the darkness with an emotion she couldn't quite read. "It was over fast."

The night air was suddenly close, close and heavy with unexpected tension. Silvia couldn't help but think about how isolated they were. In the distance, lights from a small house twinkled, but it had to be at least a mile away. Standing away from the car, she straightened up and put her hands in the pockets of her jeans. Her voice was firm. "I think I'd better be getting back."

He said nothing. Putting her feet in motion, Silvia turned and moved toward the car door. Just as she came to his side, he unexpectedly reached out and stopped her with his hand on her arm. His touch was electrifying and for a moment, there was nothing she could do but stand still and allow the current to pass through her.

It seemed like minutes but in reality, no more than a second or two passed and then he dropped his hand. "You look good, Silvia. Really good."

She laughed nervously. There was nothing else she *could* do, not with her skin still burning even though his fingers had left her arm. "You say that as though you're surprised."

"No." He shook his head. "That's not what I meant at all. I always knew you'd become a beautiful woman. I just didn't know how beautiful...or how successful."

The words were spoken with a mixture of sincerity and a hint of awkwardness, just enough to make her know that he was being honest. Or being a very good actor.

"Thank you," she said. The silence stretched between them until she couldn't stand it any longer. "You've done pretty good yourself."

"Not really," he answered. "But I can fool most of the people most of the time."

"You can't fool voters."

He smiled unexpectedly. "Is that what they tell you guys in Washington?"

His expression held echoes of the past, warm echoes, echoes she couldn't ignore. She told her heart to stop beating so fast, but it ignored her. "You've been elected sheriff of this county three times. That tells us something, doesn't it?"

"Yeah." He stopped. "That you've been keeping track."

She could see the shadow of his beard and the creases along his mouth. Remembering how that mouth once fit hers, she felt her heart begin to accelerate. "I have my sources." She answered more flippantly than she felt. "Just like you do."

His attitude shifted as she spoke, his expression turning more serious.

"I have my sources about this, too," he said, his voice almost menacing in its deepness. "And they're telling me you need to be careful here, Silvia. Damned careful with this investigation."

His words shocked her. Her stomach clenched in instant nervousness. "Is this a warning?"

"You can call it whatever you want." His gaze was piercing. "Just be careful. It may sound crazy, but there really are people here in San Laredo who don't want this murder solved."

Chapter 3

With a stack of files tucked under his arm, Rick headed for the cubicle that had been assigned to Silvia. He told himself his actions meant nothing. He simply didn't want to bother his secretary. She had better things to do than run his errands. He was going that way anyway because he needed...coffee.

Right.

He rounded the corner and muttered a curse under his breath. Who was he trying to fool? He wanted to see Silvia again, plain and simple. Since she'd driven away from him last night, the dark swallowing the taillights of her car, he'd been able to think of nothing else. She'd looked too damn good in those worn, soft jeans, her hair piled on top of her head, soft curls escaping to hang around her face. He wanted to look into those deep brown eyes some more, to stare at that shimmering hair, and imagine his hands on either side of her face. He wanted to think about how it would feel to put his mouth on hers and kiss her like he used to when they were both teenagers and had nothing but time. He wanted to...

"Did you want something?"

Silvia's voice startled him into awareness. He'd reached her office and hadn't even realized it. As his eyes took her in, he struggled to keep his emotions from his face. She had on a short red skirt and a white silk blouse. He knew little about women's clothing, but he knew enough to recognize that Silvia's was simple, elegant and terribly expensive. The kind of expensive his ex-wife had always wanted to experience. He would have let her if she'd ended up looking like this, he thought to himself, but she wouldn't have. She would have gone to the nearest boutique in Brownsville and come out looking like a hooker headed for the border.

"I brought you the case files." He dropped the folders on the edge of Silvia's desk, his attitude abrupt and brusque as if it could cover up the confusion whirling inside him. The confusion that had been with him since the moment Silvia Hernandez had walked back into his life. "Almost everything's in there."

"Good," she answered briskly. "The fresher the trail, the better picture I can get. I usually don't have the chance to get in on the investigation this early." She patted the files. "You said almost everything. What's missing?"

"There's another ballistics report I want to have done. I'm still working on that." She nodded, then he spoke again. "How soon will you have a preliminary report?"

She took her time answering him, her legs whispering against each other as she crossed them then stared at him. "It will take awhile," she answered, her own voice noncommital. "These things can't be done overnight."

"And what will we have when you do finish?"

Her eyes reminded him of the sky that had been overhead last night. Deep, dark, fathomless. "A fairly accurate psychological profile of a person who could be Bonnie Kelman's killer."

"Then all I have to do is find him?"

She stared at him, measuring his words, evaluating them as if each one meant something terribly important. It made him feel uncomfortable. Could she tell what he was thinking about her, too?

"I guess you could look at it like that." She crossed her arms in front of her and stared at him, the tension rising between them. "I try to be as specific as possible based on my experience and the facts you've given me, but I generally don't spit out a name and address."

"Too bad," he said tightly. "We do want to get the right man."

"Or woman." Her voice challenged him, dared him to give her a hard time. "You have to be open to all possibilities, you know."

"Oh, I'm open all right. I'm open to catching this son of a bitch and hanging him. Anyone who does this kind of thing to a woman doesn't deserve to live—"

She leaned closer. "And I agree...but we have to figure out who he is first, don't we?"

He stared at her. "And at this point, that's still a mystery to you."

She met his steady gaze. "At this point, yes, it is."

She'd been scared last night out on Cemetery Road. Rick had felt her fear as clearly as if it had been a living, breathing thing standing between them. He'd heard rumors. Rumors that she'd been afraid to come back into the field. That things had gone wrong with an investigation. That someone had died and she had blamed herself. There was a problem, he was sure, but the shadows in her eyes were too deep to be explained away so easily.

"Is there anything else I can get you?" he asked abruptly. "Do you need office supplies? A computer?"

She patted the black case resting on the desk. "I always bring my own. Thanks for the offer, though."

Silvia studied Rick and wondered what he was thinking. People usually gave away clues to their thoughts and emotions. There would be a hint of nervousness or a suggestion of fear...even someone who was innocent might reveal some defensiveness with their body language when talking to a psychologist. But Rick Hunter didn't show anything. His face was a granite mask.

And that terrified her.

It terrified her because she knew he was hiding something. He hadn't been telling her the truth last night and it was even more obvious now in the morning light that he was keeping something from her. She chastised herself—hadn't she already seen what damage a lack of trust caused? But she couldn't stop thinking about his warning. *There are people here who don't want this murder solved.* She'd asked him to explain himself but when he'd refused to say more, she had left quickly. She took a deep breath now and started to ask him again, but he turned and headed for the open door.

He stopped at the opening to turn and look at her. "If you need anything, call me." He reached into his pocket for something, then handed it across the desk to her. It was his business card. "That has my fax number, and my beeper number as well."

She slipped it into her pocket. "Thanks."

He looked as if he wanted to say something else, but at the very last minute, he simply turned and walked out of her office. Fingering the card, Silvia watched his broad back disappear from her view. She wished she could make him disappear from her thoughts just as easily.

With the phone pressed against her ear, Silvia stared out her lone window at the grassy expanse leading to the city hall steps. It was quite a different view from the one she had back in Washington. There it was nice and green now, the flowers blooming, tourists crowding all the public places. Here it was brown and desolate.

One ring sounded before Don picked up. "Rogers here."

"Don—it's Silvia."

"Hey! How're things going in Texas?"

He sounded surprised, but she'd expected him to sound that way. When she'd first gone out into the field, she'd called him every day. Later on, with more experience under her belt, she'd worked more on her own. This felt like it was her first trip again, though. She didn't know if it felt that way because it'd been two years since she'd been in the field, or because she was dealing with Rick Hunter. For whatever reason, her fingers had reached for the phone the minute Rick had left her office.

"Is everything okay?" Don's voice sounded concerned.

"I don't know," she answered slowly. "Things are...confused."

"Explain."

"It's safe to say the sheriff isn't happy that I'm here."

"When are they ever?"

"You've got a point," she answered. *But you don't know the whole story, that's for sure.*

"How's the case look so far? Besides the sheriff?"

"I've just gotten the files. Haven't had a chance to even look at them yet." She stared out the window. "I went to the scene last night, though."

"And it was…?"

"It was…" She started to say more, then broke off, unable to describe the feeling she'd had, especially the one that had come over her when Rick had materialized.

"Was what?"

"Worse than usual," she finally managed to reply. "It's a very lonely, isolated place. It just gave me the creeps, that's all." She took a deep breath. "Listen, Don, it's possible this killing might be related to another one, one that happened here eighteen years ago. I'm not at all sure yet, but there are some similarities, and they're troubling me."

"What kind of similarities?"

"Well, for one thing, the murders both happened at the same place."

"That's interesting, especially when you consider the eighteen-year span."

"I know. I find it…disturbing."

"Anything else?"

"Both victims were shot—late at night—with a large-caliber gun." She swung her chair around to stare out the window again. "If the situation takes off in a different direction, I may need to head that way. I thought I should get an okay from you to do some digging in that other case if I need to."

"By all means," he answered instantly. "Do what

you need to—take as much time as you want. Is that other case still open?"

"An arrest was never made."

"Then do what you can. It'd just be another feather in our cap if you can close two for them—and I'm sure they'd be thrilled."

"All right, I'll do what I can…and to that end, I need some copies of some papers I wrote a few years ago for the *Journal of Psychology Review.* I thought they were in my computer but they aren't. They must be down on the mainframe."

"I'll send Mary for them." She heard him reach for a pencil. "Give me the titles."

She explained what she needed, then heard him drop the pencil to his desktop.

"So shall I E-mail them or fax them?"

"I haven't got my computer set up yet. Just fax them." She reached for Rick's card. "Here's Hunter's fax number."

"I'll get them to you as soon as possible." He paused, then dropped his voice. "How's it going with your family? Everything okay there so far?"

A mockingbird landed on the edge of the sidewalk outside. He began to peck at an invisible spot in the cement. Silvia stared at the bird and wondered how she could answer Don's question. Carlos had been puzzling, Yolanda was older, Consuelo happy. The children…how could she tell him it was torture to see all those children? How could she explain? She shook her head and knew she couldn't.

"Ask me that one in another week or two," she said, watching as the bird took flight. "I might have an answer then."

* * *

Silvia had taken one bite out of her sandwich when Yolanda's considerable shadow fell over her table at the deli. "What are you doing eating here?" her sister whispered. "You should come home for lunch. The food here's no good."

Looking at the plate her sister held in her hands, Silvia put her sandwich back down on her own plate and laughed. "What are you doing here then?"

Yolanda grinned and squeezed into the chair opposite Silvia's. "I had to go to the courthouse to renew my driver's license," she said. "It seemed like too much trouble to go home and eat." She looked around at the suited men and women who filled the tiny restaurant. "So many lawyers! It does the appetite no good, eh?"

Silvia found herself smiling again. "You don't think much of lawyers, do you?"

Yolanda's dark eyes opened wide. "Of course I don't think much of them. What do they add to our society? Do they make things? Produce goods? No! They consume and nothing more. There's no value added in that, if you ask me."

"You don't think Carlos contributes anything to society?"

Yolanda's expression turned guarded. "Well, Carlos is different. He contributes in his own way. I'm sure he'd be happy to explain it to you if you ask him. Take it with a grain of salt, though. His main occupation is acquiring more money, and that's all he thinks about. He's—" She broke off abruptly as if she had become suddenly aware of where she was. "Let's talk about something more interesting," she said. "Tell me about Washington. I've always wanted to visit there."

"Then you'll have to come." Silvia spoke the words without thinking, then realized she meant them. In the few short days she'd been back, she'd felt a closeness to her sister that had surprised her.

But then again, that's what secrets did, didn't they? Brought some people together and tore others apart.

"Do you mean that?" Yolanda asked, her voice amazed.

"Yeah," Silvia said softly. "I do mean it. I'd love to show you Washington. Let's plan a trip for you before I leave, okay?"

The two women exchanged an almost shy look, then Yolanda spoke again. "I'd like to do something for you, too, then. Will you let me?"

"Of course. Like what?"

"I'd like to plan a family get-together. A *real* reunion." She crossed her arms and put them on the tabletop. "What do you think? Would you like that?"

Hearing her sister's enthusiasm, Silvia hid her own sense of growing dismay. "That sounds...interesting," she said. "Um...tell me more."

Yolanda's voice became excited. Obviously she had been thinking about this for a while. "Well, Mama had sisters and brothers we haven't seen in ages. One of them called me the other day from El Paso. She's eighty-nine, and when I told her you were coming, she broke down and started crying. Said she hadn't seen everyone in years, and asked if she could take the bus out here." Yolanda took a deep breath and met Silvia's eyes. "I know it's...it's been hard for you, Silvie, but things are different now. We're all older, wiser..."

Yolanda stopped, and in the silence, her unspoken words hung over the table like a fog. She took a deep breath. "When I knew you were coming back, I figured you had finally decided to let the past stay in the past, and I was so happy. I think a family reunion would be so good, don't you?''

Silvia started to speak then stopped. If only she *could* put the past behind her...

"A family reunion," Silvia finally managed to repeat. "That would be really...something, Yolanda. I'd hate to see you go to that much work, though. It's not necessary, really."

"But I'd like to do it for you, *chica*. The kids—they need to get to know their family better anyway. You're a good excuse for it."

Silvia took a sip of her tea. "So you'd invite everyone? All the aunts and uncles?"

Grinning, Yolanda nodded.

"Our cousins? And their children?"

"That's right," she said. "It'd be really fun. Please say yes, and let me do this for you."

What else could Silvia do? "I'd love it," she said, a smile that she hoped at least looked sincere lifting her lips. "But you've got to let me help. Okay?"

"It's a deal." Beaming now, Yolanda took another bite of her lunch. "So tell me about your investigation," she asked a moment later. "Is it going well so far?"

"I haven't really started yet. I need some files and things like that first—"

"But Rick's helping you, right? I mean...the two of you are working together on this?"

Silvia tensed. They *never* spoke about Rick. It was one of the unwritten rules they had practiced throughout the years over the telephone. Apparently Yolanda believed the rule no longer applied. To correct her would only draw attention to the matter, so Silvia answered the question, her voice as neutral as she could make it.

"We're working on the same case," she said cautiously, "but I wouldn't really say we're working together—"

"I haven't seen him lately." Yolanda looked out the window to their side. It faced the courthouse. "He wasn't looking very good after the divorce."

Silvia didn't know what to say so she remained silent. Her sister turned and looked her straight in the eye. "He took it hard, you know."

"Divorces can be difficult."

"She left him for another man. A rich, older man. He took her to Dallas, but it didn't last long, and she came back here. I see her all the time. Her mama lives over on Sabine Street, but she doesn't live with her.... I don't know where she actually lives."

Silvia absorbed the news. She didn't know Rick's wife. Realized she didn't *want* to know her.

Yolanda starting speaking again, her voice holding a curious note. It should have sounded a warning bell for Silvia, but it didn't, and her next words hit her with a surprising punch.

"They never had children."

Now it was Silvia's turn to stare out the window.

"He does a lot of work at the elementary school, though. He loves kids. He even has his own little baseball team. They play every Saturday and—"

"That's enough." Silvia interrupted her sister abruptly, her gaze going to her sister's face. "I get the picture."

She'd been about to bite into her sandwich, but at Silvia's words, Yolanda's hands froze, her expression immediately turning apologetic. She put the food back down on her plate, her forehead wrinkling in distress.

"Oh, Silvie...I'm sorry. I wasn't trying to be mean.... I just didn't think—"

Silvia's voice was clipped, but she knew her eyes were glimmering with unexpected emotion. "Forget it. I certainly have."

She turned her face back to the window, a knot forming inside her throat at the lie she'd just told. She hadn't forgotten a thing and both of them knew it. The past was as real for her today as it had been eighteen years ago....

When she'd lost Rick's love...and then his child.

Silvia was sitting on the porch reading the paper when Rick pulled his car up to the curb. A shaft of sunlight slanted through the arms of a nearby live oak and highlighted the red tints in her hair. When she heard the car, she lifted her head and looked toward him, her expression going from curious to guarded all in a matter of seconds. He sat motionless for a moment longer and let his gaze stay on hers, the tension between them so strong it managed to span the yard and creep into his car like an unwanted guest.

It had been eighteen years since he'd touched her, but it didn't feel that way. Sometimes, hearing a song on the radio, he could recall the silky feel of her skin or smell the clean scent of her hair as if he'd left her side only moments before. Sometimes, like today, it felt as if their past had happened in another lifetime...to another person.

He opened the door and climbed out of the car, the heat of her stare burning into his back as he reached inside to pick up the folder of reports that was his excuse for coming over. They'd been sitting in his fax machine when he'd gotten to work. For fifteen minutes, in the silence of the Saturday morning at his office, he'd stared at the curling pages. Finally—quickly so he wouldn't change his mind—he'd ripped them off the machine and strode outside to the car.

She was standing by the time he reached the porch steps.

"You're up early," she said.

He held the folder out to her. "I thought you might need these."

She came toward him, then two steps down, the faint trace of Chanel No.5 coming with her. Her brown eyes were curious as she took the folder and looked inside. "My papers…" she murmured almost to herself. "Oh, yes." She looked up. "You didn't have to bring them. They could have waited until Monday."

"It's not a problem." He wanted to close his eyes and take a deep breath, to pull in her perfume and hold it against him. But he didn't. Couldn't. Wouldn't. "I was coming this way anyway."

An awkward moment of silence, then she gestured toward the porch, almost reluctantly it seemed to him. "Would you like some coffee? I just fixed a fresh pot, and there's plenty—"

The screen door creaked unexpectedly and they both turned, Rick resisting his automatic urge to put his hand on his gun. In the shadows, equally surprised it seemed, Carlos froze. After a moment, he pushed the door open the rest of the way and came outside, the old wooden boards of the porch complaining under his steps.

What was Carlos doing here, so early on Saturday morning? Rick would have expected to see him at the city golf course, or maybe even at his office, but not here at Yolanda's this time of day on a weekend. Carlos nodded to Rick, the barest of acknowledgments, then turned to Silvia and spoke rapidly in Spanish. It was a question, his voice going up a notch at the end.

She answered him in English. "The party's set for next Saturday. She's going to hold it here." She turned back and faced Rick, a pleasant noncommittal smile on her face. "Yolanda's planning a family reunion. The prodigal daughter and all that."

Without revealing he'd understood everything Carlos had said anyway, Rick spoke. "It sounds nice."

"She should have consulted me first." Carlos's voice was tight. "I have meetings planned for that day. I will be very busy with them."

"That's a shame," Silvia answered. "Maybe you can work something out?" She turned back to Rick. "Now, how about that coffee?"

Behind her, Carlos's expression turned dark. He wasn't accustomed to being ignored—especially by a woman. Surely Silvia knew this by now, Rick thought. She'd been back long enough to see her brother hadn't changed a lot. Long enough to know he still hated Rick and still felt the world owed him more than he was getting.

"You need to change the date." Carlos wasn't ready to give up. "Please see that Yolanda knows that day is not acceptable. The following week would be better—"

Silvia turned slowly. Her voice was pleasant, but Rick could hear the tension underneath. "We can't change the date. She's already invited people. I'm busy right now, Carlos. Could we please discuss this later?"

Carlos turned his dark eyes on Rick. His stare was cold and calculating, meant to intimidate. Rick met it easily yet he couldn't help but wonder what it would feel like if he were one of Carlos's clients. One of his poor clients who didn't speak English very well and who couldn't read at all.

Rick had met one of them a few weeks ago. A brave one, a migrant farmworker, who'd had the courage to come to the courthouse and ask for Rick. He had explained in a soft voice about what was really going on in Carlos's plush offices. About how Carlos promised citizenship papers to his clients who didn't know he couldn't legitimately provide them. About how he wasn't around when the INS wouldn't accept the bogus papers, and about how the innocent and bewildered illegal aliens were then shipped back to Mexico without the chance to confront Carlos. And why did he do these things to his own people, take advantage of them like this?

For money, pure and simple. When the worker had told Rick what he'd paid for the false papers, Rick's stomach had knotted with disgust. Now he understood who had paid for Carlos's fancy house, his brand-new car, his thousand-dollar suits.

Knowing right from wrong, the poor man sitting in Rick's office had risked everything to sneak back to San Laredo and get his family, their dreams of being real Americans shattered. But later, when Rick had hunted for him, he had already disappeared. The man was smart. He wanted to stay alive.

Rick had immediately tried to get an arrest warrant for Carlos, but without the witness, it had been impossible, the county judge looking at him as if he were nuts. Carlos was well thought of in San Laredo—Rick would need more than a now absent victim and just his suspicions, the judge had explained.

So he'd get more. Carlos had to have help at the INS office for his scheme to be successful. Rick would ferret them out, then they'd all be out of business. Corrupt government officials were something he wouldn't tolerate. Not in his county.

Carlos stared at him a moment longer, then he swirled around and went inside. In the hot silence, Silvia watched the screen door bang shut. Shaking her head, she turned back to Rick. "I'm sorry—"

"You don't have to apologize for him."

"He shouldn't have been so rude but..." She shrugged her shoulders, an eloquent movement that said more than her words could express. "I think he has a lot on his mind, actually. He told me a little about his practice last night, and it seems like he's really busy. If he'll have clients here all day, I guess it would be a problem for him."

"Here?" Rick's radar went on full alert. "He brings clients here? To Yolanda's? Why doesn't he use his office downtown?"

"Some of his clients don't feel comfortable going there. He said last night a lot of times he has a lot of meetings here." She looked up at the house. "This is the kind of home they're used to. Offices can be intimidating sometimes, especially to his pro bono clients who might not be accustomed to them. This is more hospitable, more private."

Lots more private, Rick thought to himself. Especially if you were meeting with people who didn't want to be associated with you...like government officials.

Silvia looked down at her tennis shoes then back up to Rick. "You have to give him credit for being understanding," she said. "Not too many lawyers even bother to be that sensitive about their clients."

She was still defending him. Rick couldn't believe it. For a moment, because of her earlier obvious irritation with Carlos, he'd thought she'd come to her senses, but now he realized the truth. She was still defending him...probably always would.

"—coffee?"

He realized too late Silvia had been speaking. Her eyes were on his, a questioning cast waiting in their dark depths.

And that's when he realized what he had to do. Realized there was only one way to figure it all out. He had to see for himself what Carlos had going on that he didn't want to take place at his office. Just as importantly, Rick had to know who else might be involved with him.

He would come to the reunion.

If he couldn't somehow wrangle an invitation from Silvia, then he'd think up an excuse. He'd do whatever it took. A twinge of momentary guilt came into his mind, but he pushed it away. Nothing was more important than getting Carlos Hernandez. Nothing.

"I can't stay," he said abruptly. "The office is always busy on Saturday and I told my secretary I'd catch up on my paperwork."

She nodded slowly, but her eyes told him she knew he was lying. From interested and lively, they'd gone to distant and remote, their brown depths almost appearing lighter, somehow. "Some other time perhaps," she answered, her voice already a notch cooler.

"Some other time," he said.

They stared at each other for one more heartbeat, then Rick turned around and left. There was nothing left to say.

Chapter 4

After all these years, Rick Hunter was still mad at her.

Not content to just turn down her first attempt at reconciliation, Rick wanted to make his feelings really clear...and he had. His abrupt departure and cool attitude had left little room for interpretation. Watching him climb into the black-and-white patrol car, its door covered by the county emblem promising Fairness and Justice for All, Silvia was surprised by how sharply that realization stung. She'd walked out on him eighteen years ago and he'd never forgiven her. Never *would* forgive her.

If he only knew the whole truth....

For a long time she'd thought the miscarriage had been her fault. That she'd somehow willed it to happen. Alone and desperate she'd had no one to depend on, but herself and Yolanda's charity. A baby would have been the last thing she'd needed, and she knew it. Afterward, though, the guilt had come. Maybe if she'd toughed it out and stayed in San Laredo, maybe if she'd believed in Rick, maybe if she'd taken better care of herself. Maybe, maybe, maybe... She knew now how ridiculous it was to feel so responsible for something so far outside her command, but still...

Secrets. So many secrets.

Carlos's voice interrupted her thinking. "Is he gone?"

She turned and looked at her brother, a mixture of anger and understanding coming over her. "Yes," she answered patiently. "Rick's left...but I didn't appreciate your attitude toward him, Carlos. Speaking Spanish like that was rude."

He pushed open the screen door and came outside to stand on the granite gravel walk beside her. Making an elaborate ceremony out of lighting a cigar, he finally looked at her when he finished. "He has no business here. I don't think you should be seeing him."

Anger flared inside her like the match he'd just struck, but she stayed calm. Calm and cool. That was the key to dealing with people like her brother. People who had to control everything and everyone.

"I'm not *seeing* Rick," she said calmly, "but if I were, it would be none of your business. You no longer have the right to tell me what to do. I'm thirty-six years old now, Carlos." She tilted her head and smiled in what she hoped was an engaging way. "You do understand, don't you?"

"Of course." He smiled back, an easy expression that crinkled the corners of his dark eyes and deepened the brackets around his generous mouth. "But I would think after everything that has happened, you would have more sense about you, Silvia. You *are* thirty-six years old. Doesn't that mean you've learned something, eh?'' His voice was friendly, big-brother advice and all that, it said.

"I've learned not to let other people's opinions influence me,'' she answered quietly. "I've learned I have to take care of myself and not depend on anyone else to do it for me.''

A cloud of blue cigar smoke drifted across the yard, its pungent bitterness replacing the clear, crisp air of the morning scent. From inside the house, the sounds of pots and pans could be heard, Yolanda's comforting tones mixing with canned laughter coming from cartoons playing on the television set in the living room.

He finally spoke. "Not even Rick Hunter?''

She answered instantly. "Not even Rick Hunter.''

Stop here, a voice inside her warned. Leave it alone, and don't say another thing, or you'll regret it. She heard the words—and then ignored them.

"If I were to need someone, though, I certainly might turn to him. He's grown into a capable man, I think.'' To give herself time to think, she reached for the coffee mug she'd set down on the railing and took a sip, even though the brew had cooled. Over the rim of the china, she met Carlos's gaze. "I wouldn't hesitate to depend on him.''

In the smoke between them, her brother's face seemed to waver, and his eyes narrowed. On the cigar he held, his fingers tightened. The first hint of guarded tension entered his tone. "But you don't even know the man.''

"And you do?''

He held out his hands expansively. It was meant to look like a relaxed movement, but to Silvia's trained eyes, it was false and contrived. "I've lived here all my life. I've seen him in action.'' He laughed lightly, almost apologetically. "He's exactly what he was eighteen years ago, *chiquita.* A rich gringo who doesn't understand the first thing about real life. He has no appreciation—for anything. You're naive if you think differently."

Shrugging her shoulders, she spoke. "Well, everyone's entitled to an opinion."

"That isn't opinion, Silvia." He pointed his cigar at her then waved it in the air. "It's fact."

Silvia waited a moment then spoke softly. "Your opinion has always been fact, Carlos. To you if no one else."

His eyes blazed momentarily, then he dropped the remaining stub of his cigar and ground it with his heel into the gravel of Yolanda's walk. When he lifted his foot, there was nothing left but tiny shreds of tobacco. His barely suppressed anger shimmered between them.

"Are you analyzing me, Silvia? Is this what they taught you to do at that fancy school you went to?"

Something ticked inside her, a little internal noise that said any hope she'd had of reconciliation had just been revealed for what it was—useless. For some undefined reason she'd probably never know, Carlos was still as angry and defensive as he had been when he'd kicked her out eighteen years ago. The realization made her sad.

She spoke softly, gently…regretfully. "I don't think you need analyzing, Carlos. That's for people who don't know who they are. You don't have that problem."

"That's right," he retorted, his eyes sudden slits. "I am exactly what you see. A simple man. A family man. And I can't believe that you would consort with someone who broke up this family years ago. *La familia* is everything to me. I care about what happens to us. And if you did as well, you'd stay away from Rick Hunter. He's as bad for you now as he was back then.'' He stared at her a moment longer, then strode down the walk, rage stiffening his gait, his hands clenched at his side.

Three days later, sitting in an unmarked car one block over from San Luis Street, Rick pulled his hat down lower over his eyes and waited patiently. When he'd been younger, waiting for a suspect had been his least favorite thing to do. His impatience had made the minutes stretch into hours and hours into days. But not now. Now he could wait forever because the downtime gave him time to think. Time to think about things he ordinarily wouldn't think about.

Like Silvia.

In the past eighteen years he'd relived their last night together a thousand times. How could Silvia have thought he'd killed Linda Willington? As a teenager, he'd been unable to accept her distrust, had decided she had simply never loved him and that's why she hadn't provided him with an alibi that night.

Then he'd grown up.

Shouldering the responsibility he hadn't accepted then, he had finally admitted the truth. That he'd looked guilty as hell that night. That he'd told Silvia he'd done something terrible. That he'd been covered in Linda's perfume and beer.

…and that he'd had sex with Linda when he was in love with Silvia.

He had hated to accept the reality, but the truth was the truth, and he had to acknowledge that now. He'd looked guilty, and he *was* guilty. Not of murder, but of infidelity, and *that* had definitely killed any hope of a real relationship with Silvia.

The question remained, though. Had Silvia ever loved him, or had it all been an act? The bitterness, the deception, the ripped-open feeling of being abandoned by someone he'd loved—he seemed incapable of getting rid of the feelings even though he accepted partial responsibility for them. Over the years, they'd simply changed and boiled down to their essence—which was a hard core of nothing.

He'd tried to get rid of the feeling, to bring back emotion into his life, but he'd finally realized a part of him actually didn't want to. If he didn't have the hole inside him, then what would be there? Love for a woman that was lost to him? That wasn't acceptable, was it? His ex-wife had made it more than clear that she didn't think he was even capable of love.

Had she been right? He didn't know for sure, but the emptiness was so familiar, it felt as comfortable as the hat he now wore.

Until lately. Until Silvia's return. In the short time she'd been back, she'd stirred up emotions inside him he'd ignored and suppressed for years. What in the hell did she think she was doing? Her presence was not only screwing him up, it was going to jeopardize his investigation of Carlos as well, and that was something Rick couldn't afford to even think about.

His hands tightened on the steering wheel while his gaze swept over the street in front of him. In the days since he'd learned Carlos met clients at Yolanda's house, Rick had stepped up his investigation of the man. He'd put an undercover man on the job, trailing Carlos, watching his office, asking some discreet questions. Rick had been amazed at the opulent life-style his investigation had so far uncovered. Rick had been aware of the cars, the clothes, the nice jewelry, but Carlos appeared to have more assets than Rick had ever thought, much more than a small-time attorney could ever earn in a single practice. He'd been shocked.

The only really important thing he had picked up so far, though, was something he already knew. Carlos was still an arrogant, self-centered hypocrite who cared for no one but himself. Money meant everything to him.

A black BMW appeared at the end of the block, and Rick tensed. The expensive sedan belonged to Carlos. Reaching for his keys, Rick started his car's engine but didn't put it in gear. He would want to stay back, way back. Carlos was a cunning bastard—he hadn't gotten as far as he had on simple luck and hard work. He might already know he was under surveillance and be looking for signs.

Watching the BMW take off in a dusty cloud, Rick counted to twenty, then edged the nondescript white sedan forward.

Fifteen minutes later, from a vantage point so far away he could barely make out the black BMW anymore, Rick watched Carlos pull into the driveway of a small, ordinary-looking house. The garage door came up and he pulled inside, lowering the door immediately. He obviously had an opener to the garage.

Rick stared hard at the little house. Trim red brick sparkled in the baking sun, and someone had planted several rows of lantana along the sidewalk. A huge red oak shaded one side. The windows glistened in the bright sunlight, curtains moving slightly in the breeze behind them. The whole place was well tended if modest; there was certainly nothing strange about it that he could tell.

Except its location. The house sat on the last lot of Cemetery Road.

The empty stretch of land next to the house where the bodies had been found made the little home look lonely and isolated. Once the pasture had been a thriving cotton field, but the farmer who'd plowed it had sold it after Linda's murder. After the second victim, Bonnie Kelman, had been killed there, Rick had checked into the ownership of the parcel and learned a big corporation out of Houston held the title and paid the taxes. He'd dug further, to see who the person was behind the corporation, but no word so far. He made a mental note to call again. Whoever owned the field might own the house as well.

Pulling out a pair of binoculars, Rick turned his attention back to the house just in time to see Carlos step out of a door from the side of the garage and hurry across a sidewalk to disappear inside. Rick shifted his focus to the only window that fronted the road. The blinds were tilted, but as he watched, he could make out enough to tell what was going on.

Carlos walked inside, and a woman greeted him. A woman too thin and too blonde to be his wife. A woman who was now in his arms, her body pressed against his, her arms twined around his neck as he gripped her buttocks and pulled her closer. Rick strained, but it was hopeless—there was no way he could see who she was from this far away.

But he'd find out. He'd definitely find out.

Tuesday afternoon Silvia went straight to her office, looking neither right nor left. After seeing Rick on Saturday, when he'd made his feelings so clear, all she wanted was to get her job done and leave town. The easiest way to accomplish that task was to stay clear of him and the distractions he presented. Carlos had been right about that point, if nothing else. Rick Hunter *was* bad for her—for her and her investigation. She hurried inside and shut the door.

He must have felt the very same way. A stack of folders was already lying in the center of her desk, a terse note paper-clipped to the edge of the one on top. ''These are the files you requested.'' Rick's sprawling signature covered the bottom half of the paper. Clearly he'd brought them in early, sparing him the possibility of seeing her.

Trying not to think about what that really meant, she went to work quickly, scanning the documents, briefly looking at the photos, trying to get a feel for the crimes as much as anything.

Unfortunately, it was quick work. The folder on Linda's murder was excruciatingly thin because Robert Tully's old boss, Sheriff Walters, had let the case grow cold then die. Like countless murder files Silvia had read before in countless other states, this one contained the same tired excuse for a resolution—he'd blamed the killing on a drifter, an ''unknown Hispanic male.''

The day before her death, the report read, Linda had been seen talking with a migrant worker passing through town, a man in his twenties, well built and strong-looking. They were seen in front of one of the small, local diners, then later that afternoon, they both drove off in Linda's car.

The sheriff had assumed the rest. A transient, the man had killed her then fled, a seduction gone awry. Walters hadn't been able to close the case without an arrest, but he'd obviously decided the killer posed no threat to anyone else because of his interest in Linda. Linda's mother, a poor, single woman, hadn't had the resources to pursue the investigation more, and it'd finally been dropped.

No one pointed out the fact that Linda and her mother farmed a small plot of land behind their broken-down farmhouse. Linda could have been taking the man home to get something done on the farm that she and her mother couldn't have handled. Everyone had just assumed the worst…of Linda.

Silvia made a sound of disgust. The sheriff should have tried harder. Linda Willington had been a real person, someone who mattered. Her penchant for men shouldn't have affected the kind of investigation her death had received. She was as worthy as the next victim, not less.

The file on Bonnie Kelman was thicker, more complete. It was obvious Rick was in the process of conducting a very thorough investigation. There were photos of the crime scene, along with measurements and diagrams, plus a folder full of reports.

Looking through the summary first, Silvia saw that no fingerprints had been obtained. The open field where Bonnie had been found had made that task pointless. Fingerprints off bodies were notoriously hard to work with, too. Trace evidence had been negligible as well, with the weather and elements destroying anything that might have been there to begin with. The only blood found had been the victim's own. She'd had sex, but semen samples meant little without a suspect with which to match them. She'd been shot with a large-caliber gun.

Silvia scanned the papers then decided to go back to Linda's case and began at the beginning.

The photos were gruesome. Silvia swallowed hard as

she stared at them, Linda's body forever frozen at the age of eighteen, her eyes open and blank, a gaping hole obscenely located where her heart would have been. There was nothing but horror in her expression, no clue, no hints to give away whose face she'd seen last.

Her shorts, partially ripped and halfway off her body, revealed a bit more, their edges torn and shredded, almost to rags. Whoever had killed her had been angry, very angry. In her mind, Silvia tentatively labeled the scene as a mixed one. There were elements showing it had been thought out—therefore it was organized—but not too well. It was disorganized, too. It didn't appear to be a planned murder. Despite the use of a gun, she had the distinct feeling this had been a crime of passion, a crime of opportunity. The killer had taken advantage of a situation, then fled.

Silvia dropped the photos and closed her eyes. She always tried to maintain a professional distance, but even after having seen thousands of photos like this, these sickened her. What kind of person would do this to another human being? She rubbed her eyelids, but the images refused to leave.

Taking a deep breath, she went back to work, picking up the reports on trace evidence and the autopsy. One thing caught Silvia's eye immediately. The report wasn't conclusive, but the coroner had said there was a possibility of two types of semen present. And two kinds of skin had definitely been found under her fingernails. The rape evidence seemed shaky to Silvia, but what else could it have been? Sex that had somehow gotten out of hand? Consensual sex with two partners? Sex with a lover, then sex with someone else, too? The scenario seemed unlikely, even for Linda.

The evidence list offered no additional help. Everything that had been recovered at the scene of the crime was listed, including Linda's clothing and her watch that had been smashed, stopping at ten minutes before 1:00 a.m., the official time of her death. Silvia's gaze scanned the list to the bottom, her attention stopping at the last item, its description catching her eye since it was so generic.

"One piece—gold jewelry." The cramped and faded handwriting was barely legible, but Silvia was sure she'd read it right. A necklace, an earring? What? Her curiosity piqued, she thumbed through the papers, but found no other reference. Had the piece belonged to Linda or the killer? With manufacturer's stamps and limited runs, jewelry was often traceable—this could be important.

Silvia thought for just a moment, then her hand went to the phone and dialed Rick's number before she could give herself more time to think about it.

"The sheriff's not in. Can I take a message?"

Despite her concern, Silvia felt a moment's relief. "No, that's all right. You can tell me where the property room is, though. I need to check something out."

"Across the street on the first floor. Right-hand side of the hall."

"Where the library was? In the old courthouse?"

"That's it."

A few minutes later, Silvia was striding across Main Street and heading for the building that had housed the county library eighteen years ago. As she entered the dim, dusty building, she held back a groan. It still smelled musty and old, and the people behind the counters still looked at each other and every one else with suspicion. In fact, the dust motes dancing in the sunlight from the tall windows around the perimeter could have been the same ones she'd seen when she'd come here as a kid.

A decrepit sign on her right pointed to the last door down the main hall. Property Room. She headed down the hallway, her heels clicking on the peeling linoleum. A moment later, she entered what had been the main room of the library.

The shelves and desks were the same, but all the books had been replaced by brown paper sacks and small cardboard boxes. Rows and rows of bags and boxes, each labeled with numbers and dates. A mesh of wire had been stretched across the front desk to keep the area restricted.

Silvia rang the bell sitting on the counter. A second later, footsteps could be heard. She halfway expected to see old Mrs. Bailey, the former librarian, but the harried clerk who appeared was someone she didn't know.

From behind the wire, he glared at her with suspicious black eyes. "Yeah?"

"Hello, I'm Dr. Hernandez. I'm working on a case for Sheriff Hunter, and I need to see some evidence, please."

He pointed to a pile of request slips lying on the counter. "Fill that out, then I'll look for it."

His surliness was understandable. Who would willingly want to work in the dusty, remote confines of the property room? Following his instructions, she handed him the completed form with Linda Willington's case number on it then prepared to wait. It would take him a while to find the bag. After this many years, it would surely have been moved to the archives. When he didn't immediately step away from the counter, she turned back and stared at him.

He was looking under the cabinet in front of him, a

puzzled expression on his face. Under her gaze, he bent down then straightened up, a brown cardboard carton in his rough hands. "This the one you want?"

Silvia glanced in surprise toward the number on the side, then back to the man's face. "That's it," she answered. "What's it doing so close? I wasn't even sure you'd still have it. I thought you'd have to go back to get it—"

"It seems to be a popular one today. Already had somebody ask for it."

"And who would that be?"

He looked at her with an air of superiority, his eyebrows arching in a studied way. He must practice that in the mirror every morning, she thought. "That's confidential."

Mildly irritated, Silvia thought briefly of going and getting Rick. Maybe his word would be enough to breach security, but her impatience got the better of her. She reached across and scribbled her name on the fresh sign-in sheet the man had thrust over the counter.

A moment later, the clerk unlocked the wire door and motioned for her to come in. She stepped behind the counter, a strange feeling coming over her as he bolted the door behind her, locking them both inside a smaller, examination room.

He dropped the box on a nearby table, the heavy thump echoing against the high ceiling. "I shut down at five forty-five. You'll have to be finished by then."

Silvia nodded without a word, her attention already focusing on the box in front of her, her heart suddenly beating unexpectedly faster. With fingers that weren't too steady, she lifted the lid, a musky smell rising up to meet her.

It held a single manila envelope, the rape kit and a see-through plastic bag.

The rape kit would contain only nonperishable samples they'd taken from the body that night, so Silvia ignored it and reached instead for the clear plastic bag. It held the clothing Linda had worn. From the crime scene photos, Silvia recognized the pair of ripped shorts—no longer white—and Linda's pink-striped T-shirt, torn and bloody. A pair of panties and a bra were pushed to one side. Despite the holes in both of them where samples had been taken, they were neatly folded as if someone had cared. One grungy tennis shoe weighed down the bottom. That was it. Nothing gold.

Silvia turned to the envelope and shook out the contents.

A single smaller plastic bag came tumbling out.

Shock rippled over her in an unexpected wave. With shaking fingers, she reached out and picked up the plastic bag to stare at it, a small groan of disbelief escaping from between her lips. Her fingers closing tightly around the bag, she shook her head and closed her eyes tightly.

She didn't believe it. Didn't want to believe it…but her eyes couldn't lie. She opened them again and unclasped her fingers.

It was Rick's Saint Christopher medal.

The round gold disk looked as shiny and new as it had eighteen years ago when she'd placed it around his neck.

She groaned again, then bit off the sound, looking around quickly to see if the clerk had noticed. He was standing beside his counter, watching her. Her gaze hit his, then he jerked his head down and tried to look busy.

She slowly put the plastic bag back into the envelope. Dropping it into the box, she slid on the top and stood.

Rick hadn't killed Linda.

But he'd been there that night, and here was the proof.

Silvia's stomach turned over in a churning movement of anxiousness. Why? What had he been doing? What did it all mean? She thought back to the perfume, the smell of beer. Remembering it now, she sucked in her breath, a dizzying buzz sounding in her ears.

In a daze, she walked toward the counter and set the box down by the sign-in clipboard.

In spite of his earlier concerns, the clerk had carelessly flipped the page to reveal the one on top of Silvia's. She glanced down automatically and stared at the sprawling signature of the person who'd checked out the box before her, her nerves jumping, her brain going into overtime.

She'd just seen the same signature minutes before in her own office and she immediately recognized the powerful strokes slashing across the page.

Sheriff Rick Hunter.

Chapter 5

By the time Silvia made her way back to the main building, it was past six o'clock, and everyone had left. The lonely halls echoed with her footsteps, her heels beating an uneasy rhythm that matched her heart rate. She went straight to Rick's office, the golden image of the medallion burning too brightly in her mind to be ignored.

He wasn't there.

The secretary was walking out the door, locking it behind her. "He's already gone," she said, juggling her purse, her lunch sack and an empty coffeepot. "Baseball practice tonight."

Something Yolanda had said tickled the back of her mind, but the question popped out automatically, Silvia's brain somehow refusing to accept Rick had a life beyond the law. "He plays baseball?"

The secretary looked at Silvia as if she'd misplaced her brain. "No—he coaches. Little League."

Silvia nodded, remembering then, as the information soaked in slowly, that this was what Yolanda had told her. But she'd turned it off, tried not to listen. She didn't want to know things like this about Rick because it made her look at him differently. Made her think about what could have been.

If they'd had children—one that had survived—Rick might be coaching that same child right now.

The idea left her reeling, speechless almost, but she had to say something. The secretary was staring at her even more strangely now. "I...I didn't know...."

"We can always get in touch with him. If he's not in his car, we can beep him if it's an emergency, or you can leave him a message at the front if it's nothing important. He calls dispatch once or twice every evening, and checks in." She nodded toward the front of the building. "Go up there and tell Susie to have him call you."

"I...I guess I'll do that."

With the secretary's eyes on her back, Silvia headed toward the front of the building. She left the message, then went straight to her car, her legs trembling, her mind still on the image of Rick throwing a ball to a little kid. Calling Yolanda on her cell phone to let her know she wouldn't be there for dinner, Silvia headed for the local diner. Maybe a little time alone, time to think, would be a good idea.

Things were getting awfully complicated.

Ten minutes later, she pulled into the parking lot at Sharkey's and killed the engine.

Walking inside, the first thing Silvia realized was that Sharkey's hadn't changed in the eighteen years she'd been gone. The little diner where they'd hung out as teens was as grungy and tacky as ever. The same red plastic chairs sat around the same aluminum-legged tables, and it even looked as though the same grim-faced man was flipping burgers by the grill on the right-hand side. The details registered through a fog of confusion.

Silvia took the first booth she came to and sat down. The waitress appeared, and she ordered a salad and iced tea. As soon as the woman stepped away from the table, Silvia had the image again. The image of Rick and a little boy.

She'd never actually been told the sex of the child she'd lost. The nurses had started to say something, but Silvia had closed her ears. She hadn't wanted to know, hadn't wanted to connect with a child she could never hold. She closed her eyes now and rubbed them. The truth was the truth, though. She'd known all along because one of the women had later slipped and said something, and Silvia had heard her.

The child had been a boy.

She'd had Rick's son, then lost him. Grief welled inside her as fresh as if it had happened yesterday, and a moan escaped her. She picked up her iced tea glass with shaking hands and took a sip, pushing the feeling back down, way down, as she usually did.

It was history, she told herself. In the past. Over and done with. She ought to be thinking about the case and if nothing else, asking herself about that gold medallion, not thinking about Little League.

The waitress appeared with her salad. Placing it before Silvia, she turned around and left without a word. The lettuce tasted like cardboard. Silvia could have been eating that just as easily. A second later, a voice broke into her thoughts.

"Mind if I join you?"

She jerked her gaze upward, knowing it was Rick before she'd even moved. He looked tanned and relaxed, a baseball cap covering his tousled hair, his sunglasses dangling from his fingers. Out of uniform, he looked…better. That was the only word she could think of. Just better. Her heart thumped once, then once again.

"I heard you were looking for me. I called in a little while ago, and dispatch said you'd left a message."

"And you tracked me down here?" she said with amazement.

He laughed out loud. "My powers of investigation aren't that grand. No, I called Yolanda's house, and one of the kids told me I might find you here." He slid into the seat opposite her, not waiting for an invitation. "What's going on?"

His intensity seemed to reach across the table and physically touch her. It was so strong, it blocked her ability to think straight, to organize her thoughts, especially about the case. She shivered slightly under his gaze, then told herself to relax, to breathe, to forget about the way he used to hold her and kiss her and bring her to the edge of her control.

She drew a deep, ragged breath, then touched her lips with her napkin. *Concentrate,* she said to herself. *Concentrate.* "I was reading the case files today on Linda and Bonnie when I found something I didn't understand. An entry in the evidence log that I found later in the box."

Rick nodded. "And that was…?"

She wanted to ignore his question and ask her own, but the words refused to come. Instead, they got stuck in her throat where they refused to go further and stayed to burn painfully.

What really happened that night, Rick? Tell me the truth, please. Let me know.

Taking a deep breath, she finally answered him, his

eyes boring into hers. "It...it was a gold medallion. A Saint Christopher medal in yellow gold on a heavy chain. It...it looked like the one I gave you."

The words froze him into stillness. He didn't even blink.

"Was it...was it yours?" she asked.

The silence that stretched between them seemed to go on for years. Finally, he spoke. "Yes."

That was all he said. One single word. She waited for him to say more, but he didn't.

"Can you elaborate?" she said stiffly.

"What more do you want? You asked me a question, and I answered it. Do you have additional questions?"

A thousand, she thought instantly. But she kept herself to just one. "Yes, I do," she answered softly. "I'd like to know how it got there. How it got into that evidence box."

"I'm sure you *would* like to know," he replied, his own voice just as level and steady as hers. "But that's not going to happen. At least, not right now."

She blinked and tried to understand. "What are you saying?"

"I'm saying that I'm not going to answer your question. This isn't the time."

"Oh, come on, Rick—"

He interrupted her by raising his hand. "Please." His dark gaze wrapped itself around her and reached deep inside. She felt it touch a part of her that hadn't been touched in a very long time. "Don't ask me more right now. I'll tell you about it when the time is right."

"And when will that be?"

"I'm not sure," he answered. "But you'll know. I promise."

There was nothing else she could do. Pressing him

would only make things worse, and part of her accepted the fact that she didn't want to do that anyway. Not yet.

"All right," she said finally. "I'll trust you—on this."

He smiled, and a little of the tension, so thick only moments before, seemed to seep away from the table. Strangely enough, Silvia couldn't deal any better with the relaxed Rick. It put them on too different a footing. She searched for a way to get more distance between them, and found it easily.

"Can we talk about the case?"

"Absolutely."

"I was wondering, then.... Have you done any ballistic testing."

"Ballistic testing?"

"On the bullet from Bonnie Kelman. I...I'd like to know more about it."

"Of course we've ordered ballistic testing. That's SOP, you know that."

"Well, standard operating procedure isn't always followed," she said stiffly. "I just wanted to make sure you'd ordered the tests...so we wouldn't have to wait any longer than necessary."

He leaned back in the booth, his broad shoulders covering a wide section out of the middle of the red plastic upholstery. "I ordered the tests immediately after the autopsy was done, and the bullet removed. We might be a long way from D.C., Silvia, but we're not ignorant hicks. The department here is a sophisticated one. We have drug problems that demand we be on our toes."

"I...wasn't trying to imply you weren't." She rolled the paper napkin under her fingers into a small, tight tube. "It's just that I've been to bigger places with larger staffs than yours and seen mistakes you wouldn't believe. I can't do my job if I don't have all the information.''

He leaned forward and put his hands on the table, clasping them together in front of her. Her eyes automatically went to his fingers. They were broad with flat, even nails and she couldn't help but let her gaze go to his left hand, ring finger. It was bare, of course. Bare and tanned with smooth-looking skin that she found herself wanting to touch and not believing that she was actually even having the thought.

''You'll have all the information I've got,'' he said slowly, oblivious to the path her thoughts had taken. ''In fact, you can have anything I've got, Silvia. Anything. You just have to tell me you want it.''

Her heart throbbed painfully in her chest. He was talking about the case, she repeated to herself, the case, nothing more. ''I...I really appreciate that,'' she managed to reply. ''It'll make my job a lot easier...but why have you decided to be so cooperative? I thought you didn't want me here.''

''I don't,'' he said without pausing. ''But I'm a realist. You're here and that's a fact, so I might as well accept it.'' He stopped then and stared at her. ''Just tell me one thing, though. Why did you decide to come? The last I'd heard you were out of the field for good.''

She looked down at the tabletop and the scattered pieces of rolled napkin she'd somehow begun to mutilate without even knowing it. ''I didn't have a choice,'' she said finally. ''My boss told me it was time to get back out in the field or give it up completely.''

''And why did you leave in the first place?'' he asked quietly. ''You had a helluva career going. I heard rumors, but I want to know the truth about it. What happened?''

Swallowing past the lump in her suddenly dry throat, Silvia looked up and into Rick's eyes. For the first time since she'd come back, his expression wasn't guarded, wasn't veiled, as he took her in. He was telling the truth. He simply wanted to know what had happened to her…and she didn't want to think about why he wanted to know.

"I made a mistake," she said softly. "A terrible mistake…and somebody died because of it."

Her throat closed, but she forced herself to relax and continue. "I wrote a report about a killing after doing an initial investigation. I named the number one suspect as the probable killer. At the time, it seemed like a clear-cut answer. Everything about him fit the profile, except that he was too young, didn't fit into the age bracket. That had happened before and we'd still gotten the right guy, so I ignored that fact—called it an anomaly in my report—and went on about my merry way."

She shut her eyes for a moment, then opened them again. "But somehow, a reporter got hold of my findings and leaked them. The suspect hung himself in his jail cell. He was eighteen." She took a deep breath, pulled the air into her lungs as though it could cleanse the thoughts that could never be cleansed. "Two days later, the real murderer confessed."

Rick's voice pulled her back. "We do the best we can, Silvie. That's all we can do."

Her eyes flew to his. "Well, an eighteen-year-old kid is dead because my best wasn't good enough. I can't ever live that down."

"But you can't change it, either, can you? What's done is done. You have to go on and live and forget about it as much as you can."

"Is that what you'd do?"

His face clouded over, and when he spoke his voice was harsh. "I'm not perfect, Silvia. I never was, and I never will be. I can give out advice with the best of them, though. Just ask my ex...she'll tell you."

The waitress appeared at the table, a glaring smile now stretched across her face. "Hey there, Rick! I brought you the usual—that okay?" A giant plastic glass of iced tea sat on her tray.

"That's great, Janey. Thanks."

She smiled at him again, then put the glass on the table. "Getcha something else?"

He shook his head. "Thanks—this'll do it."

She gave him another megawatt smile, then threw a careless glance toward Silvia, turned around and left.

Silvia resumed the interrupted conversation. "Your divorce was not amicable, I take it?"

He made a sound of disgust. "The marriage wasn't even amicable. It should never have happened in the first place."

"So why did it?"

"I was tired of being alone. I wanted a family, a wife, a home to come to at the end of the day. It didn't exactly work out like I'd planned, but at least I gave it a shot."

His honesty surprised her, but not as much as his next question. "Didn't you ever want those things? Why haven't you ever married?"

Because I could never find a man like you. The answer popped into her head without warning. It took her a shocked second to compose another one. "I...I've been too busy," she answered lamely. "I guess I just haven't had time to miss what I didn't have."

He lifted one eyebrow as if to say "Come on." When

he spoke, his voice was polite. "It that right?" was all he said.

"Working for the DCA is very demanding. It doesn't allow for much of a social life." She looked down into her lap. That much, at least, was true. She didn't have many friends. When she'd first started at the DCA, she'd traveled too much to know her neighbors, then when she'd started staying in the office instead of doing fieldwork, she hadn't had the energy to meet them.

The one relationship she'd had, the only one that had really meant anything, had died a natural death after a year or so. He'd said she didn't share enough with him…and he'd been right. Sharing meant risk, and risk could lead to heartache. She'd already done that with Rick—risked everything—and the consequences had been devastating. She'd never totally give her heart again.

She looked up and into the dark eyes of the only man who'd had it. A curling lock of hair had fallen across his forehead, and in the dim light of the restaurant, his lips were so full and sexy, her breath caught in her throat like a trapped animal. He was virile. Powerful. Intense. A man like none she'd ever known before or since and suddenly all she could think about was how he'd touched her when they were teenagers. The desire they'd shared had been the most intense she'd ever experienced and ever since that time, she'd measured each man's touch to Rick's. They'd all come up short.

She couldn't help but wonder what it would feel like if he were to touch her now. A real touch. Not a polite handshake or a brief brush against her, but a real honest-to-goodness embrace where he took her into his arms and molded his body against hers.

Would the thrill be even greater now? She couldn't

imagine arousal any greater than she'd felt at eighteen, but Rick wasn't just any man, either. They shared a history, a past, a life that even Rick didn't know anything about. What deeper bond could there be between a man and a woman than that of having a child...even if the child hadn't lived.

He seemed to read her mind. Reaching across the table, he put his hand on her arm, the weight of his touch heavy and warm. It made her think of things she shouldn't be thinking of, and when he spoke, his voice matched it, the tones so deep and low they echoed inside her.

"I haven't been fair to you, Silvia. I gave you a hard time when you got here, and you're just trying to do your job. I'm sorry if I was rude."

Startled, by his words and his action, she nodded. "I...I understand."

"How can I make it up to you?"

She was shaking her head before he finished speaking. "There's nothing to make up for—"

"Well, I think there is. Let me take you to dinner Saturday night." He looked around the diner, then back at her, a wry expression on his face. "Somewhere a little nicer."

The invitation puzzled her. He knew the party was scheduled for Saturday, but at the same time, unbidden excitement snaked through her. "I can't," she said, pulling her arm away. "Yolanda's party is that night, remember? A party for me."

He smiled, one corner of his mouth going up just enough to make her notice. "Oh, yeah, the party, eh? One of Yolanda's bashes. Mmm, does she still make those wonderful *tamales?*"

She shouldn't do it. She knew she shouldn't do

it…but the words were out before she could stop them. "Why don't you just come on by?" she asked. "We'll eat at seven."

It had been too easy. Wrangling an invitation from Silvia to the party had been like taking a candy bar from one of his first-grade baseball players. Rick felt like that was exactly what he'd done. Guilt laid over him like a heavy blanket.

He made his excuses in his head. What else could he do? He had to see who was going to be at that party. If Carlos was in bed with the INS, Rick had to know. He told himself there was no other reason. He didn't just want to spend more time with Silvia, to get to know her better, to hear about the rest of her life. He didn't want that. He *couldn't* want that.

In separate cars, they pulled up to the curb outside Yolanda's house, a single light glowing in the living room. For a minute, all Rick could think about was how they used to do the very same thing when they were dating. He'd pull up to the house, then they'd sit in the car and talk until they knew Silvia had to go inside or risk the wrath of Carlos for coming home too late.

And talk wasn't all they'd do.

To dispel the heated memories that suddenly came into his mind, Rick threw open his car door and walked to Silvia's car just ahead of him. Opening her door, he helped her from the car then they started up the walk together. "You didn't need to follow me home," she said. "I think it's pretty safe around here."

It was extremely safe. She had a better chance of getting hit by a meteor than she did of running into a mugger in San Laredo, but Rick had wanted to see if anyone had been at the house, anyone he'd be interested in. He told himself that was the only reason, but he knew he was lying. "You can't ever be too careful," he answered calmly, "not this late at night."

As they reached the porch, though, Rick's denials broke down, and suddenly all he could think about was how she used to smell when he'd put his arms around her, right here, in the darkness. Sweet. Clean. So sexy it made him ache with desire. Just like he was aching now.

There was nothing he could do to alleviate the feelings. He had to ignore them. Turning to tell her goodnight, a sudden movement by the window caught Rick's eye. Without moving his head, he cut his eyes toward the glass just in time to see the curtains twitch. Someone had been waiting for them. Someone who was watching now.

It took him just a second to make up his mind. If Carlos Hernandez thought Rick and his sister were getting closer again, it just might somehow tip the scales. Angry men couldn't concentrate. He knew. They got careless, made mistakes, and all Rick needed was for Carlos to just make one—just one mistake. He could arrest him and put him away.

With that thought in mind and nothing else, Rick found himself reaching out for Silvia. Her eyes widened slightly as his intentions became clear, then before she could do more, he pulled her toward him. In another second, his lips were on hers, his arms around her body.

Nothing had changed. And everything had.

Her mouth was as warm and pliable as he remembered, but the figure in his arms had shifted. Pressing against him was the body of a woman—fully developed with hips that dipped in all the right places and curves that filled his mind with more possibilities. She resisted for just a second, then a small groan escaped from the back of her throat and she leaned into him.

Rick's body responded instantly, and his arms tightened even more as her lips parted slightly. He suddenly felt as though he'd been injected with something—some kind of magic elixir that heightened all of his senses at once. Without warning, the night air smelled fresher, the low sounds of a bird calling sounded sweeter, and when he opened his eyes and stared at Silvia, her skin seemed to be glowing in the pale wash of the moon overhead.

"Wh-what are you doing?" she said, her voice husky and raw.

"Kissing you," he replied.

"I know that, but wh-why?"

Why? He could think of a thousand replies. Because she'd never left his mind. Because he wanted her. Because he'd thought of this moment for all his adult life. But even as those answers came to him, he knew he couldn't voice them because he had too many questions of his own that were unanswered. Questions like, why did you doubt me? Why couldn't you have trusted me? The realization of why he'd taken her into his arms in the first place—because Carlos was watching—entered his mind so late it startled him. But he couldn't tell her that, either.

"I wanted to see if it would feel the same," he said finally, his eyes never leaving hers as though he could convince her this was the truth by the sheer force of his expression.

Her eyes seemed dazed, almost bewildered. She made no move to pull away from him and he realized she probably couldn't. Just as he was incapable of moving himself.

"Does it feel the same?" she asked, almost breathlessly.

"You tell me," he answered. Without thinking, he lifted one finger to caress the side of her cheek. Her skin felt like nothing he'd ever touched. "What do you think?"

The caress brought her out of her trance. "I...I think this is crazy," she said, stepping back away from him, the boards of the porch protesting as Rick wished he could. "I...I think we both got a little carried away and I think it shouldn't ever happen again." She straightened her skirt and patted the buttons on her blouse. Finally she looked up at him. "That's what I think."

He met her gaze, her mussed hair and swollen lips making him think of Sunday mornings and warm beds with crumpled sheets. Something he hadn't thought of in a very long time. Something with associations that suddenly scared him. Something that made him think of wives and long-term relationships.

"I think you're absolutely right," he answered in a suddenly thick voice, "but it's a little too late to take it back, isn't it?"

Chapter 6

By Saturday, Silvia was a complete wreck. She couldn't sleep, her stomach was upset, and concentrating on anything important was impossible.

Around four that morning, she got up, made herself a pot of coffee and stepped out on the porch with the first cup steaming in her hand. The street was silent and deserted, the empty quiet something she definitely needed in order to straighten her tangled thoughts.

Rick Hunter had some kind of power over her—that was all it could be. When he came near, her heart would go still until she thought something was wrong, then it'd leap against her ribs and pound with frantic speed. It was frightening, really. She could actually feel her blood coursing through her veins, her pulse almost animallike in its intensity. During her internship while obtaining her Ph.D. she'd done some therapy work, and one of her patients had described his panic attacks with sickening detail. His breath would stop in his chest, his heart would pound erratically, he'd almost pass out. The attacks had been horrifying to the man, and he'd been completely incapacitated with them.

Now—finally—she understood the feelings he'd been trying to explain.

Being around Rick had the same effect on her.

If she needed a perfect example, all she had to think about was the jewelry. Why hadn't she pushed him harder about the medallion the minute he'd refused to say more in the restaurant? It was the reason she'd been looking for him, dammit, and when he'd said he didn't want to talk about it, she should have told him that wasn't acceptable. Instead of doing that, with minimal fuss, she'd simply accepted his answer and said nothing more, had done exactly what he'd asked. Why? Was she scared of what he'd say? Scared of what the truth might mean?

He hadn't killed Linda Willington but something had definitely happened that night. What? Did the jewelry have something to do with the crime...or simply something to do with Linda and Rick? Why would it be there if it wasn't important to the case?

Why had she invited him to the party?

Why didn't she trust him?

Why, why, why...

A red line of dawning light eased above the roof of the house next door and a car turned the corner. Driving slowly and pausing before each house, the driver aimed the newspapers he was delivering with careful precision. When he reached Silvia's porch, he dropped the morning's issue three feet from where she was standing. She waved her appreciation, picked up the paper, and went inside. Her questions would have to wait.

Like they had for eighteen years.

* * *

The day went by as fast as the night had dragged. When Silvia looked up from her desk, and discovered it was one o'clock, all she could do was groan. Yolanda was going to kill her—she'd promised she'd be back at the house by noon and not a minute later. She'd offered to help with the party preparations and here she was, still sitting at her desk, still working. Gathering her things, Silvia quickly went out to her car and headed back to San Luis Street.

The curb in front of the house was already lined with cars by the time she got there. Groaning again, Silvia found a parking spot in the driveway and hurried up the walk. Before she was even inside, she could hear the laughter and talk of the women crowding around the kitchen table, their hands covered in *masa* and meat as they prepared the *tamales* for the feast that evening. Children were everywhere as well, screaming and laughing and chasing each other around and under the table like a room full of puppies.

The talk died when Silvia entered the kitchen, and for a moment, her heart failed. Sensing her discomfort, Yolanda immediately rushed to Silvia's side and began to fuss good-heartedly at her for being so late. Within seconds, as Yolanda introduced her to everyone and slipped an apron over Silvia's head, the conversation resumed with even more intensity. Smiling shyly at the women around her, Silvia soon felt as much a part of the festivities as anyone.

Which was really a strange sensation because she'd never really felt that way before...as if she belonged.

It was strange...and wonderful.

"Come on," Yolanda called out at the end of the table, grinning at Silvia as the afternoon passed. "You girls are too slow. How can we feed fifty people tonight if you don't roll faster? No wonder your men are all so skinny…you never have enough food to feed them right.''

One of the cousins at the other end began to protest. Silvia recognized her as one of Carl's sister's daughters. ''That's not true, 'Landa. Our men are skinny 'cause we keep them busy in bed!''

''Ohhh…'' The other women began to laugh, some nodding their heads, others covering their mouths as their amusement took hold of them.

''You should be so lucky, Elena,'' Yolanda answered, laughing herself. ''Your man doesn't even know what a real woman is…you're too skinny yourself! He needs a real woman like me to hold on to at night…to keep him warm in bed. You bring him over to my house, and I'll show him some real lovin'!''

Silvia giggled along with the rest of the women. Yolanda outweighed the girl by a good fifty pounds, and she had silver in her hair to boot. Everyone knew how devoted she was to her own husband, too. On the other hand, she was as beautiful as any of them there. She could still turn heads, and they all knew it…including Yolanda.

''Oh, no,'' Elena said, dramatically putting her hand on her chest and clutching it there. ''No way, Tia 'Landa. I'd lose him forever, then my heart would be broken. He's the only man I'll ever love.''

They all laughed, but one of the older women, standing beside Yolanda, simply nodded her head, her hands folding the corn husks that held the filled *masa.* Her name was Patricia, Silvia remembered. She was Yolanda's mother-in-law.

''That happens,'' she said, her voice more serious

than the rest. "There's always one man who steals your heart. He's a thief in the night. He slips in before you know what's happening then you belong to him. If he changes his mind and goes to another woman, it's too late. He takes your love with him and you can't ever love someone else." Her eyes were knowing as she took in the others around the table which had now fallen quiet. "One man and one woman. You're lucky, Elena, if you have the one God meant for you. Some women never find him."

Something tightened inside Silvia's chest. Her hands, covered in *masa,* grew still, as did those of most of the women in the room.

A teenager by Elena leaned closer and spoke. "But how do you know when you've met the right one, *abuelita?* Sometimes one comes that makes your heart beat fast, and he fools you."

The older woman smiled softly. When her gaze went around the table once more, it seemed to stop and linger on Silvia. She told herself she was imagining it, but she wasn't sure, especially when the grandmother finally answered the teenager's question. "If your heart's still beating that fast, twenty years later...then you know he's the one."

"Twenty years!" The teenager's voice made her feelings plain. "That's a lifetime!"

"That's right, *chica.*" This time her smile was almost serene. "Sometimes a lifetime is what it takes."

The giant plastic bowl of *tamales* was almost overflowing an hour later when Carlos entered the room. The talk died just as it had when Silvia had entered, but this time it didn't resume. The women all ducked their heads and suddenly concentrated on their work.

"What a domestic scene." Carlos walked to the edge of the table where Silvia stood, his black eyes taking in her apron and *masa*-covered hands. He leaned against the counter behind him and crossed his arms. "I wonder what your bosses back in Washington would say if they could see their fancy consultant now."

Silvia met his gaze with a level look. It was sad, really, that her success threatened him so much, but then again, that was the way it had always been with Carlos. He was a prosperous attorney, a man respected in town, but nothing had changed. Deep down, he was still the insecure teenager who always fell short when he compared himself to everyone else he knew.

"I'm sure they'd be surprised," she said evenly, keeping her opinions about his personality to herself. "Cooking isn't my forte and that's certainly no secret around the office."

He reached into the bowl of meat and plucked a morsel out. "Then how do you ever expect to catch a man, *hermana?*"

"Maybe I don't want one," she said, flushing slightly. Around her the women had finally resumed their conversations, but they were muted ones at best. Carlos had definitely spoiled the fun. "Not every woman feels she has to have a man to feel alive."

"Oh, really?" His expression darkened with some indescribable emotion, and his voice dropped in tone. "Well, if you feel that way, then how would you explain the little scene I saw on the front porch last night, eh? The one where you and our esteemed sheriff were wrapped in each other's arms. I could be mistaken, but it looked to me as if you were 'feeling alive.'"

Silvia felt her face flame. In the bowl of *masa* her fingers curled with anger. "Were you spying on us?"

"I didn't have to spy—and neither did the neighbors. You weren't exactly discreet."

She didn't want a scene—not now and not here—but she couldn't let him think he was intimidating her, either. She turned and spoke quietly, so quietly he was the only one who could hear her. "I thought we had already discussed this once, and I'd made myself clear. Obviously I was mistaken—you didn't understand."

His face darkened, but he said nothing.

"I don't need advice on how to run my life—from you or anyone else. I've lived by myself for years and managed just fine." She kept her voice level, but there was no mistaking her anger. "In case you haven't noticed, I'm a grown woman."

"Then I suggest you act like one instead of embarrassing the family like you did when you were a teenager." Putting the palms of his hands on the table, he narrowed his eyes and leaned closer to her. "Grown women control themselves. Why don't you try doing that for a change?"

For one long moment, they stared at each other. Looking into her brother's eyes, Silvia felt her emotions run the gamut from embarrassment to defensiveness to anger. He had no right—that was her main thought. No right to say what he had and definitely no right to spy on her and Rick. And to think, she'd wanted to reconcile with him, to understand and forgive his actions of so long ago. How could she have been so naive?

She opened her mouth to answer him, but reading her intention, Carlos didn't give her the chance. He gave her a final superior look, then turned and left, the back door banging noisily shut behind him, her own glare burning a hole through the screen. Immediately, all around her, the women's chatter turned louder.

Yolanda stepped toward Silvia, a concerned look on her face. "What did he say to you?" she demanded. "I can tell he upset you. What'd he say?"

Taking a deep breath, Silvia shook her head. "Nothing. He said nothing...at least nothing worth repeating."

"He's always making life so difficult." Yolanda cut her eyes toward the end of the table where Lydia stood. "Why she ever married him, I have no idea. He doesn't deserve a woman that good."

Silvia stared at Carlos's wife. She was quiet, unassuming—definitely nonthreatening. "He couldn't have married any other kind," she said wearily, her anger draining unexpectedly, as quickly as it had come. "He'd have to have a woman he could bully, or it'd never work. Are they close, or do they fight? Does she just give in to him?"

"Carlos is close to no one but Carlos, and yes, they fight. I hate it, especially when they do it in front of the children." Her lips formed one thin line. "I have heard rumors, too..."

Silvia looked at her with curiosity. "Rumors? About what?"

Obviously realizing she'd said too much, Yolanda shook her head as though to clear her thoughts. "About nothing important," she said with a smile. "Let's just finish these *tamales,* then we can start on the *menudo.* We have a party to cook for!"

Yolanda finally declared the cooking finished an hour later, and the women all left to clean up for the party. Silvia decided to put the quiet time to good use. At the small desk in her bedroom, she pulled out her report and tried to work a little bit more. The pressure was on—not from anyone else, but from herself. She wanted to figure out the case and leave San Laredo before things got any more complicated. With Carlos constantly acting obnoxious and Rick never leaving her thoughts, nothing good would come from staying longer.

But she couldn't concentrate. The crime scene photos blurred before her eyes, and the medical reports made no sense whatsoever. It was obvious she couldn't focus her thoughts, and it was pointless to even try any longer. Slipping out of her room, Silvia made her way down the hall to the bath to get ready for the party.

When she came out thirty minutes later, the house had already begun to fill. Looking around, Silvia was glad she'd taken the time to change. The women coming up the porch were all wearing their heels and Sunday best, and the children beside them were dressed as well, the little boys sparkling for the moment with slicked back hair and clean white shirts, the little girls wearing frilly polyester dresses in rainbow colors. As Silvia entered the living room, already noisy and crowded, Consuelo's husband, Johnny, caught her eye in particular. He wore a dazzling white *guayabera* with jeans pressed so stiffly the creases looked capable of cutting steel. Under the broad rim of his black straw cowboy hat, he looked proud of himself and of his wife, his bronzed skin glowing in the evening light from the windows, his hard, callused hands on either of Consuelo's shoulders as they entered the room. He'll make a good father, Silvia thought instantly.

As good as Rick would have made.

A giant lump formed in the back of her throat and suddenly it was hard to breathe. Suddenly she didn't want to be there a second longer, didn't want to be reminded of what she could have had...and didn't. She wanted to leave so she wouldn't have to see that she'd sacrificed the children, the family, the closeness—everything for nothing but a career she could no longer handle. For an empty refrigerator and an even emptier bed. For no kind of life at all.

Moving through the crowd like a ship parting the waters, a second later, Yolanda grabbed Silvia and prevented her from fleeing. It was almost as if she'd known what Silvia was thinking as she determinedly began introducing her to everyone in the room. After a while, the names and faces began to blur and get confused, but it didn't really matter at that point. At least it kept her from thinking of what she didn't have.

"She's so beautiful," one of the teenagers was saying as Rick walked up to the crowded front porch. "Do you think she buys all her clothes in New York? Washington's really close to New York, you know. I bet she goes to those fancy places on Fifth Avenue."

Another of the teenagers tossed her hair over her shoulder. "She probably orders them from Neiman Marcus or someplace like that. She'd be too busy with her career to shop all the time. My cousin in Houston does that. She says it's what career women do now. They get catalogs from all the fancy stores, and they order everything from them...from their office when they aren't working."

Opening the front door, Rick made his way into the crowded room, leaving the teenagers behind. When his eyes found Silvia across the crowded room, however, there was one thing he was sure of...she had not ordered her clothes from a catalog. The short white skirt fit entirely too well, the soft material clinging discreetly to the curves of her buttocks, the hem stopping just short of her knees. The black silk blouse she wore with it looked way too expensive as well, a single top button undone to reveal only a shadow of cleavage.

The teenagers were right about one thing, though. Silvia *did* look incredibly beautiful, gorgeous and self-assured. The years had taken her youthful prettiness and turned it into a deeper kind of beauty, a kind that he found even more appealing. It left him feeling tongue-tied, though, and unsure of how to approach her. He stared and wondered just what in the hell he thought he was doing there.

Obviously feeling his gaze, Silvia lifted her head a moment later, her eyes searching the crowd. When she finally focused on him, her gaze opened, exposing something he hadn't seen before. Something unguarded and unexpected. Something suspiciously reminiscent of longing, but for what? He immediately told himself he was acting ridiculous, imagining her emotions…but was he?

Crossing the room, she came up to him. "You made it!"

"I wouldn't have missed it for the world. I've been thinking about Yolanda's cooking all day."

A big fat lie—he'd been thinking about Silvia and nothing else.

"Well, that's good…because we have a ton of food." Silvia paused and smiled timidly, an expression that shot straight into his gut. "You have to help me out, though. Yolanda tied me down and forced me to roll *tamales* all afternoon, and I'm sure no one's going to eat the ones I rolled…they look terrible. Would you choke one or two down so I won't be totally embarrassed?"

She was being gracious, he realized. Obviously sensing his own awkwardness, she was doing her best to make him feel more comfortable...and it was working.

"I'd be delighted," he said with a smile. "Which ones are they?"

"I think you'll be able to figure that out." She looked down for a moment, then lifted her gaze to his, her dark eyes a little more serious. "I'm glad you came, you know. Really glad. I hope you can stay for a while."

He looked at her, remembering the kiss they'd shared, and suddenly he knew she was telling the truth. She wanted him there. She needed him for some strange reason. Something was going painfully wrong for her and he could help. Part of him felt like a bastard—she needed him and he was using her—but the other part of him, the professional side, said it was working out just like he'd wanted, what was the problem?

He looked at her and said the only thing he could. "I'm glad, too."

She smiled again then, and looking as young and beautiful as she had all those years ago, she made a path through the crowd for them, leading him into the dining room. "Grab a plate," she instructed, "and fill it up. We're eating out back under the trees. I'll get our drinks and meet you there."

He nodded and began to work his way around the table, heaping his plate high with just a sample of the food covering the table—*tamales, menudo,* beans, rice, *tortillas.* She hadn't been kidding about the *tamales,* he realized as he reached that bowl. There were quite a few pushed to one side that looked like a child had rolled them. They seemed painfully lonely. He took them all.

Silvia had two cold beers in front of her and a plate

halfway full when he found her under the pin oak tree near the back of the yard. She laughed when she saw his platter. "I see you found my *tamales*. My signature rolling style is distinctive, isn't it?"

He grinned and slipped onto the bench beside her. "It is unique," he agreed, "but I'm sure they'll taste just fine. It's what's inside that counts. Right?"

Picking up their silverware, they began to eat and talk about the weather, about her family, about the way San Laredo had changed. Ordinary conversation, he thought, but more. Much more. The shadow he'd seen earlier in her eyes began to lighten a bit.

Then a burst of wild shrieking pulled his gaze away from Silvia to a corner in the yard. The kids had assembled a makeshift baseball diamond, and a rowdy argument had broken out near the patio seat cushion marking home plate. A boy about seven or so was rolling in the dirt, clutching his knee and screaming dramatically while two others were standing over him about to come to blows. One of the mothers was quickly making her way to the scene to resolve the situation, her hands on her hips, her dark hair swinging behind her as she strode toward the conflict.

Without thinking, Rick looked down at Silvia. "Motherhood and its rewards, eh?"

Her expression took on a startled complexity before he nodded his head toward the kids. "You have to be a diplomat and a policeman and a doctor all rolled up in one."

"I...I suppose you do." She looked toward the fracas. "I never really thought about it, I guess."

Sunlight drifted through the leaves of the tree overhead, a pattern of light and dark dappling her face. They suddenly seemed isolated in the crowd, alone as only two people can be who had known each other as they had.

"You haven't?" he said softly. "Not ever?"

She turned to look at him. Her gaze held a painful darkness that he recognized. He'd seen it in his own reflection.

"You've never wondered what it would have been like?" he asked, knowing it wasn't wise but being unable to stop. "If things had been different, we might be out there right now separating our kid from one of his cousins. Haven't you ever—"

She spoke abruptly, her voice harsh. "There's no purpose in thinking about things like that. The past is over. It's done with. I don't think it's productive to talk about—"

Before she could continue, raised voices interrupted her. This time, though, they weren't childish. It was a man, an angry man, and he was getting angrier.

"What the…"

"Who is that?"

They spoke at the same time and exchanged a puzzled look. A moment later, as the voice grew louder, they both rose. Rick saw what was going on a second before Silvia did.

"It's Carlos," he said tightly.

"Carlos…" Silvia frowned, a knot of confusion marring the spot between her eyebrows as she looked over Rick's shoulder. "And Lydia… What in the world…?"

The couple was standing beside one corner of the house, hidden from the eyes of the party crowd, except for Rick and Silvia. Carlos was hovering over his wife, his arms raised, his hands fisted in anger. As Rick and Silvia watched, he moved even closer. The evening breeze wasn't strong enough to carry his words, but it was more than obvious he was berating his wife about something. As his voice grew in volume, she shrunk back against the house, almost cowering while she tucked her arms around herself protectively.

"This is crazy," Silvia said, starting forward. "I'm not going to stand by and let him bully her like that."

Rick agreed completely. Within seconds they were approaching Carlos and Lydia just in time to hear the last of Carlos's hateful words. "...and when are you going to learn to keep your stupid mouth shut? You have no business talking about things you don't understand—"

He broke off abruptly as Silvia moved to Lydia's side and wrapped a protective arm around her. "Are you okay?" Silvia asked.

"What's going on?" Rick spoke before Lydia could answer Silvia. "Got a problem here?"

"We're just having a little discussion, and everything's fine. We don't need any interference." Carlos's voice was tight, his jaw clenching and unclenching. He shot Rick a nasty look. "Especially from you."

Chapter 7

Rick held his hands up, palms out. "Not trying to interfere. Just seemed like you guys needed a little help, that's all...." He glanced toward Lydia. Her tear-streaked face held an expression of fear and uncertainty that turned his stomach. "Are you all right?" he said softly.

"She's fine." Carlos answered before his wife could open her mouth. "Perfectly fine."

Rick turned and looked directly at Carlos. He smiled, but there was ice in his voice. "I believe I asked your wife that question...not you."

"It—it's okay." Lydia spoke quickly. She obviously didn't want Carlos to have the opportunity to say more. Her smile was tremulous. "I...I did something stupid inside. Carlos was just explaining..."

Silvia interrupted. "Explaining? He was using a rather loud tone of voice."

Shaking her head, Lydia swiped the handkerchief

Rick had handed her across her cheeks. "No...really. It...it was all my fault. I shouldn't have been..." Her words died, and she handed the square of white back to Rick. "Thank you for your help."

"Which we really don't need." Carlos stared coldly at Rick. "So if you'd be so kind as to leave us alone now, we'd like to finish our conversation. It's private."

Rick ignored him, and moving closer to Lydia, he accepted the handkerchief then replaced it with a business card which he'd removed from his wallet. "If you ever need any help, the people here know how to listen."

Carlos grabbed the card before Lydia could take it. It was from a women's shelter.

"What the hell do you think you're doing?" he growled. "My wife doesn't need anything like this."

"Maybe not," Rick answered. "But it never hurts to know there are people who care."

"You're overstepping your boundaries, Hunter," Carlos growled.

"I think someone around here's doing that, but it isn't me." Rick moved closer to Carlos, his bulk menacing. "Beating up on women is what's overstepping the boundaries, Hernandez. I don't put up with that kind of behavior like your family apparently does. It's against the law, you know."

Carlos's jaw twitched, and his eyes sparked in the darkness. "I think it's time for you to leave."

The two men moved closer together, an unseen signal of tension and challenge coming on between them. "Keep this kind of behavior up, and you'll be the one leaving, Hernandez—"

She couldn't wait any longer. Silvia jumped forward, her eyes sweeping over her brother's face and onto

Rick's. Her words took both of them in. "This isn't helping anyone, including Lydia," she said tightly. "You're acting like a couple of teenagers."

Her dark eyes and sharp voice jerked Rick back from the edge of the cliff. Taking a deep breath, he tried to ignore the anger curling inside him like a flame about to explode and acknowledged that she was right, more than right.

But God, how he hated to see a woman beaten up like this. Whether it was emotional battering or physical, he hated it. And the fact that it was Carlos doing the beating added fuel to the fire, Rick had to admit.

Silvia spoke again, this time more quietly, her arm still around her sister-in-law's shoulders, her eyes locking on Rick's. "I can take care of things here so maybe Carlos is right for the moment." She took a deep breath, held it, then let it out slowly. "Maybe it'd just be best for you to leave now."

His stare clashed with hers. Inside his chest, the tight feeling of anger Rick was so familiar with grew even tighter. All he could hear was that she was agreeing with Carlos…defending him. Again.

There was nothing else he could do. He nodded once, then turned around and left.

Staring out her office window Monday morning, Silvia raised her right hand to her forehead and slowly massaged her temple. It was a futile attempt to dislodge the headache echoing inside her skull. The headache that had been there since Saturday night.

What in the world had Rick thought he was doing? He couldn't have really believed he was helping, could he? Handing Lydia that card had been a gallant thing to do, but not a smart thing. Not smart at all.

And Carlos— Dear God, he was the real culprit in all this. Did he always talk to Lydia like that? With no respect or regard for who she was? Silvia knew it was foolish of her to even ask the question—the whipped-puppy look in Lydia's brown eyes told the story. She was a victim. Carlos's victim. When Silvia had tried to counsel her later, she'd insisted everything was fine between them, and Silvia didn't really need to interfere. She'd told Carlos exactly how she'd felt about his behavior, though. It wasn't acceptable, she'd said. Simply not acceptable. He'd turned and stalked off without another word.

What a mess.

Dropping her fingers, Silvia knew there was only one answer to the entire situation—she had to leave. Just like she'd left eighteen years ago. Of course, she'd been forced to flee then, but no one would have to force her now. All she had to do was finish her report, then go back to her life in Washington. She'd leave her family, the children, the brown eyes of Lydia and she'd go back. She would do everything she could, then she'd leave. Not too admirable, but necessary to her survival. She'd go back. Back to her quiet little existence in Washington that didn't contain the emotional land mines San Laredo did. Back to a life that excluded Rick Hunter.

With renewed determination to reach that goal as fast as possible, she turned to the reports about Bonnie Kelman spread over her desk. Despite everything going on at home, or maybe because of it, Silvia's mind had been turning to the case constantly, and without her even knowing it, a picture had begun to take form. A vague form, but a form. Pulling out first one report then another, she organized the papers before her and the form took on more substance.

First the ballistics report: the fact that a gun had been the weapon of choice was significant in and of itself. Unlike a knife, it meant the killer did not have to be a physically large person, although, of course, he could be. Larger men liked larger guns; they could handle the recoil and the weight of the gun, and the scale of those pistols fit their hands better. In addition, the guy had to have been a pretty good size because Bonnie had been a large woman herself. She'd fought her attacker...but still lost.

The fact that a large-caliber weapon had been used was important, too. Women felt more comfortable with small pistols, like a .38. She picked up the photo of the slug from Bonnie Kelman. A man would be more likely to choose something like a .41, the gun that had apparently been used. The lands and grooves on the spent bullet were consistent with that size caliber weapon, but mistakes could be made, and of course the gun had never been found.

Silvia chewed on the end of her pen as her eyes went over the spiraling notches pictured on the slug. The most important thing it told her was something she'd have a tough time explaining to Rick, a feeling that she could only base on experience and her former cases. People who selected large-caliber guns generally had power issues. Control was something of paramount importance to them, and anything that would give them more control and leave less to chance—like a larger-caliber gun—was something they would want.

She pulled a yellow legal pad closer to her and wrote on the first line: "Dominant male with prevailing unresolved power issues.'' She paused for just a moment then made another note. "Large in size.''

Which brought Silvia to another point. Bonnie had fought the man...but she'd known him, too. The sex she'd had, moments before her death, had been, most likely, consensual. Unlike Linda's case, there had been no signs of rape here, ambiguous or otherwise. Bonnie had let the man make love to her, then he'd turned around and killed her.

But before he'd killed her and probably during the time they'd made love...he'd beat her.

Silvia pulled out the autopsy report. In gruesome detail, it outlined the bruises and contusions which had covered the victim's body. Some were antemortem and some postmortem. A few of the now yellowing splotches had had to have been suffered a week or more prior to her death because her body had had the chance to begin the healing process. In the reports about her, Bonnie Kelman hadn't seemed like the kind of person to be involved in rough sex, but again...how did you ever know? Silvia had been called in once on the death of a senator's wife, and she certainly hadn't expected what she'd seen there, either.

Silvia sat back and rubbed her eyes, then stared off into the sunshine outside her window. Men who beat women were bullies. And bullies were bullies because they were insecure. They were always trying to cover up inadequacies, real or imagined, that had hindered them all their lives. They knew deep down they couldn't win over someone their equal so they had to select someone weaker, someone like a Linda Willington.

She pulled the pad closer. "Pathological self-doubt resulting in passive-aggressive behavior.'' She studied the words for several seconds, then added another line.

"Alienation from others with no close personal ties. Abusive family of origin?" Studies had shown that killers like this rarely had a circle of friends. They felt isolated, all alone. Sometimes it was self-imposed, but more generally they'd come from a dysfunctional family that supported that kind of behavior. They'd been abused as children.

She stared at the list.

She slowly put down her pen then dropped her head into her hands. It was more than possible that the same person who'd killed Linda Willington had also killed Bonnie Kelman. There were too many similarities to ignore, and Silvia had to ask herself about the links between the killings.

Whatever they were, though, those links did not include Rick. No way. The portrait she'd just drawn was of someone totally opposite Rick's type. How in the world could she have ever thought...?

She shook her head. Yes, she'd been eighteen. Yes, she'd been scared. And yes, he'd definitely *looked* guilty, but how could she have thought he'd been involved in something like this? How could she have ever thought he was this kind of man? If she had only known then the things she knew now.

But it was too late to go back, wasn't it? Whatever she and Rick could have shared in the past had been destroyed, and it could never again be recovered. Between the two of them, they'd obliterated their relationship and all it could have been. It was history. Over with. Finished.

The time had come for Silvia to accept that.

Rick angled one booted foot on the curb and stared at Barbara Williams. She was still an attractive woman, but wouldn't be for much longer. She'd played fast and loose with her looks and the rest of her body as well. Pretty soon, that carelessness would begin to harden the lines of her jaw, to slacken the skin around her eyes. For the moment, though, she could still turn heads...as she was right now.

With amusement, he watched a teenage boy stumble into the grocery store behind them, his feet tripping over the doorway as his eyes roamed over Barbara's generous curves.

"I don't know what you're talking about," Barbara was saying, replying to Rick's previous question. "I'm not even sure I know the man, Rick. And even if I did, what does it matter to you? What I do now isn't any business of yours...."

She was lying, out-and-out lying, but why?

He started to tell her he knew what she was doing, but just as he began to interrupt, Barbara's words faded into the back of his consciousness and ceased to make sense. Right behind the teenager, going into the grocery store, was Silvia. He caught a glimpse of dark, flowing hair and a tantalizing flash of elegant leg, then she was gone.

He wanted to run after her, to ask her to ignore the way Saturday night had turned out, to beg her to talk to him. The conversation they'd been sharing just before the incident with Carlos was one Rick wanted to finish.

But the other part of him was still mad at the way she'd handled the situation with her brother. Why did she always feel she had to take Carlos's side? Why couldn't she stand up to the man, for God's sake?

And to top off matters, leaving like that had completely destroyed Rick's opportunity to see who might have arrived later to talk with Carlos.

The whole evening had been a disaster.

At Rick's side, Barbara continued to talk, totally unaware she had none of his attention...which was certainly nothing new. Two seconds later, while he was still staring at the door to the grocery, Silvia came back out. She casually scanned the street with her gaze, then jerked it to a stop as her eyes locked on Rick's. Her stare slid away from his to take in the woman beside him.

Rick felt a tightening in his gut. The two women were night and day, but sometimes that's what it took, didn't it? To get the memory of one woman out of your mind, you tried to replace it with someone who was just the opposite. It never worked, of course, but he hadn't understood that...until it was too late.

Suddenly making up his mind, he looked down at Barbara and interrupted her abruptly. ''I've got to go, but I'll be calling you. I want to talk to you about this some more.''

She started to protest, but he took off before she could say more. Whatever she had to say didn't matter, anyway. He *would* call her, and she *would* tell him what he wanted to know.

He caught up with Silvia just as she reached her car and stuck her key in the lock of the door. Placing his hand on the roof where the window met metal, he prevented her from opening the car and escaping. The heat of the day rose off the pavement at their feet and came between them as she shifted her body slightly—an effort to pull away from his closeness.

''We need to talk,'' he said without preliminary.

Her full, red lips compressed into a line of something that looked like anger. For just a moment, while he stared at those lips, all Rick could think about was kissing her. Luckily, her sharp words focused his attention once more. "There's nothing to talk about yet. My report isn't finished—"

"I don't mean about the case. I mean about us. About Saturday night."

Her eyes widened almost imperceptibly before she got herself under control. "It's history...Saturday night, I mean."

"No. It's unfinished business." He took a deep breath which was a major mistake. Chanel No.5 filled his senses. "I don't like unfinished business." And too much of it still hung between the two of them.

She blinked at his words, her sweeping dark eyelashes brushing against her cheekbones before she lifted her eyes to his once more. She knew his thoughts. They were hers as well. "Some business stays that way. It has to."

"Not to my way of thinking."

She took a moment to respond but when she finally did, it caught him by surprise. Her eyes suddenly flashing, her voice going up a notch, she spoke with unexpected emotion. "What exactly is it you want from me, Rick? I came here to do a job and before I knew what was happening, things went crazy. First, you tried to run me off, then when that failed, you kissed me. Finally, on Saturday night you picked a fight with my brother and stormed off when I intervened. What's going on? Give me some answers."

"Answers?" He drawled the word out, to give himself some time as much as to rattle her. "I'd like some of those myself. Why don't you start first?"

Under his scrutiny, she seemed to lose her steam. "I...I can't. I don't have any."

"Well, try for just one." His fingers clasped the edge

of the roof, but he ignored the burning metal as it bit into his skin. "Why did you defend Carlos the other night? Don't you see how he's taking advantage of his wife? Are you blind to what he is? What he does?"

She stared into his eyes and read the message behind his words. *Why have you always trusted your brother and not me?*

"I know exactly what kind of man Carlos is," she said finally, "and after you left, I told Lydia she needs to do some serious thinking about their relationship. I offered to help her any way that I could, too, but I did it outside of Carlos's hearing." Her jaw tightened. "You stepped way out of line Saturday night. Carlos thinks of his family in a very proprietary way, and you offended his limits when you approached Lydia with that card."

"Offended his limits? Is that what I did when we were dating? Offended his limits?" Shaking his head once, Rick narrowed his eyes and glared at her. "Damn...all this time, I just thought he was a controlling bastard, jealous and envious. Somebody who just didn't want you to do better than he did. Just didn't want you to have love...if he couldn't."

She stiffened visibly then deliberately ignored his reference to their past. "If you hadn't handed Lydia the card, the whole thing would have blown over."

"Somehow I doubt that. I really doubt it." He clenched his jaw and held back the other question burning inside him. *And would it have blown over eighteen years ago if I'd been let out of jail and you'd still been around?*

"I'm not defending his actions, and I did talk to him about his behavior," she finally said with a sigh. "All I'm saying is, he did what he always does. Family means more to him than anything, and you challenged that.''

''Family means more to him? Are you crazy? He was yelling at his wife—''

''It might not seem logical to you—''

''It's not logical, period.''

''Well, it is to him. He thinks he's protecting things, keeping things safe. He isn't always right, but I think he tries to do what he believes is best...even though he might not have all the details at the time.'' For just a moment, her eyes darkened with some long-ago memory, some secret she held that he'd never know about.

His frustration ballooned. If things had gone differently, he'd know what that look meant, dammit. ''Why in God's name are you always making excuses for him?''

''Why are you always attacking him?'' she countered.

He let her question ride for just a second and then he couldn't hold back any longer. ''Because he deserves it,'' Rick retorted. ''Because he isn't the man you think you know. Because if he thought as much about his family and what it means as you think he does, then he wouldn't have a girlfriend on the side, now would he?'' As soon as the words were out of his mouth, he regretted them, but it was too late to pull them back.

''A girlfriend!'' A nervous laugh escaped before Silvia realized he was serious. As the reality sunk in, her eyes turned suddenly wary, two dark pools of apprehensiveness. ''Wh-what are you saying?''

He sighed heavily. ''Your brother has a mistress, Silvia. Her name is Barbara Williams, and she lives out on Cemetery Road. That was her I was talking to when you came out of the store.''

She jerked her gaze over her shoulder, but Barbara was long gone. Swinging back, she glared at him and spoke. "I don't believe you."

He shrugged. "Then talk to her yourself. I'll give you her phone number. Her address is—"

"You're lying."

"I'm not." He held his hands out, palms up. "I'm telling you the truth, Silvia. There are things about your sainted brother that don't add up and they never have." He dropped his hands. "He's a tyrant—a tyrant and a bully and that's just the beginning," he added darkly.

The name-calling seemed to jar her, to jolt some kind of memory. Her black eyes darkened even more, and the barest hint of unease danced forward in them, before it fell back, out of reach. She lifted her right hand and briefly touched the hollow at the base of her neck. His eyes followed the movement, felt the skin beneath her touch.

"A bully?" She repeated the word, softly as if she were thinking.

She was loyal, he'd grant her that. But loyalty was often blind. He forced his gaze up to hers, his voice soft when he finally spoke.

"You didn't learn as much as you should have when you picked up all those fancy degrees." He paused then spoke again, a hardened tone this time. "Because your brother is not what you think he is, and I'm going to prove it."

Carlos was sitting on the front porch when Silvia drove up. Parking her rental car in the driveway next to his BMW, she cut off the engine and sat still for just a moment, the heat building inside the closed vehicle like an oven coming to temperature.

Had Rick been telling the truth? Was Carlos involved with a woman besides his wife?

A moment's conversation came into her head. Yolanda saying "...I've heard rumors..." What kind of rumors had she been talking about, Silvia now wondered. The kind that connected Carlos with other women?

There was only one way to find out.

She grabbed her leather briefcase from the seat beside her and stepped out into the evening heat. It was only marginally cooler than the inside of the car. Crossing the front yard, she tried not to notice her blouse sticking to her shoulder blades or the trickle of sweat running down between her breasts.

"Hello, little sister." Carlos greeted her as she stepped up on the front porch. Despite the heat that had her rumpled, he looked cool and composed, his white shirt starched and pristine, his expensive gabardine slacks spotless and creased. "Hard day at work?"

"You might say that," she answered. Dropping her case, she took the chair beside him and reached out for the beer he was offering her that he'd pulled from a nearby cooler. It was imported, of course. She took the drink and tried to imagine him with another woman. The image came much too easily.

She took a deep swallow from the amber bottle then carefully put it on the table between their chairs. Looking him in the eye, she didn't bother with niceties. "I heard something today about you. I'm hoping it's not true."

He arched one black eyebrow. "And what would that be?"

"That you have a mistress. On the other side of town near Cemetery Road."

He didn't say anything; he didn't move. Finally he raised his bottle to his lips and took a drink that was longer than hers had been. The bottle was almost empty when he placed it near her own. "And who is this mistress supposed to be?"

A long time ago, she'd learned to listen to the first thing someone said when questioned. It revealed everything—especially when they didn't answer. She let her breath out slowly, a sinking sensation coming into her stomach. "I was told her name is Barbara Williams. Does that ring a bell for you?"

He laughed quietly. "Oh, yeah. It rings quite a few." Looking over at her, he seemed almost amused. "Don't you know who she is?"

Silvia shook her head. "I have no idea. I've never heard the name before."

"Well, then, before I enlighten you, let me make a guess as to who told you this snippet of gossip."

"That's not important." The words came out too fast.

"Oh, I beg to differ. It's very important. In fact, it's probably the most important thing you're going to learn in this whole conversation." The dying sun shone directly on his face, highlighting his arrogant expression and burnishing his skin. He looked exactly like what he was—a very successful, very competent lawyer. But there was more. A hidden cruelty had lightly etched itself in places she hadn't really seen before. Or maybe she'd seen it and denied it. Rick's words echoed in her mind. *He's a bully.*

"Just tell me the truth," she said sharply. "Are you having an affair?"

"Why would I be having an affair with Rick Hunter's ex-wife?"

A leaden silence fell onto the now almost dark porch.

It was broken only by the distant sounds of life going on—a car starting, a child crying, a dog barking. Someone had just cut the yard, the sharp, green smell reaching Silvia's nose with an almost bitter intensity.

"What are you saying?" Her throat was dry—the words croaked out.

"Barbara Williams was married to Rick Hunter. I bet he failed to mention that little fact as he filled your ears with this filthy gossip."

"What makes you think I heard this from Rick?"

"Where else would it come from?"

They stared at each other in the growing darkness. A deep shadow made it almost impossible for her to see his face now. She could hear the derision in his voice, though.

"Why do you let him do this to you, Silvie? Why do you always buy the trash this man is selling?" The chair creaked, and as he leaned forward, Carlos's face came into view. "I may not be the politically correct man of the nineties, but I'm not an adulterer." He looked directly into her eyes. "And I have always been faithful to my wife. Always."

"Then Rick is lying."

"Oh, yes. He's definitely lying." Carlos leaned back and rocked once more into the shadows. He disappeared, his voice turning him into nothing more than a disembodied question. "And I think you need to ask yourself why."

His voice lingered in the stifling air for a few more minutes, then Carlos rose and went inside without speaking another word. Silvia watched the screen door bang shut behind him, confusion sweeping over her. Carlos appeared to be sincere but things weren't adding up, were they? Despite her conversation with Rick earlier, there were niggling doubts in the back of her mind about her brother. Things Yolanda had said…things Silvia had heard… And if he was telling the truth, then that meant Rick was lying. Why would Rick do that? Was he playing some kind of game?

When he'd walked up to her in the parking lot, she'd been uneasy, and when he'd begun to speak, she'd only gotten more nervous. Something about him set her on edge, put all her senses on alert. She'd known he was holding something back, but she didn't know what.

Secrets. Would there always be secrets between them?

The rumbling sound of a car slowing down in the street took her attention away from her thoughts. A second later, the engine died as it apparently parked. She stared out into the darkness, the sound of a car door slamming, then heavy steps coming up the sidewalk. From out of the shadows, straddling the sidewalk in front of her, Rick suddenly loomed, his feet apart, his hand on the butt of his gun.

"The new ballistics report just got back." He stared at her, stony-faced. "We need to talk."

Chapter 8

She looked like a startled deer, caught on the porch and unable to flee. "Wh-what's it say? The report?"

"I'd like to discuss it somewhere else, if you don't mind. Somewhere a bit more private." He tried to keep his voice level and even. He'd let himself get upset this afternoon and he'd lost control.

Like he was always doing around her.

She seemed to recover slowly, as if she couldn't reconcile his presence in the growing darkness. Finally, almost reluctantly, she spoke stiffly. "I'd be happy to discuss the case with you, but first I'd like to know why you didn't tell me the truth this afternoon."

His gut tightened. "I did tell you the truth."

She walked down the first porch step and came closer, up the sidewalk, toward him. Her eyes were huge and filled with anger, although she was struggling to contain it. Beneath the suit she wore, her body held tension. "Have you ever heard the term *lying by omission?*"

He wanted to pull her into his arms and replace her indignation with the same kind of an aching desire he was experiencing. He spoke instead, his jaw tight. "I believe I'm familiar with the term, yes."

"Then you'd have to admit you lied to me this afternoon—because you didn't tell me who Barbara Williams really is."

He stayed silent.

"She's your ex-wife, dammit!" She raised her right hand and thrust it through her hair, pushing it away from her face in a movement of frustration. "Why didn't you tell me?"

"It's not relevant."

She dropped her hand and stared at him. "Not relevant?" she repeated slowly.

He shook his head. "I don't care who your brother is sleeping with, Silvia. I only told you about Barbara because I'm tired of you thinking he's perfect when he isn't. And as far as Barbara goes, she and I haven't been close for years. Hell, we weren't even close when we were married."

It took her a second to absorb the information. "But Carlos says it's a lie."

"Of course he would," Rick answered calmly. "Being an adulterer wouldn't exactly fit his image, now would it?" He waited for her to come back at him, but she didn't. She couldn't. Deep down, and he wasn't sure why, she knew he was telling the truth, even if she couldn't admit to it yet. He could see it in her eyes. "This isn't why I came here, Silvia. We need to talk about the ballistics test, and I don't want to do it here. Come with me."

She hesitated a moment longer, then finally spoke, her voice weary and still edged with anger. "All right...but let me change first. I feel like I was born in this suit."

Rick waited on the porch. Five minutes later, when she came back out the screen door, he almost wished he hadn't given her the time. She had on a pair of well-worn jeans and an oversize white sweater. Her hair gleamed from the brushing she'd obviously just given it, and her face glowed, evidence of a recent scrubbing. She looked like she was seventeen, and Rick's heart tumbled all the way to his boots.

"Ready?" she said.

If there had been a way to get out of it gracefully, he would have turned and fled, but all he could do was nod.

She passed him, trailing a cloud of perfume, then climbed into the cruiser without waiting for him to open the door. He hurried behind her and got into the driver's seat. Ten minutes later, they were pulling into the driveway of his mother's house.

Silvia turned puzzled eyes on him.

"She's visiting her sister in Houston. I thought this would be as good a place as anywhere else."

He'd wanted to take her to his house, to get her away from Carlos's prying eyes and into the quiet of the country where they'd be undisturbed, but when she'd come outside in those jeans, he'd known instantly what a mistake taking her home would be. He couldn't risk it. He'd turned without thinking down the street leading to his mother's house.

She climbed out of the car and trailed behind him as he automatically headed to the summerhouse out back. The house had been built beside a small, man-made lake, and his parents had erected the small building the summer he'd fallen in love with Silvia. They'd spent hours lounging inside the open but private structure with its screened-in walls, swings and outdoor fireplace. No one would disturb them here.

"So what's the deal?" she asked as they reached the structure, and he held the screen door open for her. "What's going on with the ballistics test?"

Part of him was listening to her question, but the other part of him was just realizing what a mistake he'd made. Bringing Silvia here was the *last* place he should have thought of. Seeing her snuggle down among the cushions and tuck her feet underneath herself brought back a flood of memories he couldn't hold back. They'd spent so much time here, so much love-filled time.... He would have been better off taking her to his house. Where was his head?

"Tell me what's going on," she repeated, looking up at him.

Sitting down on the bench opposite hers, he forced himself to concentrate, to ignore what his mistake of bringing her to this place probably really meant. "The new test I ordered finally came back," he said. Looking into her eyes, he spoke calmly and quietly, exactly opposite of how he was feeling. "The gun that was used to kill Bonnie Kelman was also the gun used to kill Linda Willington."

Her hand went to her throat, her eyes grew huge. "Are...are you sure?"

"Positive. The barrel's got a burr on the inside of it, right-hand, bottom side. The mark it makes is distinctive. Both bullets show it. Just to make sure, I took everything down to Brownsville, to Jack Simpson's office. He has a comparison microscope."

"And…"

He shrugged. "And the match was perfect. I've got the photomicrographs to prove it. Those are admissible, you know. You don't get much more sure than that."

Silvia nodded slowly, the heavy scent of roses filling the night air like expensive perfume, their fragrance as jolting to her as the news Rick had just delivered. She'd had doubts about Rick back then. If the murders were definitely linked, she had one question to ask herself.

Did she have doubts about him now?

The answer came swiftly and confidently. No. Absolutely not. She knew beyond the shadow of a single doubt that Rick had nothing to do with this murder…or that one.

But something had happened that night, and she would never be able to sort out the Kelman murder if she didn't know what had happened to Linda. It was just that simple.

She took a deep breath, feeling as if she were about to leap into the deep, dark waters of the nearby lake from a hundred-foot height.

"I need to know the truth, Rick. I need to know what happened that night between you and Linda."

She didn't look in his direction, but she sensed when he stood and moved across the concrete floor. Reaching her side, he paused, his proximity taking away her logic, her air. Without saying a word, he reached down and lifted her chin with one finger. She finally lifted her gaze and stared at him.

"Do you really want to know?"

She tried to pull away, but found she couldn't. All her muscles had suddenly turned to wood, and they wouldn't work. No, part of her screamed silently. *I never want to know the truth because if you tell me what happened that night, then I'll have to tell you what happened to me, won't I? And I can't ever do that.*

"I have to," she answered softly. "The two cases are related, and I can't go on with this investigation unless I know the whole truth."

"Go on with this investigation...or go on with your life?"

She felt her defenses crumble. He knew her too well. Or was it himself he knew too well? Looking into his dark gaze, she spoke, her voice husky. "Just tell me."

He sat down, right beside her, his thigh pressing hotly against her hip, almost pinning her to her position. Glancing toward him, she could hardly make out his face, and she was glad. That meant he couldn't see hers. Couldn't see the fear. Couldn't see the longing.

He took a deep breath and jumped straight in. "I was on my way to your house, and I was in a hurry because I was running late. I...I don't really remember why now, but I took the shortcut down Cemetery Road. I was excited about being out of school, about my scholarship, about everything we had planned between us. The thought had even crossed my mind that we might somehow get..." He stopped and licked his lips. "That we might somehow make our relationship more permanent. Then I saw Linda. She ran to the center of the road and waved me down. There was nothing I could do but stop."

Silvia closed her eyes, let his voice carry her back in time. Out on the lake, a loon cried out.

"'I've broken down,' she said. She had on a pair of white shorts and T-shirt. It was pink with white stripes and it fit her like it had been painted on." He swallowed and looked out into the darkness. "I wouldn't have even gotten out of the car, but then she told me you were with her. That she'd given you a ride home after seeing you downtown. I pulled off to the side of the road, jumped out of the truck and started looking around, but you weren't there.''

He shook his head, regret filling his voice. ''It scared me. I didn't know what was going on, and I panicked.'' In the darkness, he cut his eyes toward Silvia. ''She was crazy, you know. I...I was almost afraid she might have done something to you.''

Silvia spoke, but she didn't recognize her own voice. ''...and then?''

''And then I realized what had really happened. It wasn't you she'd seen downtown, but me. She'd left early, before I did, then used the same shortcut through the cemetery to try to get ahead of me. She'd been drinking. Heavily.''

Silvia closed her eyes and willed herself to ignore the rising tide of nausea in the back of her throat. She could smell the beer and the Jungle Gardenia.

''The minute I realized what was going on, I turned around to get back in my truck. I didn't want anything to do with her, Silvia. I swear to God, this is the truth.''

The words lodged somewhere deep inside Silvia, somewhere around her heart. ''But...''

There was a moment's silence, then he continued. ''But she came up from behind me. She was laughing and acting silly and saying something about sacking the quarterback. Before I knew what was happening, she'd jumped on my back and knocked me down. We rolled into the ditch on the side of the road.''

He stopped for a moment. Silvia could hear his breath coming in ragged spurts, as if he'd been running. After a few seconds, it slowed and he shifted on the cushion to look at her in the darkness. Placing his hand on her leg, his fingers squeezed her thigh, but he hardly seemed to notice. It was almost as if he needed courage from the touch, the courage to go on.

"I tried to get up, but she grabbed me—by the chain holding the Saint Christopher medal you'd given me. I didn't want it to break so I leaned back down. It didn't matter, though. The links had already snapped. I scrambled around, trying to find them and fight her off at the same time." His knuckles gleamed, and his voice went hoarse, as if it hurt to say the words. "I got mad, Silvie. Mad because she'd made me stop, mad because of everything she was doing. She grabbed me and started rubbing me and things went crazy after that. Just crazy."

He stood abruptly, the cushion from his side slipping off the bench and falling to the floor with a thud. Silvia hardly noticed the sound. She felt numb, thick, halfway beyond caring.

"We had sex," he said, looking out into the hot, heavy night. "I'm not going to lie and tell you it was rape or anything like that. She was a willing partner, and I was, too." He swallowed hard. "And I've regretted it ever since. Being unfaithful to you was the worse thing I've ever done. I should never have gone near her, and I have no excuse for my behavior."

The space she was in seemed to tilt, to go off its axis and lean slightly to one side. Staring at his profile, the angles and planes hard and unforgiving in the dim night, Silvia fought to regain her emotional balance and to take in the words, to fully understand what they meant.

He'd been unfaithful to her. When she'd been young and naive and trusting—and so in love with him it hurt—he'd made love to another girl. A mixture of jagged relief and pained betrayal came over her, the emotions as sharp and penetrating as if it had just happened. The intensity of the feelings was shocking, especially after all these years. A second later, she felt a stab of guilt, equally as strong.

She hadn't exactly been open with him either, had she? And had no plans to be, either. Ever.

He turned around and came back to where she sat. Dropping to one knee, his stare locked on hers, he took both her hands in his, his heated touch shocking against her freezing fingers. "I had sex with Linda, but I left her alive, Silvia. I swear to God, I left her alive. I did not kill Linda Willington."

For what seemed like an eternity, in the dark silence between them, Silvia sat still, then finally she nodded her head slowly, her mouth dry, her heart pounding a slow, heavy rhythm against her ribs. "I know you didn't kill her, Rick. You couldn't have—you just couldn't have. I...I thought about it so much all these years. I obviously didn't trust you that night—"

His fingers tightened on hers. "And I didn't deserve it. I'd been unfaithful to you."

"But I could have helped—"

"By lying? That would have been the worse possible thing you could have done. For you *and* for me. It would have made me look more guilty, and I didn't need help in that department, believe me." He stood up then sat down beside her once more. She felt the space around them compress, turn warm. It made her more aware of him than ever, despite what he'd just told her.

She spoke again. "But...but you weren't even indicted. There wasn't enough evidence for that."

"That's right." He nodded. "And I guess you know why—you read the file. There was a clear indication someone else had been there as well. Two kinds of skin under her nails, two kinds of semen.''

"The migrant worker?"

Rick looked out toward the pitch-black lake, his expression neutral. "That's who they assumed it was. She'd been seen in town with the guy. Also her watch had been smashed in the attack, and it'd stopped around 1:00 a.m. A witness finally came forward and said they'd spotted my truck just about that time on Mulberry Street."

"Mulberry Street—?"

"After I left Linda, I stopped there. To think...to try to organize my thoughts. To decide what I should tell you about...about what had happened."

Silvia leaned closer, to look at him. "And you had decided..."

He turned and met her gaze. "I had decided I had to tell you. I didn't want there to be any secrets between us. Not ever..." He stopped and looked at her, his dark eyes pulling her into him. "And not now, either."

She stood so suddenly, he had to move back to avoid her. She couldn't help it—she had to get away from what he'd just said.

Despite her obvious unease, he stood and came beside her. His voice was a hoarse whisper, but it couldn't disguise the longing behind the words. "For years I've lived with the guilt of knowing I did you wrong. I made a stupid, stupid mistake and you deserved more, a helluva lot more. If we never talk about this again, though, I want you to know one last thing."

She looked up at him and waited.

"I loved you." His eyes glittered painfully in the dim light. "I loved you with all my heart. Despite my craziness, you've got to know that no other woman has ever come close to meaning to me what you did back then.''

She swallowed against the sudden tightness in her throat. ''I...I loved you, too,'' she whispered.

''But you left?''

''I had to... I just had to.''

His fingers came to her face and cupping her jaw, he lifted her head. ''We could have worked something out.''

''I...I don't think so.''

He leaned down to her level, his breath warm and sensual against her cheek. ''We had everything going for us, baby.'' His voice deepened. ''Everything. It was perfect.''

She blinked. ''I think your memory may be rewriting the past. Nothing's ever perfect.''

He shook his head and leaned even closer. ''It was...and I can prove it.'' His lips then closed over hers, and he wrapped his arms around her, pulling her into his embrace.

The past swept over her in a rush as his familiar body curved into hers, his hips pressing against her at the very same place, his hands finding the sweet spot in the middle of her back. For just a second, Silvia thought about resisting. He'd just told her he'd been unfaithful— How in the world could she still feel the way she did about him?

The answer came easily—because her body didn't really care. Eighteen years was eighteen years, and he'd just told her he'd loved her more than he'd ever loved anyone else. What woman wouldn't respond to hearing that? It was almost as if they needed to reaffirm that feeling, to experience the emotions again, and somehow cleanse the memories, restore them to what they should be.

She allowed her arms to snake around his neck, and her fingers to tangle in his soft, curling hair. Breathing deeply, she took in the clean, fresh smell that was so familiar and yet so strange. And in the back of her mind, while all this was happening, she acknowledged what she'd been trying desperately to ignore anyway. From the moment she'd returned, even before then actually, she'd known it would all come down to this.

To her body and his, locked together in an embrace and aching with needs that no one else could possibly fulfill.

His tongue parted her lips, and he deepened his kiss, his hands drifting lower, to cup the arch of her buttocks and pull her even closer. She couldn't hold back a moan, and the sound came between them. In response, Rick lifted his mouth and began to string a series of nips along the curve of her neck. Like priceless pearls, they warmed her skin.

And made her want him even more.

He ended the torture a second later and pulled back slightly so he could look into her eyes. "I've been thinking about this since the minute you walked into my office, Silvie. Tell me you have, too."

She couldn't lie to him. Not about this. She nodded. "I...I have."

"There's no way we can stop it now. You realize that, don't you?"

Again she nodded. "I wouldn't want to," she said hoarsely. "Even if I could."

With an intensity she could feel, he nodded his agreement then pulled her even closer, his hands slipping under her sweater, skimming her breasts, warming her skin, teasing her nipples through the lace of her bra.

Through her jeans she could feel the hard evidence of his desire, and her own aching need bloomed inside her. How many times had she felt him respond to her like this? And how many times had she dreamed of it since then?

Without another word, he picked her up and carried her to the tangle of cushions they'd abandoned moments before. A flurry of clothing fell to the floor, and then he was looming over her, his tanned, lean body stretching past the length of her own, his fingers warming the skin of her stomach and fluttering lower, searching for the most sensitive parts of her body.

For a passing second, she panicked. What if he could tell? What if her body betrayed her, and he realized she'd been pregnant? In the part of her brain still working, she realized she was being silly. The darkness would turn her faint stretch marks into shadows, nothing more, and other than that, he'd never be able to tell. A moment later, her concern evaporated anyway, consumed by the heat of desire burning between them. He was touching her, caressing her, bringing her to the point where nothing else mattered.

And then he entered her.

It was as if she'd never left, as if they'd never suffered the long absence or endured the missed years. There was no fumbling, no struggling, no grappling to find their rhythm. It came to them as naturally as breathing, and Silvia marveled as the ease of it. She'd forgotten how good making love could feel—with the right man.

And then she forgot everything but Rick. The feel of his skin beneath her fingers, the scent of his body on hers, the hard driving force pulling her higher and higher until there was no place left for either of them to go. Suspended for one long second, at that peak of experience, she felt nothing but heat at the center of her being, heat and power and the agony of too many lonely years, years wasted without being with Rick. Years lost, never to be recovered. Years gone...just like her baby...

A moment of climax flashed inside her, like a brilliant light of heat and desire. She coasted on the incandescence, her breath stopping, her heart pausing. Then she felt herself drifting down again, down into the warmth of Rick's arms and his love. Down into the reality of what would always be between them.

She buried her face against his chest and let the tears slowly slide from her eyes.

Hours later, as Rick parked the car back on San Luis, Silvia acknowledged that a giant knot of tension seemed to be the only thing holding her together. She was fragmenting—her brain couldn't assimilate everything that had happened tonight, all the information, all the emotions, all the feelings. Bits and pieces fell in and out of her mind like birds flying around inside a barn. It was crazy.

He turned in the front seat to stare at her. His gaze had a physical presence as it made its way over her face. A second later, as his fingers took her chin and forced her to look at him, the connection was made for real.

"I'm sorry I waited so long to tell you the truth, Silvia. I should have done it sooner...but I guess I just didn't have the courage." His voice was quiet. "It wasn't fair to you, I know."

"You couldn't tell me anything if I wasn't here to hear it."

He nodded, his gaze pressing into her in the darkness of the car. The silence built and then he spoke...softly, gently, carefully. He didn't want to scare her off. "It was Carlos, wasn't it? He made you leave, didn't he?"

She jerked her head around and faced him. "You knew?"

"I figured it out. Afterward." His hand fanned over her face, cupping her jaw. "I'm so sorry, Silvia. That everything happened the way it did."

She swallowed. "There's a reason for it, I'm sure."

"Is there?" His breath was warm against her cheek, a teasing touch that made her wish for more. He pulled her closer to him, his arm around her shoulders, the clean, calming smell of him filling her with a longing she couldn't deny, even though they'd just spent the last two hours making love.

"What do you think that reason is?" he whispered against her forehead, pulling her even closer, his lips moving against her skin.

"This isn't reason," she whispered back. "This is madness."

And it was. She'd been a foolish woman to let tonight happen, a lonely, foolish woman. What had she been thinking? That making love with Rick would solve everything? That it would bring them closer and finally put the past that separated them to rest? If that's what she'd thought, she'd been mad, absolutely mad. There was no way she could ever be as honest with him as he'd been with her tonight. No way. And what kind of relationship was built on lies?

As if sensing her thoughts, Rick pulled back slightly, and stared into her eyes. "I loved you so much it damn near killed me when you left. You knew that I loved you, didn't you?''

There was nothing else she could say. Part of her heart broke off at the realization, but she had no other choice. She had to push him away.

She spoke quietly, knowing how much she was about to wound him. ''You loved me—but you still made love to Linda, too?''

His eyes blazed with sudden emotion. ''We didn't make love, Silvia. We had sex. There's a big difference.''

''Is there?'' She took a deep breath. She had to push him harder. ''Then what do you call what we did tonight?''

He moved back as if she'd slapped him...just as she knew he would, his eyes filling with confused hurt.

She looked away. She had to—she couldn't bear to see what his gaze revealed. It meant he cared too much, and she couldn't have him caring at all.

''I thought you might call it the start of a new relationship,'' he answered, his voice turning gravelly, his anger beginning to simmer just below the surface. ''A clean start with something good and new between us. I got the impression a few hours ago that you might feel the same way. I guess I misread it, huh?'' He scorched her with his eyes a moment longer, then turned away, rage radiating from him like heat from a fire.

''Let's just say I think we both made a mistake,'' she answered thickly, turning away from him and feeling sick. ''I don't think it should have even happened.''

His voice was pained when he spoke once more. ''Well, you can rest assured it won't happen again.''

She watched the taillights of the car disappear into

the night a few minutes later. Feeling hollow, she congratulated herself on reaching her goal so easily.

She'd made him mad. Made him wish, once more, that she'd leave town and leave his life.

She'd gotten exactly what she wanted.

So why did she feel so bad?

Chapter 9

Cursing softly, Silvia glanced down at her watch then sighed. She hadn't even wanted to come into the office today, but she was expecting a call from Don at noon, and she had to be here to take it. He was so impossibly busy they had to set up phone appointments. She could never reach him on her own so this was the only way.

She swung her desk chair around and looked out her office window. It was raining, a soft patter against the glass that had taken off a bit of the heat. She watched a single drop begin at the top of one pane then trickle down. Along the way, it gathered a few of the other beads into itself, growing larger and larger, until it broke up once again.

Just like the lies we tell, she thought aimlessly. They start out simple, then grow until they can't be held together anymore. Then they tear apart until there's nothing left. Nothing at all.

If only Rick had told her the truth that night. If only

she had trusted him and listened. If only he'd never stopped when Linda Willington had flagged him down. Everything would have been different. Silvia could have told Rick about her pregnancy, and they might have worked things out. Instead, how many lives had been flung apart, changed forever, ended even?

And now they'd compounded the mistakes. By letting their bodies rule their brains. There was no chance of a real reconciliation, of a real relationship, ever developing between the two of them. How could there be?

The phone rang, and Silvia reached out automatically. Don Rogers's calm, deep voice greeted her at the other end, putting an end to her thoughts.

"Silvia how's everything going? The case looking good? Did you get a link?"

Knowing Don's time was short, Silvia outlined her preliminary report as quickly as she could.

"So the ballistics report confirms the two murders are related?"

"It seems to."

"Tell me more."

"Well, there's the gun itself and the location of the crimes for one thing."

"And the scene?"

"It's hard to catagorize. The murders took place out in an open field, a real deserted area. I'd label it a mix between organized and disorganized, really. And the contamination— It was incredible, made things impossible. If there was a suspect we might be able to trace mud or seeds from the area back to him, but as far as him leaving any traces of his presence behind—forget it."

"So all you really have are the autopsies and the ballistics."

"Basically, yes."

"And the victimology?"

"As mixed as the scene. The first woman could be categorized as high risk because of prior behavior, but the second woman was a model citizen—mother, wife, hardworker. It's crazy."

She could hear his chair squeaking, knew he was turning to look out his own office window, a view much different than her own. He spoke slowly. "I know you don't have a lot to go on, but if you can do something with this, Silvia, your problems here are going to shrink. I could use it as an example. I could get you some better cases. Get you back on top." He paused, a silent beat coming over the phone line. "I could keep you out in the field where you belong."

She drew a shallow breath and stared out her own window. "I'm not sure the field is where I belong."

"Because of one little problem? C'mon, Silvia—"

"It wasn't one little problem," she said tensely. "It was someone's life. But that's not the only reason. I...I'm just not sure this is what I want to do anymore, Don. *Can* do anymore."

"Not what you can do—" he broke off abruptly. "That's crazy, Silvia. You're the best I've got. Don't tell me you can't handle it anymore. I won't even believe you. You're made out of stronger stuff than that. Besides, you'd go crazy living anywhere but Washington. You need to be in the middle of things, where it's all happening. You know that as well as I do."

She sighed and looked out the window again. Steam was rising off the sidewalk. The rain had finally stopped. "That might have been true in the past, but I'm not so sure anymore." The face of one of her nephews flashed into her mind. She'd watched him at the party last Saturday as he'd chased one of his cousins, his chubby little legs pumping away as he'd run down the edge of the yard, screaming with delight. His face was replaced with Rick's, an image she couldn't dislodge as the memory of his hands on her body came over her. When she finally spoke, her voice was low and throaty. "I'm just not so sure anymore."

"Is thees the sheriff? Sheriff Rick?"

Rick cradled the phone between his shoulder and neck, shuffling papers as he answered. "Yeah—this is Rick Hunter. Who's this?"

"You don't need to know who I am—but you *do* need to know what I'm about to tell you. That is, if you care about catching Carlos Hernandez."

Rick's hands grew still, and his attention focused. He grabbed the receiver with his fingers and pressed it against his ear. "And what could I catch him doing?"

"Something illegal. That's all the man does." In the background, a burst of Spanish filled the silence then the man spoke again. "He got people coming to his house. His house on San Luis Street, tonight. They're not good people, but they should be. You might want to see who they are."

The words stopped, then the phone went dead. Rick looked at the receiver, then spoke anxiously into it. "Hello—hello? Are you there?"

Nothing but silence answered him.

He slowly put the phone back down. *They're not good people but they should be.* The INS? Who else could it be? he wondered.

Without thinking more of what he was about to do, he picked up the phone again and dialed.

"Hello?"

He closed his eyes as Silvia answered, her voice carrying with it her skin, her touch, her fragrance. Forcing the image from his mind, he spoke in a coolly professional tone. "I'd like to bring the new ballistics report by the house tonight. I think you need to see those photomicrographs. Are you free?"

Her voice turned frosty when she realized it was Rick on the other end of the line. "Why not just bring them to me right now? You're in the office, aren't you?"

He knew exactly what she thought he was doing. That he wanted to come over and make up, to try to get her to change her mind and believe they could start all over again and begin a new relationship. If he looked too far inside himself, that's probably exactly what he wanted to do, too.

He'd pull out his revolver and shoot himself in the foot before he'd walk over to her office and ask her to forgive him. Pain like that, he didn't need.

"I—I'm leaving in just a few seconds. I wouldn't have time," he answered brusquely.

"I can run over there—"

He tapped his pen against a white folder on his desk. A white folder labeled Ballistics. "Well, the truth is, I don't actually have the copies in my hand. I have to go get them, and then I'm going to be out of the office the rest of the day. I'd rather just come over to the house. Is seven all right?"

She hesitated, and he could imagine the look on her face. Her eyes, filled with puzzlement. One corner of her lip pulled in between her teeth. Her fingers fiddling with the top button of her blouse. He closed his eyes, but all he could think of was how soft her skin had felt, how full her lips were.

God, it was like some kind of fever, he thought wearily.

"All right," she said slowly. "I'll see you at seven."

He hung up before she could change her mind, then he jumped out of his chair, stuffed his hat on his head and fled his office. He didn't want her calling him back and canceling.

He didn't want to sit still any longer and listen to his heart.

Yolanda met Silvia at the door, a cold beer in each hand. "It's five o'clock. You ready to let down your hair?"

Silvia smiled and reached for the Corona. "More than ready. You must have read my mind on my way home."

"Bad day, huh?" Yolanda settled into one of the porch rockers and indicated Silvia should do the same. "Mine was nuts, too. The school called and said Carlota skipped yesterday's classes. I had to ream her out when she got home...and I hate to do that. She's usually a pretty good kid."

Silvia took a long swallow from her drink, her mind still on Rick and the night before. "But skipping school— That's not too good," she said absentmindedly.

"She gets bored, I think, but that's no excuse." Yolanda frowned. "And just last night she announced she wants to be a shrink—like her Tia Silvia. I guess it hasn't soaked through all that hair spray of hers that she has to go to school to do what you've done. She just sees the surface, you know. I told her you'd worked hard, had sacrificed a lot..." Her voice died quietly.

Looking down at the wooden floor of the porch, Silvia shook her head, the words finally soaking in. "Oh, God, Yolanda, she wants to be like me?" She looked up. "I'm the last person she should be emulating. The very last one. *You're* the successful woman in our family. The smart one. On Saturday when I saw all the kids, all the family, all the closeness... I think you made the better choices. Not me."

"We both made choices," Yolanda said stubbornly. "And they were both good ones."

Silvia knew her eyes were bleak. "But look what you have now."

"This little dump?" Yolanda grinned. "Oh, yeah, it's a wonderful house."

"That's not what I mean and you know it. I'm talking about your family, your husband." Silvia rubbed her eyes, then looked once more at her sister. "I...I can't stop from wondering what my life would have been like if I'd married Rick. What I might have now..."

"That was a choice you didn't have. Carlos didn't let you." Yolanda spoke quietly but with feeling. They drank in silence for a few more minutes, then she spoke hesitantly. "If things were different here...I mean, if this case was solved and you were free to do anything in the world, what would you do?"

Silvia said the first thing that popped into her mind. "I'd get my life in order. I'd decide what's really important, and I'd concentrate on that."

"On what's really important... Does that mean Rick?"

The denial was on Silvia's lips before she could think about it, but as she started to speak, she stopped. What was the use? If nothing else, making love to him had opened her eyes. She *did* care for him, had always cared for him, but that was it. They couldn't have more.

standing. "But he's a lawyer, Yolanda. This kind of thing, he'd surely understand. He would have gone with you, directly to the police."

"Maybe...but I'm not so sure." She wore a stubborn expression. "The thing is— I know I made a mistake and now I want to fix it. I want to tell someone so I'm telling you."

She took a deep breath, then began. "I found out accidently. Bonnie didn't really want me to know. She was married, had a nice little family." Yolanda shook her head. "I didn't understand it, that's for sure, but Bonnie was Bonnie. Kinda wild beneath that schoolteacher look, if you know what I mean."

"And what was it you found out?"

Yolanda looked up, her pained eyes meeting Silvia's. "She was having an affair. Seeing someone behind her husband's back. I found out because she had told Jack, that's her husband, that she was spending the night with me only she never came here. He called here unexpectedly that night, looking for her, and I had to do some pretty fast talking as soon as I realized what was going on.

"The next day, when I confronted her, she fell apart and told me the truth. She said she had a boyfriend, and she'd wanted to spend the night with him. I told her never to do that again, to use me like that. I didn't appreciate it."

"And what did she say?"

"She said it wouldn't be happening again because she was going to break up with him...if she could."

Silvia's nerves jumped. "If she could... What did that mean?"

Yolanda took a deep swallow of her beer, then spoke, the words coming out slowly, haltingly. "She

"I'm not sure what it means anymore, 'Landa. not sure at all."

Yolanda nodded. "Well...maybe you can figure t out after the case is over.... So with that thought mind, I thought I should probably mention this. I' been holding it back, but I...I can't do that anymore

Silvia swung her curious gaze to her sister's fac Yolanda's expression was a mixture of anxiousness a impending relief.

"What is it?" Silvia asked, her interest increasir tenfold.

"I...I knew Bonnie Kelman," Yolanda said quietl "And I think I know why she was killed."

For a moment, all Silvia could do was stare at he sister. Those words were the last thing she'd expected from Yolanda. "Wha-what are you saying?"

"I...I think I know why Bonnie was killed. Not who did it," she added anxiously, "but maybe why they di it."

"Yolanda..." Silvia couldn't hide her dismay. came out in her voice. "Why didn't you say somethi before now? This could be important."

"I know...I know." Yolanda's dark eyes were fi with contrition. "But all I could think about was Carlos would do. First, he'd make fun of me. S didn't know what I was talking about. Then if I sisted, he'd get mad, and start screaming about ho it would make the family look for me to get inv He'd do what he always does when he gets mad something. He'd take it out on Lydia—and I c stand that." Her expression pleaded for underst her forehead wrinkled, her mouth twisted. "Y how he is."

Frustration came over Silvia, frustration an

said...that she was...afraid of him. She said she knew things about him that other people didn't and if they found out, he'd be in big trouble." She drank again, then looked at Silvia. "She said she was thinking of turning him in to the police."

"Oh, God..." Silvia leaned back against her rocker, the hard wooden slats biting into her spine. She stared at her sister. "Who was he?"

Yolanda shook her head. "She wouldn't tell me. Said she couldn't."

"Couldn't or wouldn't?"

"Couldn't. She was emphatic about it."

Silvia felt her shoulders slump.

"I know, I know," Yolanda said, reading her body language. "When I decided not to tell Carlos, I thought about going straight to the police, but then I started thinking about what would happen. I knew they'd start asking me a bunch of questions, and it wasn't really going to help anyway. She had a boyfriend, but I couldn't tell them who. And just because she was seeing someone...that didn't mean he'd killed her. I knew that Jack would find out, too, if I told."

Yolanda looked up, her eyebrows meeting in a pleading expression. "She's got a fourteen-year-old daughter, Silvie, and a twelve-year-old son. Do you know what it'd do to them to find out their mother had a boyfriend? They were completely destroyed by her death. I couldn't kill their good memories of her, too."

Silvia couldn't contain her incredulousness, and the words slipped out before she could stop them. "You thought it'd be better to let a killer go free?"

Yolanda's face crumpled, and she began to cry. Feeling instantly awful, Silvia jumped from her rocker and put her arms around her sister. "Oh, God, I'm sorry,

Yolanda...I shouldn't have said that." She patted her on the back and held her close. Yolanda hiccuped into teary silence and looked up.

"No, you're right. Absolutely right. I should have ignored my concerns and just said something. Instead I kept quiet, and who knows what might happen because of it." She sniffed. "Is there anything I can do now? Can I go to Rick? Tell him everything I know?"

Silvia thought for just a moment, then spoke. "Well, that will have to be done, of course, but in addition, Rick will have to talk to Jack again and find out if he knew who Bonnie was seeing. You understand that, don't you?"

"Yes...but I think it'd be better if you talked to him, instead of Rick." She hesitated then drew a deep breath. "I think he might open up more to a woman. You won't threaten him like Rick does. You could get behind his facade because he thinks so little of women."

Puzzled, Silvia stared at her sister. Jack Kelman had obviously talked to Rick after the murder and said nothing to him about the boyfriend, or Rick would have already been checking this out. There was merit in Yolanda's suggestion. "Why do you say that?" she asked anyway.

"I don't know..." Yolanda hedged. "I just think he would." Almost as an afterthought, she added, "He's not a nice man."

Silvia flashed back to the report she'd read. The photos of old bruises. "Did he abuse Bonnie? Actually hit her?"

Yolanda flinched, then nodded. "I...think he might have slapped her once or twice. He's a big guy, tries to act real macho, if you know what I mean."

But he wasn't a killer. Rick's report had placed the

husband at work on the night Bonnie had been killed—on an offshore rig. And he'd been living in Saudi Arabia when Linda had been killed—didn't even know her as far as they could tell.

Silvia's mind tumbled the facts, studied them. "San Laredo's so small." She murmured the words, almost as if to herself. "Wouldn't someone else have seen Bonnie and her friend—known what was happening?"

"Not necessarily." Yolanda's voice grew stronger, more positive. "Bonnie was very resourceful, and she said they never went to public places. Ever. He had as much to lose as she did if anyone found out."

"He was married, too?"

"She wouldn't say. She just said he had a lot to lose, if anyone found out about them."

"But it's Rick's job to uncover things like that." *Unless he didn't want it uncovered.* The thought came out of nowhere and struck her silent.

"Then maybe you should ask him about it?" Yolanda tilted her head toward the sidewalk. "Here he is."

Silvia stood abruptly, the rocker swinging back against the house with a dull thud. She'd been so engrossed in the conversation, she hadn't even heard the cruiser pull up. Now here he was, standing at the edge of the porch, staring at her with those fathomless dark eyes. How much had he heard? How much did he know?

"Am I interrupting something? I can come back later...." He waited for her answer, his gaze burning into her own as if he wanted to expose everything between them.

"That's not necessary," she said coolly. "We were just finishing."

Obviously sensing the tension between them since it

was impossible not to, Yolanda jumped up, her rocker creaking a protest. "Well, I guess I'd better go in and start supper." Her voice was just a little too bright, a shade too enthusiastic. "Can you stay, Rick? We're having pot roast."

He shook his head. "No thanks, Yolanda. Maybe another night."

Yolanda nodded. "You come back next week. I'll do *enchiladas* for you. How's that?"

"Sounds great."

He smiled at Yolanda then, and Silvia couldn't hold back the shiver that ran down her spine. He was so sexy. The way his eyes crinkled when he grinned like that, the way his hat shadowed his eyes, the way he held himself, so full of coiled energy. If she lived to be 110, she'd never get tired of staring at him. A second later, Yolanda disappeared inside, leaving them alone once more.

Walking up the porch steps, Rick sat down in the rocker Yolanda had just vacated. Placing an envelope on the small table beside it, obviously the report he'd mentioned earlier, he looked up at her.

There was nothing else she could do. She sat down beside him.

Looking toward the driveway and the black BMW parked there, he spoke. "Carlos here?"

"Yes. Yolanda said he was meeting some people here later."

Rick nodded but said nothing else, and in the silence between them, the tension built until it was almost unbearable. Silvia couldn't help but think that instead of silence, there were things they should be sharing with each other...but neither of them could. Which seemed outlandish considering their intimacy. She did the only thing she could, the thing she usually did when the rest of her life was going nuts. She turned to the case.

"Yolanda just shared something with me I think you need to know." As quickly as possibly she relayed the conversation.

He took in the information quietly. "And does she have any idea who this boyfriend might be?"

Silvia shook her head. "No, none at all. Bonnie wouldn't tell her—said she couldn't. Obviously we're going to have to go back and interview the husband. Yolanda suggested I do it. She thought he might reveal more to me, and she may be right. He won't be as defensive because I'm 'just a woman.'"

"Sounds like a good idea," Rick answered. "If he was aware of the affair, he obviously didn't tell me about it so maybe you'll have better luck."

"He is clear, right?"

"Ironclad alibi. He's a rig worker, and he was on the rig. Offshore."

"What's he was like?"

"Quiet. Didn't say two words hardly. Said they got along just fine, and there were no problems in the marriage. Standard stuff."

"And you believed him?"

"No." Rick looked over at her. "I didn't believe a word he said. They fought like cats and dogs according to the neighbors and there were old bruises on her body. But the guy had an alibi, and I checked it out."

Silvia stood then wandered to the end of the porch and the swing that hung there from chains over the rafters. Looking out into the yard, she realized she wasn't looking forward to interviewing Jack Kelman.

She heard Rick rise and a second later, he was standing beside her, his powerful presence enveloping her.

He seemed to read her mind. "Is this what you want for the rest of your life?" he said unexpectedly. "To talk about murders and death and crime all the time?"

"No," she said softly. "It isn't what I want." She looked up at him, her eyes meeting his gaze, her heart thumping against her chest. "I didn't know that until I came back here, though. Until I saw the kids I don't have, and the family who's not around, and the life I've led for my career. Until I realized what I didn't have."

"You didn't know it'd turn out this way?"

Reaching out, she put her hand on one of the chains holding up the swing. Being this close to Rick made her dizzy and short of breath. To steady herself, she forced her eyes on the faint tan mark along his forehead where his hat rested. A moment later, her gaze dropped to his. His right eye still had a dark dot just to the left of the iris. She used to dream about his eyes.

"What did you think would happen?" he pressed. "Did you think you'd leave here and marry someone and have a family?"

"I didn't think," she answered. "Carlos didn't give me time to think. I just left. I went to Houston and lived with some cousins for a while. It was a bad time, a very bad time. I...I was in pain and—" She stopped suddenly, the words dying in her throat.

"In pain because you thought I'd killed Linda?"

"In pain because I felt like I'd betrayed you."

"And all this time...I was the one who'd betrayed you." Unexpectedly, he reached out and put his hand over hers, the chain rattling softly in the now dark night. The tension between them hummed with intensity, but it had changed, gone to a different level, a more personal one. "And after I'd been cleared... Why didn't you come back then?"

Silvia's heart went into knots. Her throat froze. "I...I couldn't."

"Because...?"

"Does it matter now?"

"Yes, it matters," he growled. "It matters a helluva lot to me." He took his hand from hers and moved closer, putting both his hands on her face. She stood mutely, her lower body leaning into his even as she knew it shouldn't. "I want to know the truth. I told you my truth...now it's time for you to do the same. If you didn't come back here because you hated my guts, that's one thing. If you still loved me...then that's something else. I want to know."

"Oh, Rick..." Suddenly she wanted to lay her head against his shoulder, to confess, to share the burden of sorrow she'd carried on her own for so long. She actually opened her mouth to answer, and at that very moment, the screen door banged open. She and Rick both looked up. Carlos was outlined in the light spilling from inside the house.

"I'm expecting some clients," he said tersely. "Do you think you two could take this somewhere else?"

Beside her, Rick tensed. Every muscle in his body seemed to bunch and grow tight. His voice was flat and without emotion when he spoke. "We aren't bothering you, Carlos. Why don't you just go back inside and leave us alone?"

"Are you ordering me around on my own property?" Carlos's voice was indignant, instantly angry. "What makes you think you can do such a thing?"

"I believe this is Yolanda's house." Silvia spoke mildly but her heart was thumping. "Not yours."

Carlos's burning gaze zeroed in on her. "You are

disrupting this household again. Just like you did before. I should—"

Rick moved forward, Silvia's hand in his. "Should what? Throw her out again? Cut her off without anything? Rip away the support of her family and friends and expect her to survive at eighteen?" He tightened his fingers around Silvia's. "She's not a helpless kid anymore, Hernandez. You might have a little more trouble trying to ruin her life now."

"I want you out of here," Carlos said from between gritted teeth. "Now."

Rick turned to Silvia. His eyes were blazing with anger but behind the expression, there was something else. A challenge almost. "What do you want?" he asked. "Do you want me to leave, too?"

Silvia's chest tightened, a band of tension closing around it so tightly she struggled to breathe. At the other end of the porch, Carlos seemed to fill the area with an anger so intense it almost seemed to reach out and wrap itself around her throat, making it even more impossible to breathe. Finally she answered. "I don't think that's necessary."

A second later, the door banged shut. She took a deep shuddering breath and then Rick's arms went around her.

She'd never been an easy sleeper. Silvia fought with it, wrestled with it, took forever to finally calm down, relax, and let herself go. This had gotten worse since she'd returned, and tonight was no exception. At 2:00 a.m. she gave up and rose from the bed. Throwing on a robe, she stepped outside to the back porch.

What had happened here tonight? Why had she stood up to Carlos? Why had she let Rick stay until midnight then allowed him to kiss her goodbye with a passion that left her reeling? It'd taken everything she had to make him leave, at all. The only thing stopping her, besides Carlos, had been the fact that she'd known had Rick stayed, if they'd made love again, she would have told him about their child, their child she'd lost.

She closed her eyes and wrapped her arms around herself. They offered a poor substitute for the ones that had been around her before. Her hand went up to her mouth, to trace her lips. They still held the feel of Rick's—encompassing, demanding, full of memories.

What was he doing to her? Every time they were together, they seemed more and more incapable of keeping their hands away from each other's bodies. It had taken all Silvia's willpower not to pull Rick into her bedroom tonight and to take his clothes off, to feel, once more, his body pressed against hers and making love to her like no other man. She'd made herself promise that it wouldn't happen again, but she was beginning to think it was a promise she was physically unable to keep. Making love with Rick was all she could think about.

She opened her eyes and stared into the night. Once Carlos had left them alone, they'd turned to each other in the darkness and embraced tightly, Rick's touch bringing her to the very edge of her desire even through her clothing. It'd seemed impossible for them to break apart, but the lights of a car had sliced through the darkness, and they'd been forced into dropping their embrace.

A moment later, the car had parked against the curb, then two men had climbed out, their voices clearly speaking Spanish as they'd gone up the walk then knocked on the front door. Carlos had opened the door and ushered them in, the two men never even glancing into the corner of the porch. If it hadn't been for their arrival, who knows what would have happened?

Rick had left shortly after that. Which was a very good thing because they had both realized what was going on. That their passion was taking them full circle. That they were coming back to the place neither of them had ever intended to revisit. It must have been inevitable, she thought, staring out at the darkness. Nothing—not his anger or her sharp words, not even the secrets she still kept from him—could douse the passion they still felt between them. She shook her head. It was crazy. Absolutely crazy, and she was completely powerless to fight it.

How could she still have these kinds of feelings toward him?

A sudden movement in the darkness caught her attention. Instantly on alert, she narrowed her eyes and glared out into the backyard. A moment later, a match flared, and in the instant's light, she saw the face of her brother. Had his meeting just now ended?

She started to ask him, but he spoke instead, his voice coming out of the darkness. "Thinking of your lover?"

She blushed, embarrassed by her obviousness and angered that he hadn't revealed himself before now.

"Why do you care so much?" she said coolly, walking toward the glowing ember of the cigar he'd lit, the cigar she could now smell. "If I didn't know better, I might think you had a problem with Rick."

"Oooh...is this some of that heralded mind reading that you supposedly do so well?" His voice was mocking. "I'm scared, Silvie. Really scared..."

He was sitting on the table, his feet resting on the bench beneath him. She sat down on the bench, next to his expensive leather boots, hand-tooled and polished. She looked up at him.

"What is it, Carlos?" She spoke softly. "Tell me your problem with Rick. All these years... Why do you still hate him so much?"

"I don't hate him. I just don't think he respects you, Silvia. And I never have. Men who don't respect my family do not have *my* respect."

Pausing, he drew on the cigar, smoke rising above them. He savored the taste for a moment, then spoke again. "My problem with him now, however, is different. He's involved in things he shouldn't be. I didn't tell you this before because I didn't think you'd believe me. You probably don't believe me now, either, but I can't stand by and let you continue to see the man without knowing what you're getting into."

"And what is that? What exactly is it that you think I'm getting into?"

"Trouble," he answered. "Rick Hunter is closer to the wrong side of the law than the right."

"Are you saying he's involved in something illegal?"

"I'm saying he's going down...and when he does, he's going to take the people around him down, too. I don't want that for you."

Silvia spoke without thinking. "Since when have you cared what happens to me?"

"I've always cared, Silvia. Always. That's why I've done the things I've done. I just wanted to do what was best for you."

"Throwing me out at eighteen was best?"

"It taught you to be strong, didn't it?"

"The hard way," she answered, her voice bitter. "I

had to experience things before I was supposed to. Things eighteen-year-old girls shouldn't have to face."

"But look at you now. You have real strength and you're smart."

"But not smart enough to understand Rick Hunter?"

He paused again, the tip of his cigar flaring as he pulled on it. The acrid smoke burned her throat as it filled the darkness between them.

"You're letting your hormones interfere with your brains. If I were you, I wouldn't be alone with him…at his office…in his car…." He leaned closer, his voice turning sincere for once, almost pleading with her. She pulled her head up sharply and met his gaze.

"You must listen to me, Silvia. Rick Hunter is dangerous. If you value your life the way it is, then for God's sake, stay away from the man."

Chapter 10

Jack Kelman answered Silvia's third knock on the door. Silvia had called him the day before and told him she was coming, but she halfway expected him to refuse to let her in anyway. Even over the telephone, he'd been everything Yolanda had said he was.

Reticent to the point of rudeness and resistant to go through yet another interview, he'd insisted Silvia come late at night. For a man whose wife had just been murdered, he seemed awfully hesitant to help find her killer. After a while, Silvia had explained he didn't really have a choice in the matter, and he'd reluctantly agreed to see her.

When he opened the door, he looked exactly as she had expected. He wore pressed khaki pants and a spotless white shirt. His shoes were buffed to a high polish, and it was obvious he'd just shaved and showered.

It was easy to see, with her psychologist's eye, the man Jack Kelman really was. He wanted everything under control. That's how he expected things, and that's how Bonnie had probably done them...or else she'd had to suffer the consequences.

Silvia smiled and pretended she didn't know the intimate details she did know about his life. "I'm Dr. Hernandez. You must be Jack Kelman?"

"That's right." He stared at her, measuring her from top to bottom, then he finally held the door open wider, as if she'd passed some kind of test only he knew about.

She stepped inside, and without a word, he turned and entered the living room at their right, expecting her to follow.

The room was as orderly and neat as the man, with polished wooden floors so bright and clean Silvia could see herself in them. Free of knickknacks and clutter, everything was in its place and where it belonged, no loose magazines lying about, no children's dirty socks or toys scattered underfoot. The upholstered furniture, as antiseptic as the atmosphere, was equally spotless. Silvia sat down in the chair he indicated, and he took the couch on the opposite side, against the wall.

"I don't know what else you people need to know." With his words and his attitude, he immediately tried to gain control of the situation, but Silvia wasn't surprised. In fact, any other attitude would have shocked her from a man like Jack Kelman. "I told everything I knew to that Hunter fellow already."

"I know. I read the report, and you were extremely cooperative. It really helped a lot." Silvia made her voice as sympathetic as she could. After all, the man had just lost his wife. "And I'm sure you must be tired of repeating the details. I know I would be. Questions like these just make your grief even worse, don't they?"

He seemed startled by her reply, as if grief weren't

an emotion that had been involved. "I...I guess so," he said. He uncrossed his arms, warming under her gaze. "I had to convince 'em I wasn't anywhere near here when it happened. Had to get my boss to call from the rig. Couldn't believe somebody'd actually think I could do something like that...to my own wife and everything."

Silvia nodded, keeping her expression neutral. "That must have been hard for you."

"Hard? It was stupid, that's what it was." He crossed his arms again, and his legs, too. "Don't have any idea why someone would think I'd kill the woman. We had a good marriage," he said stubbornly. "Just as good as my old mun and my ma had."

She studied him for a moment, then spoke, her voice deceptively quiet. "Would Bonnie have agreed with you, Mr. Kelman? That your marriage was good?"

He had mean, narrow eyes, and they jumped to hers at the question. "What's that got to do with anything?"

"It has a lot to do with everything. In an investigation like this we have to examine everything, all her friends, her total life." Silvia leaned forward, her elbows resting on the arms of the chair. "Sometimes when women aren't getting what they want from their marriages, they turn to other people. It's a natural reaction, you know...to turn to someone else for comfort or love."

His jaw twitched. When he spoke, the words came out from behind clenched teeth. "You saying you think my wife was fooling around?"

"Was she?"

His face immediately turned red, and his fingers tightened so hard on the sofa he crushed one corner of the cushion beneath him. "Why are you asking me something like that?"

"Because it's important...just like I said. We have to know everything about your wife if we're going to catch who did this."

His face turned even redder, his voice an angry bluster. "These are stupid questions, and you're wasting my time. Instead of sitting here jawing like this, you ought to be out there finding out more about the killer, dammit!"

"But that's exactly what I am doing, Mr. Kelman," she said quietly. "By finding out more about your wife." She paused and took a steadying breath. She didn't want to lead him to say something that wasn't true, but she had to know.

"If there was anything—and I mean anything—in Bonnie's life that we don't know about right now, it could be very important. A friend you've forgotten she had, a meeting she might have mentioned...anything at all. Are you sure there's nothing else you can tell us—"

He jumped to his feet. "What the hell do you want me to do? Make something up?"

"Of course not. I'm just asking you if there's anything else you might have thought of that you want to pass on to us. You have an obligation to tell us everything you know—"

"I don't have to do anything." The angry words erupted as he turned from her, but some of his earlier belligerence was seeping away, like air from a suddenly deflating balloon.

"Do you know what obstruction of justice means, Mr. Kelman? If you know something about this crime and you aren't coming forward, you could be in big trouble yourself." She let the silence build again, then spoke so softly the words could barely be heard. "Are you sure there isn't anything else you can tell us? Something important you know you might have forgotten to pass on? Something—''

"All right! All right! I'll tell you, dammit!'' He spun around, his shoulders tight, his hands in fists by his side. "If I had known earlier, I would have kicked her out. I didn't find out until she was dead, though.''

"And what was it you found out?''

"That she was a slut! A whore who didn't respect her marriage vows.'' He spit the words out, disgust all over his face. "She had a boyfriend. She was sneaking around, seeing someone else behind my back.'' He shook his head with contempt, his feelings more than obvious.

"So why should you help find her killer, right? That's what you thought, isn't it, Mr. Kelman?''

"You're damned right, that's what I thought.'' His eyes blazed. "From the way I see it, she deserved what she got.''

His bitter words rang in the sterile emptiness of the room. Silvia stared at him. Ironically, he'd probably loved his wife. Loved her a lot. Men like this felt so insecure, the attention of their spouses was the only thing holding them together. Now that Bonnie was gone, he was coming undone. Despite that knowledge, Silvia couldn't dredge up any sympathy for him. He was a brutal, angry man.

"We've got to find out who she was seeing,'' Silvia said finally. "If he's not her killer, he might have more information that would help us.''

Jack Kelman's expression didn't change. He stared at her with stony eyes, his face a granite carving of unrelenting hostility. Something was going on behind the mask, though, and finally he spoke. "Stay there,'' he growled. "I've got to get something.''

He came back a moment later with a small notebook covered in floral fabric. Handing it to her, he spoke gruffly. "Turn to the last page." He moved away from her and stood looking out the window.

The handwriting was small and neat. Silvia could read it easily. "I'm meeting him at noon at the house. He's so different from Jack, so gentle but so powerful. I've got to break it off, though. I'm getting scared, and I don't want to know the things I know about him."

Her breath catching in her throat, Silvia looked up and spoke to his back. "Why didn't you show this to Sheriff Hunter?"

"I hadn't found it then."

"Do you know what house she's referring to? Did she mean here?"

"Who knows?" He looked out the window again, his profile holding a stubborn silence.

Holding the diary, Silvia rose and moved to his side. "Does this diary identify the man, Mr. Kelman?"

"No." Shaking his head, he swallowed, his throat moving painfully. "She doesn't ever mention his name. She just said he was somebody important, somebody powerful." His voice was bitter, but laced with pain and regret. "A man who was really somebody...a man totally different from me."

Drained by the ordeal of talking to Jack Kelman, Silvia angled her car against the curb outside Yolanda's house and cut off the engine. Laying her head against the steering wheel for just a moment, she wondered where it was all going to end. Who had been Bonnie Kelman's lover? And how did he tie in to Linda Willington eighteen years before? The more details Silvia uncovered, the stranger the case became.

A second later, the tap of a horn made her lift her head. Her gaze shot to the rearview mirror just in time to see Rick climbing out of his cruiser and heading toward her car. She rolled down her window and looked up at him. "I couldn't possibly be speeding," she said. "I'm too tired to be going fast."

"Not to mention the fact that you're parked." He smiled, his eyes narrowing in the process and sending a shiver directly up her spine. A moment later, his expression shifted, the amusement leaving. "Did I see you coming from Jack Kelman's just a minute ago?"

She nodded. "I wanted to talk with him as soon as I could."

"Good." His voice was so deep it almost seemed foreboding. "Come for a drive and tell me what he said."

The warning Carlos had issued her echoed in her head. *Don't be alone with him.*

She hated herself for the thought, but what else could she do? "I...I'm really tired, Rick. Do you think it could wait?"

He leaned his elbow against the roof of her car and looked down at her, his voice a casual drawl. His expression didn't change. "I'd like to hear what the man had to say. Come with me. I promise I'll have you back in an hour."

His fathomless dark eyes pulled her closer, and with a sigh of resignation, Silvia did what she'd known she was going to do all along. She got out of her car and followed him back to his cruiser.

Brushing against her, he opened the side door and she climbed inside, her pulse leaping at his closeness and the scent of the shaving lotion he wore.

The minute he closed the door, she felt trapped. The

front seat was narrow and crammed with equipment, hardly leaving her room to move. When he opened the opposite door and got in behind the wheel, the space shrunk even more.

He drove slowly, one finger on the wheel, the deserted streets making her feel as if they were the only people awake. It was a strangely intimate impression, bringing to mind their time in the summerhouse, the time she couldn't get out of her head.

He took a left and glanced toward her. "Well? What revelations did Jack have for you?"

His voice rippled over her. She pushed away the sensation and tried to focus. "He confirmed what Yolanda had suspected—Bonnie Kelman was having an affair."

"Damn!" Rick's eyebrows raised in surprise. "With whom?"

"I have no idea. He told me he doesn't know, and I believe him. He gave me her diary, though."

Rick shook his head. "God, I can't believe I missed this...."

"You didn't miss it. I think he didn't know until after he'd spoken with you. Any way you cut it though, Jack Kelman would never have told another man his wife was seeing someone behind his back. He's the kind of guy whose ego is more important than anything else."

"How'd you get it out of him?"

Silvia shrugged, her eyes going out to the darkness beyond the car. He was driving away from town, away from the lights. "I made him madder than he usually is," she answered. "It was fairly easy after that."

"I'm impressed."

"Please don't be. It's not a skill I enjoy using, but when you've heard as many lies as I have, you finally learn how to get at the truth when you need it."

He turned down a county road, the gravel crunching under the car's tires. "I know what you mean. I've learned a few of those tricks myself through the years, but I guess my radar wasn't on with Jack."

"Don't be so hard on yourself. Kelman's not an easy man to read."

"So who do you think she might have been seeing?"

In the dark, Silvia looked across the seat at him. "I have no idea...and the diary doesn't give a name."

He shot his eyes toward her for a second, before concentrating on the road again. "Don't you think that's strange? That she wouldn't write down the guy's name?"

"Not really. She couldn't risk it."

"Risk it?"

"He was someone 'important.' She was scared for anyone to find out who he was. Apparently she felt threatened in some way by him."

"But she was having an affair with the guy? That doesn't make sense. How could she be seeing him and be scared of him at the same time?"

Silvia glanced toward him, her heart hammering an uneasy rhythm she couldn't ignore. "Some women find that very attractive. They like to be scared—it turns them on."

His eyes met hers in the darkness, then she pulled her gaze away. Quickly...before she could say more.

They discussed the interview a little while longer, but finally there was nothing left to say. They rode in silence for a few more minutes, each lost in thought.

After a while, the car slowed, then rolled to a stop. When he shut off the engine, total silence enveloped them. Rick turned toward her, his arm stretched out over the top of the seat, his head nodding toward the field at her right.

"Do you recognize where we are?"

She stared out the window, her eyes adjusting slowly to the darkness, a full moon helping by rimming the area with silver light. Out of the shadows, something tall seemed to take form. She studied it for a moment, then her breath caught in her throat.

"It's the tree," she whispered. "Our oak tree."

"I didn't think you'd remember." He dropped his fingers to her neck. They played warmly on her skin, his voice a silken cord, pulling her closer to him. "Want to go see if it's gotten any bigger?"

As teenagers, they'd spent hours sheltered under the branches of the enormous tree, kissing, hugging, telling each other their secrets. It had been their special place, but she'd forgotten about it. Deliberately, she was sure, because remembering it all now, the pain was sharp and intense.

"C'mon," he whispered. "I haven't been here in years. Let's go look."

Drawn by forces beyond her control, Silvia nodded. They exited the car and holding hands, made their way through the field, the moonlight giving them all the illumination they needed. She knew it was wrong, knew where it was leading to, but suddenly she didn't care. The moment had a life of its own and to interfere would have been to disrupt fate itself.

Stepping into the circle of the tree, they ducked underneath the huge branches, some of them so heavy they touched the ground, their circumferences larger than Silvia's body. In the still, silent greenness she felt as though she were inside a cathedral. Standing quietly, she drank in the fecund smell of leaves and growing grass, and she remembered.

Remembered the teenager she'd been. The love she'd had for the man standing quietly behind her. The grief she'd felt when she'd lost her child.

Hearing a rustling sound, she turned around. He'd come prepared. A plaid wool blanket covered the soft ground beneath the tree, and he was sitting on it, patting the spot beside him.

"Come here," he said softly. "Come sit down beside me."

Her heart tumbled with nervousness, but she walked to the blanket and sat down. "You planned all this, didn't you? You didn't really want to talk about the case."

"You're absolutely right." Reaching out he traced the line of her jaw with one finger. "I could care less about that case right now, Silvia. All I want to do is think about us."

"There isn't an us, Rick. There can't be. Everything we had is in the past."

He palmed the side of her cheek, his thumb rubbing back and forth over her skin to create a thrilling warmth. "And the other night? What about that?"

"It was a mistake," she answered, "and you know it. That should never have happened."

"You're not trying to make me mad again, are you?" His fingers went to her lips and traced an outline around her mouth. "If you are, forget it. I figured out your little trick. We're two adults now, Silvia. We could have a relationship again. There's nothing between us but the truth now."

"Oh, Rick..." She turned her head, looking out over the field.

He moved closer to her. Putting his hands on her shoulders, he massaged her gently, his thumbs rotating against her resistance as though he could dissolve her opposition by sheer physical power.

"You can't deny the attraction between us," he whispered, his lips moving against her hair. "It's always been there, Silvie, and it's never going to leave. Surely you can admit to that."

She groaned, his touch warming her through the blouse she wore. "The mere presence of physical attraction does not necessarily make for a successful relationship."

"You're sounding like a shrink," he murmured. Turning her around to face him, he stared into her eyes. "Don't be anything but a woman with me, Silvia. Right now, right here, that's all I want from you. Just be a woman...and let me love you." Without giving her the time to answer, he lowered his head and kissed her.

Part of her knew it was wrong—she'd regret this later when she had a chance to really think about what she was doing—but the other part of her just didn't care. For a few minutes, she wanted to pretend she was eighteen again. Eighteen and in love and drunk with the possibilities of what life had in store.

She melded against him, her body fitting into his as easily as it always had. He groaned at her acquiescence and drew her closer to him, pausing only to discard the clothing that impeded his touch.

Overhead, in the still night breeze, the leaves rustled, and patterns of silver light moved across their bodies, bringing the moon even closer. He knew exactly where to touch her, his fingers roaming over her body, his lips following close behind—brief, searing caresses followed by long, drawn-out kisses.

She returned the favor, her hands dancing over his hard, lean body until he grabbed her fingers and stilled them to end the unbearable torture, pressing his body on top of hers, his long legs stretching out on either side of her body. Again, they found their rhythm quickly, Rick bringing her to a climax a second before he found his own.

Moments later, Rick's heavy weight against her, his murmured groans still warming her, Silvia was conscious of only one thing and one thing only. She was falling in love again.

And making the biggest mistake of her life.

The Little League field was crowded with cars, kids and activities of all kinds. It looked like a scene of mass confusion to Silvia, but as Yolanda edged her Toyota down the narrow shell road that marked the outer boundary, Silvia could tell her sister knew exactly where she was going. She'd obviously made the trek a thousand times before.

Yolanda glanced toward her. "Are you sure you want to spend your Saturday doing this?"

"Why wouldn't I?" Silvia smiled. "It's not every day my nephew gets to the play-offs!"

Yolanda chuckled. "Well, that's true, but this is hardly Yankee Stadium. I don't imagine you're used to such mundane chores on a Saturday."

"You'd be surprised." Looking out the window at all the children and their parents, Silvia again felt the tug of what her life had been missing. Ignoring the bittersweet feeling, she made her voice light. "When I'm not hunting mass murderers, I really lead a pretty simple life."

"Actually, now that you mention it, you'll probably

feel right at home.'' Yolanda maneuvered the small car into a parking spot and turned off the engine. ''When you hear the parents start screaming, you'll think you've discovered a convention of serial killers.''

''I thought this was supposed to be fun.'' Silvia spoke with dismay. ''They scream at their kids?''

''No!'' Yolanda grinned from across the seat. ''They scream at the coach—who else?''

Laughing, they stepped outside the car and went to the trunk to gather the various bags of supplies Yolanda had insisted they would need. Sunblock, hats, a cooler full of soft drinks, bags of chips. With their arms loaded down, they headed toward the stands. Raul, Yolanda's youngest, was sitting on the bench waiting for his game to start. When he saw his aunt and mother arrive, a big grin split his face and he waved so hard, his arm looked as though it might fly off his body.

Settling onto the hard, wooden bleacher, Silvia smiled and waved back, her decision to come to the game reinforced once more. Although she'd wanted to come, until this very moment, she hadn't really realized how badly she'd needed this as well. Needed an ordinary day in the sunshine, a day with her family, with kids, with confusion. A day without murder and death and violence that couldn't be explained.

A day that would force Rick from her mind.

She needed it—especially after their night of love-making when she'd lost the last bit of her reserve. When they'd made love until the sun had come up. When she'd realized she was losing her heart again.

The game got underway with a minimum of confusion, Raul coming up to bat quickly. Silvia found herself on her feet, her hands sweating with anxiety as she and Yolanda both cried out their encouragement. She didn't know if he could hear her, but she gave it her best.

"C'mon, baby," she cried. "Let's go! Hit a big one—right over the fence. C'mon!"

He swung wildly at the first two balls, then seemed to settle down. On the fifth pitch, his bat connected soundly with the ball, the noise of leather hitting metal coming up into the bleachers with a satisfying *thrack*.

Silvia and Yolanda went nuts, screaming and jumping up and down. Abandoning his spot, the little second-base man ran out and grabbed the ball, pitching it wildly in the direction of first base. Scrambling to catch the ball, the first-base man collided with his coach and they both went down in a tumble of dust and howls of surprise.

Raul went straight into the fray. When the dirt began to settle, he realized he hadn't touched base. With Silvia and Yolanda now laughing so hard they were crying, they watched his desperate scramble toward the canvas-covered bag...but it was too late. The first-base man grabbed him by the ankle and tagged him.

A few seconds later, still laughing, Yolanda and Silvia sat back down, Yolanda reaching into the cooler at their feet. Pulling a drink from the ice for herself, she reached back inside and got a second one for Silvia. As she handed the dripping can over, her eyes went beyond Silvia's shoulder then turned round with surprise.

Automatically turning to follow her sister's gaze, Silvia felt her heart click.

Rick stood at the bottom of the bleachers, a baseball cap covering his eyes, his uniform identifying him as a coach for one of the older teams. Yolanda had told Silvia he coached, but for some reason, she hadn't expected to see him. Her heart did a little flip. He looked incredibly handsome, tanned and fit.

And he was talking to Barbara Williams—his ex-wife.

Silvia couldn't look away. She watched the two of them talk, Barbara's face turning up to Rick's, his expression serious and intense as he spoke. A moment later, he reached out and put his hand on her shoulder, clearly trying to make a point.

She reached out as well, her manicured fingers touching his lightly, a smile on her face. A second later, in response to something he'd said, she shook her head, her hair flying over his hand still resting on her shoulder.

They talked for a few more minutes, then Barbara backed away, her tanned legs flashing in the summer sunshine, her hair gleaming in the light. Smiling her goodbye, she turned around and left quickly. Silvia's eyes went back to where Rick stood. He watched his ex-wife leave, his unreadable gaze steady on her disappearing figure.

Watching him watch Barbara, something twisted deep down inside of Silvia, something hot and immediate. She told herself it wasn't jealousy because she didn't have the right to claim such a ridiculous emotion, not where Rick was concerned. Yes, they'd been intimate, and yes, there was a history between them, and yes, dammit…she might be falling in love with him again. But jealousy? It couldn't be.

But it was…and she knew it.

Chapter 11

"Let's go down to the field." Standing up, Yolanda stretched. "I want to talk to Raul's coach about practice next week. Raul might be late, and I want to make sure he knows why."

It was three games later and almost five o'clock. Nodding, Silvia stood. Rick had disappeared after his conversation with Barbara, and she hadn't seen him since. Obviously his own game had concluded, and he'd gone home.

She couldn't help but wonder about what she'd seen.

What had he and Barbara been talking about so intensely? Barbara's alleged boyfriend, Carlos? Rick hadn't seemed angry, but he'd definitely been intent on something.

Trying to put it all out of her mind, Silvia looked at Yolanda. "You go ahead," she answered. "I'll pick up everything here, then meet you back at the car."

"Sounds great." Yolanda started down the bleachers,

stopping to talk to the other parents and grinning over their obviously complimentary remarks. The Blue Devils had won their championship. They'd head to Austin now for the state finals.

Making her own way down the steep wooden steps, Silvia headed back toward the car. She was halfway across the parking lot when she saw him. He hadn't left after all. There was another field behind the one where Raul had played. Rick had probably been there all day.

A swarm of children was crowding around him. They were singing and laughing, and hanging off his broad shoulders as if he were part of their playground equipment. One of them was holding up a trophy almost bigger than he was. Obviously Rick's team had had a successful day, too.

Talking to each one in turn, laughing with them and making sure no one got slighted, Rick was clearly enjoying himself, and Silvia couldn't help but be shocked. There was no trace, no hint, of the grim-faced man in the uniform she was so accustomed to seeing. Her reaction was swift and strong, one thought stabbing her through with an intensity almost too painful to bear.

He would have been the perfect father.

The child she'd carried and lost would have had a wonderful dad, a caring, loving, attentive father. Rick would have been there always with unconditional love and support, and he would have seen that the child lacked for nothing. Their family would have been as special and wonderful as it could have possibly been.

As if her thoughts had an energy of their own and had gone out to touch him, Rick's gaze turned up and went over the children's heads. For a moment, he searched the parking lot, then he saw her. His eyes widened slightly in surprise, then he smiled and motioned for her to come closer.

Like a moth drawn to a flame, she moved toward him.

"What are you doing here?" Laughing as the children clamored over him, Rick ruffled the hair on one while another one pulled on his belt. The change in him was remarkable—even his eyes looked lighter around the children, more alive, less intimidating.

She motioned to the field behind her. "I came to watch Raul."

"Ah...the Blue Devils! They won, didn't they?"

She nodded, her heart in her throat. "It...it looks like you did, too."

"We won!" the kids around him screamed, then began to chant, "Pizza! Pizza! Pizza!"

He grinned at her. "I bribed them for a win. Guess I'm going to buy out the Pizza Hut. Want to come along?"

She answered quickly, without giving herself a chance to think. "I can't... I...have to work on my report."

"It's Saturday night," he replied. "C'mon, I won't tell anyone you took an evening off." He looked down at the screaming kids, still milling around his knees and tangling with each other in the dust. "Besides, you wouldn't leave me alone with all these heathens, would you? I need some help here—some psychological assistance!"

"Let's go, Coach! It's time to eat. We want our pizza!"

The kids pulled at him, but Rick stood still and waited for her answer. "It's just pizza," he said finally, a gleam coming into his eyes. "Pepperoni or sausage—not a lifelong commitment."

"All right," she said, knowing all along she was helpless to do anything but agree. "Let me put this stuff in Yolanda's car. I'll meet you there."

"Ride with me. I'll take you home afterward." He paused, his dark eyes pinning her down. "Unless, of course, there's someplace else you'd like to go. Somewhere more private."

She knew exactly what he was talking about—their time under the oak tree had obviously been on his mind, too.

"No...no. Th-that would be fine," she answered. "If it's not too much trouble."

"It's no trouble at all," he said, holding his hand out to her. "Let's go."

By the time the pizza party ended, it was almost nine. Under a moon that was still full, Rick led Silvia out to his truck and opened the door for her. She brushed past him, Chanel No.5 filling the thick night air.

He hid his groan in the sound of the slamming door. Dinner had been torture. They'd sat, side by side, for more than two hours, surrounded by third-graders and their grateful parents. Being that close to Silvia for that long and not being allowed to touch her had been almost unbearable.

He planned to remedy that situation immediately.

She noticed as soon as he turned right out of the restaurant's parking lot instead of left.

"I thought you said you'd take me home," she said suspiciously. "This isn't the way to San Luis Street."

"I know. It's the way to my house."

Her voice rose. "You said—"

He glanced toward her, across the cab. "I said I'd take you home...I just didn't say whose home."

They went a few more miles before she spoke again. "I don't really think this is a good idea."

"I'm sure it's not a good idea," he replied, pulling the truck into a wide, curved driveway, "but we're here, so it's too late to go back." Killing the truck's engine, he turned in the dark to stare at her. "But if you really want me to take you home, I will."

She returned his stare for one long moment, then she reached for the handle on the door and threw it open. His heart did a double take then he followed her, scrambling across the seat and into the humid night air.

Opening his front door, Rick stepped back, and Silvia walked slowly into the living room. He started to turn on the lights, then stopped. There was enough moonlight coming in through the wide glass windows for him to see her perfectly.

Every curve, every line, every delicate feature of her face and body was bathed in the silvery streams of light. She'd made the decision to come inside, but now like some kind of wood nymph who wanted to flee, she turned around hesitantly and stared at him.

"I shouldn't have let you bring me here," she said.

"I couldn't think of anything else all the way through dinner." He moved into the room to stand beside her, to breathe in her silky perfume. "Your being here is my reward for being so patient."

"I'm your reward?" She shook her head and laughed nervously, her dark hair moving in the moonlight, enticing him to run his fingers through it. "If you only knew..."

Stepping up to her, Rick cradled her face in his hands, her skin smooth and soft beneath his touch. "If

I only knew what?'' he asked. He thought of the dark shadows her eyes always held, the way she never spoke of her life beyond here. ''Have you got some kind of horrible secret you're hiding?''

Almost abruptly, she pulled out of his arms and stepped away. Moving to the windows, she stared out into the woods that covered his backyard.

He came up behind her and put his arms around her. For a moment she resisted then she leaned against him, her weight barely noticeable, her warmth instantly sensual. The clean smell of shampoo and soap rose from her hair and enveloped him. It took a moment for him to realize she was trembling.

''What is it?'' he said softly. ''What's wrong?''

She shook her head, unable to speak.

''You can tell me, Silvie.'' He put his hands on her shoulders and turned her around to face him. There were tears glimmering in her eyes, and it shocked him. The only other time he'd seen her cry was the night Robert Tully had carted him off. ''What is it?''

Her eyes were huge as they met his. ''Just hold me,'' she whispered. ''Don't ask me anything else. Just hold me.''

He stared at her a moment longer. What was wrong? Why the tears? He thought briefly of pressing her, but what was the point? When she was ready to tell him whatever she wanted to tell him, she would…and not a minute before. She was a stubborn woman, but he almost admired that trait. It was part of what had made her as successful as she was. With that thought, wrapping his arms around her and bringing her as close as he could, he closed his eyes.

Just hold her? He could do that for the rest of his life.

The thought no longer shocked him. Last week, when he'd first realized it, he'd spent the greater part of three days trying to convince himself it wasn't true. Trying to tell himself they didn't have a possible future together, trying to tell himself their past would only get in the way.

The more he'd thought about it, though, the more he'd come to realize he didn't really have a choice in the matter. Sometime between seeing her that first day in his office, so professional and uptight, and seeing her under the oak tree, her hair tousled, her lips swollen from his kisses, he'd accepted the fact that they were bound together and always would be. The connection between them had withstood years of separation and nothing short of death would probably ever cut the ties. That was just the way it was.

He put his hand on the back of her head and gently caressed her hair. Murmuring against his touch, she drew even closer, lifting her head finally to gaze at him, her eyes sultry with longing. "Take me to your bedroom."

He didn't have to think twice. Lifting her easily, he made his way to the back of the house, the darkness no hindrance. When they reached the edge of the bed, he gently set her on her feet.

"Let me undress you," she whispered. "I want to do it."

Unable to speak, all he could do was nod. Her fingernails gleamed as they reached out for his shirt buttons. One by one, she undid them, slipping her hands inside to his chest when his shirt finally hung open. Her touch was at once warm and comforting...but more exciting than he'd ever thought possible. Spreading her fingers over his skin, she pressed her palms against him. A second later, she put her cheek against his chest.

He groaned as her silky hair brushed his nipples. "I can hear your heart beating," she whispered.

"Is it still there? I thought I'd lost it." He met her gaze in the darkness. "A beautiful woman came into my office a month or so ago and stole it. I thought it was gone."

She didn't answer him. All she did was rise up on her toes and kiss him, her arms twining about his neck, her breasts pushing into his bare chest. Pressing his mouth against hers, he reached between them and undid her blouse. Her lacy bra followed and then they were standing skin against skin.

It was hard to pull his mouth from hers, but he did. Dropping to his knees he began to kiss her breasts, first one and then the other, pulling her nipples into his mouth and lightly brushing his teeth across their hardened points. She groaned, and he pulled her closer, his hands on her buttocks. Burying his face between her breasts, he breathed in her perfume, her skin, her essence.

They quickly discarded the rest of their clothing, a scrambled pile of cotton and silk, lace and leather lying at the edge of his bed. Falling to the coverlet, their arms still locked around each other, Rick pulled Silvia on top of him.

"I want you," he murmured against her neck. "This is all I've been thinking about for days."

"Me, too," she confessed, her words muffled as her lips moved over his jaw. "At home, in the car, at the office. It's terrible…it's like I'm eighteen all over again, and sex is the only thing I can think about."

He pulled back slightly and looked at her. "This is more than sex, Silvie. A lot more."

"I know," she answered, her hair falling in a curtain on either side of her face. "But I don't want to talk about that. Not right now."

He nodded and pulled her toward him. She was right. Words weren't necessary. Not here. Not now.

They had the rest of the night to talk.

He brought her closer to him and slid his hand over her thigh, her skin velvety beneath his touch. Murmuring, she turned toward him and began to kiss him, tiny caresses with her mouth, up and down his shoulders, his chest, his stomach...and then lower.

Groaning, Rick used every ounce of his strength to hold back, but she was making it almost impossible. Her fingers dancing over him, her hair brushing against him, the scent of her perfume rising in the heat between them. He wouldn't last much longer.

She raised her head and looked at him. There was desire in her gaze, a hunger he knew no other man had ever been able to see. She wouldn't have allowed anyone but him to see such naked longing, longing that had nothing to do with sex and everything to do with love.

It went straight into his heart. He pulled her up, then rolled her over. Looming above her, he stared into her eyes once more.

"I love you," he said, each word a separate acknowledgment. "I have always loved you. You know that, don't you?"

He wasn't sure, but in the darkness he thought he saw her eyes glistening once more. She nodded her head.

"I...love you, too." Her voice broke. "Even in the bad times...I loved you."

There was nothing left to say after that.
Their bodies did the rest.

She woke up before he did.

The clock beside the bed glowed with eerie greenness, the numbers almost pulsing in the darkness. It was 3:00 a.m. Lifting the covers, Silvia gently slid from the bed and padded toward the pile of clothing spread over the carpet.

The first thing she found was Rick's shirt, and picking it up, she slipped her arms into the sleeves and walked toward the hallway at the same time. Behind her, Rick murmured softly in his sleep and turned over.

The living room was still bathed in silver light, but from a different angle now. While they'd been making love, the moon had gone over the house and was pouring sterling through the front windows, the back bathed in darkness, trees looming overhead.

She made her way slowly across the tiled floor, staring at the furniture, looking at the books scattered across a nearby table. Everything was comfortable, livable. It wasn't the home of the man she'd thought Rick was. But then that shouldn't have been a surprise, should it?

She'd been wrong about a lot of things as far as Rick was concerned.

Lifting the collar of his shirt toward her face, Silvia breathed deeply, inhaling the scent it still held, the scent of Rick. She'd been so close to telling him tonight, so close it had hurt. Leaning her head against the bookcase where she stood, she remembered his gaze as he'd held her. His eyes had been so sympathetic, so patient. She'd almost been ready to believe he would understand her silence about the child she'd lost.

But something had stopped her. A tiny voice in the

back of her mind, a voice that had said, "Are you crazy? You were pregnant with this man's child and never told him. He's not going to understand that one, *ever*. How could he?"

Opening her eyes, Silvia moved toward the desk that took up one corner of the living room. A huge black leather chair, worn but obviously well liked, rested behind it and she sat down, the leather whispering against her fevered skin.

He'd looked so perfect out at the ball park, playing with all those kids. Her heart tightening painfully inside her chest, Silvia remembered the laughter, the smiles, the teasing voices. The children liked him as much as he liked them—and kids knew about that kind of thing. They could sense if they were loved or not.

Lifting her eyes to the window beside her, Silvia stared out into the darkness. At the very least, didn't he have the right to know about what could have been? Didn't he deserve the truth of her pregnancy? What had she been doing all these years, keeping the secret from him? If she'd thought she was protecting him, what had made her think he needed that? Who had really needed emotional protection? Whose heart had been bruised and broken?

The answer came swiftly and without warning, the sudden clarity of it stealing her breath, putting her in shock.

She'd never been protecting him.

She'd been protecting herself. Herself and no one else.

She lifted a hand to her throat, her pulse pounding beneath her fingers, her throat going dry with the self-realization.

All this time she'd been telling herself she'd been

keeping the grief from him, sheltering him from the slash of the painful truth, but that really hadn't been the case, had it? She hadn't been protecting Rick...she'd been protecting herself. And now, after all these years when she didn't really need the protection any more, it had evolved into something else, something closer to an excuse, an excuse to keep her emotions hidden, to safeguard her heart. If she continued, it would be the wedge that came between them and destroyed the possibility of a new relationship as well.

A sound escaped from somewhere deep in her throat, something halfway between irony and hysteria. She muffled it instantly, glancing toward the bedroom, her hand over her mouth. What kind of psychologist was she, for heaven's sake? Why hadn't she been able to see this before now?

She knew the answer to that one, of course. It was always easy to diagnose other people's situations, impossible to understand your own. That's just how it worked.

She glanced back toward the bedroom. She'd just have to tell him. That was all there was to it. The time had come for her to trust Rick, and she really had no other choice. She couldn't hide any longer, not behind her own denial, not behind her unwillingness to trust.

She actually stood up and took two steps toward the bedroom before stopping. What was she doing? Was she just going to rush in there, wake him up, and say, "Oh, by the way, I was pregnant with your child when I left here." Frozen with indecision, she stood beside the end of the desk and realized it couldn't work that way. She'd have to plan it out, think it through. She couldn't dump news like this on a man without thinking about the best way to do it.

In the darkness, she reached out, her fingers caressing the pages of the leather notebook open on Rick's desk. She'd have to pick the right time, think it through, analyze how she'd do it. There was a real chance for them to succeed now...but she had to do it right. Just right.

She stared at the notebook beneath her hand, her thoughts as unfocused as her gaze. A moment later, through the fog of her thinking, something strange about the calendar registered dimly in the back of her mind. Looking at it upside down, she stared a moment longer, her puzzled forehead finally clearing.

It wasn't current. It was an old notebook, from several months ago. Squinting at the date, Silvia's brain suddenly clattered into awareness, her pulse pounding rapidly.

It was open to the day of Bonnie Kelman's murder.

Ignoring her commands, her fingers froze on the edge of the desk. They wouldn't bring the notebook closer, closer so she could read the entries that day. For one long moment, she sat there, then she reached out, pulling it toward her with jerky movements. Swinging it around so she could read it, she felt her knees go weak.

"B.K.—Cemetery Road, 11:00 p.m."

The words swam before her eyes. B.K. had to be Bonnie Kelman, who else? Why had Rick met her on Cemetery Road the night she was killed? Did anyone know about this? Mentally reading the reports, she couldn't recall seeing notes about this, nothing at all. If he'd met her that night, the night she'd died, Rick had told no one else about it.

Silvia stared out into the darkness.

Secrets...so many secrets...

Chapter 12

Silvia leaned back in her office chair and wearily rubbed her eyes. Before her, the computer screen she'd been staring at for the past four hours wavered in and out of focus. She was exhausted and confused.

The killer of Bonnie Kelman and Linda Willington was still a murky figure to Silvia, someone she just couldn't pin down. She'd read the reports until she practically had them memorized, she'd gone over the endless details until she was blind, she'd thought about it all until her brain felt like oatmeal. She just couldn't get a handle on it.

And she knew exactly why.

The larger part of her waking thoughts were occupied with Rick, not the case. She couldn't get him out of her mind. All she could think about was how to tell him what she'd kept from him for the past eighteen years.

After he'd woken up last night, and they'd made love again, she'd been so confused she'd almost forgotten to ask him about the diary entry. When she'd finally mentioned it, he'd told her Bonnie had requested a meeting with him, but had never shown up. He had no idea what she'd wanted to talk about.

Silvia had nodded, then given it no more examination that night. Nothing was in her brain except the touch of his hands, the smell of his skin, the feel of his lips. She wanted all of that...and more for the rest of her life, and if she didn't handle the situation just right, she would lose everything.

Again.

There was nothing else to do but go home.

Ten minutes later, pulling up to the house, she was surprised to see Rick's cruiser. Her heart pounding with anticipation, her body already aching for his again, Silvia climbed from her car and headed up the sidewalk.

As she opened the front door, angry voices met her, spilling out of the kitchen with a savage intensity. She ran toward the back of the house.

"I'll get you, Carlos. Sooner or later, I'll get you. You'll make a mistake and I'll be there to see it. And when I do—"

"When you do...what? I'm not without friends in this community, you know. Friends in high places. You're biting off more than you can chew, *tonto*, if you think you can tie me to this—"

The furious words of both men stopped abruptly as Silvia reached the kitchen, her startled gaze taking in the scene with shock.

Rick stood on one side of the kitchen table, his eyes blazing with anger, his body tense and poised. On the other side, Carlos was poised like an angry cat, his hands fisted at his sides, his own expression taut with rage.

"What in the world is going on here?" Silvia looked at Rick and then at her brother. "Have you two gone crazy?"

Carlos looked at her, his eyes glittering. *"Loco? Sí, tu amante está muy loco, hermana."*

Rick answered before Silvia could. "You're the crazy one here, Carlos, not me. You can not get away with this. I'll be there when you screw up and then you're going down."

"You can't prove any of this." Carlos's expression was smug. "Where's your evidence? Where's your so-called victims?"

Silvia shot a look toward Rick. "Victims? What's he talking about—?"

Rick ignored her. "They're hiding right now. Hiding from you." Rick's jaw twitched angrily. "I'll find them, though. If I have to go down to Mexico and drag them back, I'll do it."

Carlos grabbed his jacket from the back of a nearby chair. Staring at Rick, his animosity filled the room. "You're blowing hot air, Hunter. You've always been full of it, and this is a perfect example. If people really knew about you..."

His gaze bounced to Silvia's face. "Ask him for the truth. Ask him to explain. To explain how he's been using you to investigate me. Maybe you'll finally understand what I've been trying to tell you."

With one last baleful glance in Rick's direction, Carlos turned and slammed out the back door of the kitchen. A second later, the powerful engine of his BMW could be heard racing out of the driveway and down the street.

In the dead silence that followed, Silvia turned slowly to Rick. "What was he talking about?" Her fingers curled around the back of the nearest chair, the carved wood biting into her skin. "Tell me."

Rick's dark gaze locked on hers. She could feel the will behind the stare, feel the power he was exerting to make her believe him.

He took a deep breath, then spoke. "I'm investigating your brother, Silvia. He's been working with corrupt INS officials to cheat illegal aliens sneaking over the border, and I'm going to prove it."

Her mouth dropped open and she stared incredulously at Rick. "Che-cheat illegals? My God, that's the last thing Carlos would do—"

Rick crossed the open space between them so quickly she didn't know how he did it. One minute he was on the other side of the table and the next he was standing beside her, his gaze blazing with anger.

"I'm not making this up, dammit. I have proof!"

"What kind of proof?"

"A victim, how's that? He snuck back into Texas just to tell me what was going on." Rick took a deep breath and spoke again. "Your brother is taking advantage of people who can't read—people who trust him because he's one of them. After they sneak over the border, he's giving them official-looking papers with a fancy gold stamp on it and telling them it makes them legal, makes them citizens! When they realize they've been screwed, it's too late to ask for help. They're already back in Mexico, courtesy of his border patrol buddies who've picked them up and returned them."

Silvia's pulse was pounding so loudly she could hardly even hear Rick. "I…I never heard of anything so ridiculous in my life," she sputtered.

"I haven't either," he snapped. "But it's a working scheme and he's getting rich." His mouth curled with disgust. "He's splitting the money with the border guards who send them back. I suspected it all along but that night I saw the agents here, I knew I was on to something. Their presence confirmed what I'd been thinking."

Silvia blinked, her heart thumping, her throat going tight. She didn't want to believe what she was hearing, but she couldn't ignore it. "You saw them...here?"

"Yes."

Their gazes locked, and for just a second Silvia caught a glimmer of something in his eyes...something that almost looked like guilt. She processed the information and then put it together with everything else. Her heart slowly went numb.

"You...you've been watching him, haven't you? Every time you came here—that night we were sitting on the porch, and the night of the party, too.... That's why you've been coming around, isn't it? So you could see who Carlos was meeting?"

"It was *one* of the reasons I came. The other one was you."

He could have been speaking Urdu for all the sense the words made to Silvia. She stared at him unblinkingly, her breath grinding to a stop as she slowly realized the enormity of what it meant. The kisses, the lovemaking, the words of desire—all false, every one of them.

"All this time..." she whispered. "I...I...thought it was us. I thought we were... You said you wanted to start a new relationship, and I believed you—"

"And I do want to do that." He came closer, his face an unreadable mask. "Believe me, these two things are not related, Silvia. My investigation of Carlos has nothing to do with our relationship. They're two separate issues. Completely different. I know what it must look like, but you have to realize there's more to it than there appears."

Her heart cracked. Slowly. Agonizingly. "How can you say that?" she whispered. "Every time you came over here...every time we were together... I thought you were coming because of us—not anything else."

"I *was* here to see you, but I wanted to see what Carlos was doing, too." Rick's eyes darkened. "I knew it wasn't the best thing in the world to do, but it was an opportunity I couldn't pass up. I couldn't look the other way if he met someone while I was here, too. I couldn't pretend it wasn't happening and not take advantage of the situation. What would you have done? What should I have done?"

"You should have trusted me," she cried, her pulse thundering. "You should have told me what was happening, and we could have worked something out together. I could have helped."

"And you wouldn't have told Carlos?"

"Of course not. If he's doing something illegal, I'm not going to protect him. My God, Rick, what kind of person do you think I am? Why couldn't you just have trusted me?"

His eyes turned darker, then narrowed. "You're not exactly in a position to talk about trust, are you?"

"I wasn't. Neither of us was," she replied. Her breath came in sharp, quick bursts, her emotions at the breaking point. "But that changed last night. After I really realized what I was doing."

"Last night? What the hell are you talking about?"

Her heart felt as though it were being ripped from her chest. "After we made love, I finally realized we couldn't have a real relationship without trust, and I was ready to tell you everything! I wanted to tell you but I knew I had to find the right time, the right moment. I couldn't just blare it out!''

His forehead knit. "What on earth are you talking about?''

The words spilled out like water from a dam, uncontrollable, raging, too big to ever be contained. She couldn't have held them back now if she'd had to.

"I was pregnant," she cried out. "I was carrying your child when Carlos made me leave!''

The sudden silence was deafening.

Blindly, Rick fumbled for the counter behind him. His hands gripped the edge as he stared at her with disbelieving eyes. Beneath his tan, his face paled into a pasty shade that could only come from shock.

"I...I was three months pregnant the night Linda Willington was killed...the night you came to the house, and Tully took you away. I...I was going to tell you that night, talk it over with you. See what you wanted to do, but then everything happened, and I couldn't do it.... I went to the jail to tell you, but I left. There was nothing you could have done....''

"I can't believe this." His voice was thick and hoarse, his eyes two dark spots of pain. A flurry of emotions came and went across his face, then one settled in to stay. Her heart breaking, Silvia recognized it. It was hope.

"And the child..."

She shook her head, the pain almost as fresh and awful as it had been eighteen years before. "I lost the baby." She choked on the words. "It happened in Houston. I...had cousins there. Yolanda made the arrangements, and I went to live with them—there was no other place for me to go. One night, I woke up bleeding."

He groaned, a grief-filled sound that tore at her with painful claws, his face crumpling. Unable to look, Silva turned away, her own grief almost overwhelming. "I tried to stop it. I lay really still, I talked to myself...I did everything I could, but it wouldn't stop. The bleeding kept on and on, and finally the bed was soaked. I cried out for my cousins, and they called an ambulance. By the time it got there," her voice cracked, the words turning almost impossible to understand between the sobs, "it...it was too late. I'd lost the baby."

Her words dying, she fumbled for the chair and sat down without looking, her face hidden in her hands, the tears coming so fast and furious there was no way to stop them. "There was nothing else I could do," she sobbed. "I tried...but I just couldn't do it. I couldn't make it stop...."

Another moan brought her head up. Leaning against the kitchen counter, Rick had raised one hand to his face to cover his eyes. Maybe if he didn't see her, he wouldn't hear her. Was that what he was thinking?

She looked at him, a bleak emptiness coming over her. "I'm sorry," she whispered. "I should have told you sooner...but I couldn't. I just couldn't."

He dropped his hand, his voice incredulous. "What were you waiting for?"

"I...I thought I was protecting you," she said, her voice miserable. "But what I was really doing was protecting myself. I hadn't realized that till the other night. I was going to tell you...but the right time hadn't come yet."

"In eighteen years? You couldn't find the right time in eighteen years to tell me we almost had a child together?'' He swallowed hard, the column of his throat moving with a jerky motion. "A child...my God, Silvia. All this time..."

Swiping the back of his hand almost angrily across his eyes, he turned away from her and stared out the window over the kitchen sink. "I would have tracked you to the end of the earth if I'd known."

She said nothing. What could she say?

The kitchen clock ticked loudly. In the stuffy silence, the aroma of Yolanda's vegetable soup from lunch still hung in the air, and for a just minute, Silvia thought she might get sick.

After a while, Rick turned around and stared at her, his eyes empty and cold. "You had no right to keep this to yourself. We could have worked something out."

"How?" She jumped to her feet. "What would we have done?"

"I don't know," he replied angrily, "but I would have thought of something."

"It was too late!" she cried. "There wasn't anything to work out two days after I left here! I lost the baby immediately."

"You still should have told me," he said stubbornly, angrily.

"Why? There was nothing you could do by then. It was...it was already over."

"Over?" His voice trembled with emotion. "Over? It wasn't over, Silvia." He took a step closer to her, his whole body trembling. "We created some-thing...something wonderful. The child didn't live but our love could have and later...who knows? We wouldn't have ever been able to replace that child, but we might have been able to have other children, to have a family." His expression tightened. "It could have been different."

"It still can be."

"Oh, no...not now." He held his hands up, almost as if to ward her off. "*Now* it's definitely too late."

"But you just said—"

His eyes opened wide with sudden fury. "You don't trust me! You never have. How can you love someone you don't trust?"

"Why should I trust you?" she screamed back. "Every time I start to, something else happens! You lie to me, you cover up! You haven't told me the truth about anything. What makes you expect to hear the truth from me?"

They stared at each other, Silvia's angry words still ringing in the silence, Rick's expression more stony and cold than ever. The tension was so thick, Silvia halfway expected to actually see it, to taste it, to have it rise up like some kind of malevolent cloud and smother them.

He finally spoke, his voice so cold it made her shiver, each word as precise and as cutting as the sharp edge of a scalpel.

"You're absolutely correct. It's completely irresponsible of me to expect the truth from you. There's never been truth between us. Never. Truth or trust." He shook his head. "I was the biggest fool in the world to ever think there could be."

She listened to the sound of Rick's car as he pulled away from the house, his tires squealing angrily. Numb with shock, Silvia couldn't seem to focus. What had she done? What had *he* done?

Dragging one of the kitchen chairs out from the table, she sat down heavily, her legs suddenly too weak to hold her up any longer. He'd been using her. Using her to spy on Carlos. All this time, she'd resisted the idea of them getting back together, then when she'd finally decided they might actually have a chance—she found out the truth.

A new relationship wasn't what Rick had wanted anyway. He'd wanted her brother...behind bars.

Rick's denials echoed in her mind. *These are two separate issues, Silvia. Our relationship has nothing to do with Carlos.* She dropped her face into her hands. Did he really expect her to believe that? How could she?

And his face when she'd blurted out about the pregnancy— My God, she'd never forget that look as long as she lived. He'd gone through denial, anger and grief almost simultaneously. How could she have been so careless of his emotions?

She raised her eyes and looked bleakly out into the night. He'd been pretty careless of hers, hadn't he? She shook her head slowly, tears welling in her eyes. Through the years, they'd done nothing but hurt each other. How had she ever thought they could build a new relationship?

In the street, a car door slammed, and Silvia's heart jerked. For just a minute, she thought it was Rick, coming back, then she heard an angry step outside on the porch, and she recognized the sound. It was Carlos.

The screen door flew open, and her brother came into the kitchen. His black eyes scanned the room, then came back to her face. "He's gone?"

Silvia nodded and studied his angry expression at the same time. Was this the face of someone as brutal as Rick claimed? Someone who could cheat their own people, their people who had nothing to begin with? Who could promise something as wonderful as citizenship, then laugh as the dream was jerked away?

He seemed to read her mind as his eyes flashed with rage. "Did Hunter tell you his lies? Try to make you believe I'm some kind of monster?"

"He told me what he thinks you're doing."

"And you believed him?"

"I don't know what to believe," she answered wearily. Her emotions were raw and exposed, as rough as if sandpaper had been dragged across them all. "Why don't you tell me your side."

"There's no side to tell. Only the truth."

"Then give that to me."

"You can't handle it."

Her eyes went to his face. "Try me."

He leaned over the table and pinned her with a steady look. "Rick Hunter's been after me for years and not because of some trumped-up citizenship scam. He's after me because of one thing, and one thing only." He paused and drew a deep breath. "He's after me because I know who killed Linda Willington."

Her mouth went dry. "You know…"

"That's right." He nodded. "I know who killed her, and I've known for years."

He paused, drawing out the moment for effect. It worked, too. Her stomach lurched with anticipation.

"Who?" she whispered.

"Who else?" he answered, lifting one brow. "It was him—Rick."

"Oh, Carlos." Shaking her head, Silvia stared at her brother. Why did he insist on this obsession? This hatred? "You know that's not true—"

"It *is* true. He raped her that night, then he had to kill her so she wouldn't tell. His rich father managed to take care of everything for him, and he was never charged, but that's exactly what happened. Exactly.''

''It wasn't like that—''

''Oh, no? Were you there? Did you see it?''

''Of course I wasn't there, but neither were you! Rick told me what happened—''

''He told you what he wanted you to believe, and you believed it. Just like you've believed everything he's told you about Bonnie Kelman's death.'' He drew a deep breath and stared at her. ''He killed Bonnie Kelman, too.''

''No...no...'' Her heart lurching to an uneven stop, Silvia shook her head. ''You're going too far, Carlos. You don't know what you're talking about....''

''I don't?'' Crossing his arms, he stared at her. ''Do you have a motive for Bonnie's killing?''

''No, but I will soon—''

''I can give it to you right now. Rick is taking kickbacks from county contractors. When the bidding process begins on anything in this county, he tells his friends the low bid before it's announced, and they submit something lower. When they're awarded the contract, they pay him off. Bonnie Kelman knew about his little scheme, and he killed her because she was going to reveal it.''

''That's crazy! Where's your proof for these wild accusations?''

''My proof came directly from Bonnie. She told me, Silvia. I was her attorney, and she came to me for advice about how to handle what she knew. Her lover had told her about what he was doing, and she wanted to turn him in, but didn't know how.''

''She specifically said her lover was Rick?''

Carlos nodded once, his expression serious.

Dizzy from the bombardment of information, Silvia closed her eyes, but the barrage didn't end. A date book entry swam before her darkened vision. *B.K.—Cemetery Road, 11:00 p.m.* Then Jack Kelman's words— *She was seeing somebody important, somebody powerful...a man who was really somebody.* From Bonnie's own diary— *I don't want to know the things I know about him.* Logic told Silvia one thing, while her heart argued for another.

"Think about it," Carlos said quietly, interrupting her thoughts. "How would I have known Bonnie had a lover if she hadn't told me?"

Silvia started to say "Yolanda," then she remembered. Her sister had specifically said she had not told Carlos. She'd known he would have made everyone's life miserable, including her own. Silvia's heart sunk another notch.

"Why haven't you told anyone?" Her voice was dead, devoid of emotion.

"I wanted to make sure I had the facts straight, but I was just about to go to the D.A. when you came to town." He hesitated for a moment. "I...I knew you had feelings for Rick. That's why I tried to warn you away—I didn't want you hurt again. But you didn't listen."

He let the words soak in, then he spoke again. "Hunter's out of control, Silvia. His rage has finally gotten the better of him, and he's making other people pay."

Shaking her head, she felt compelled to try one last time. "You hate him because he's always had everything you didn't. You're making up these stories just to make him look guilty."

He made a scoffing sound. "Rick Hunter has nothing

I want, little sister, and he never has. If someone's making up lies about him...I'm afraid it's you, not me.''

Shaking his head, Carlos held out his hands. "How much more proof do you need? You saw him the night Linda was killed— He was a wreck, he smelled like beer, his medal was gone... Now you won't believe the proof you've got in this case—all the reports, what I'm telling you, the fact that Bonnie had a boyfriend! What the hell else do you need, Silvia? When are you going to wake up and realize this man is no good?''

Her throat closing against itself, Silvia turned and looked out into the empty night. Down the street a television blared, its muted sound blending with Yolanda's chimes as they moved gently on the front porch.

"He's been lying to you for years, Silvia, lying to you and using you. Had he told you about this fictitious charge against me before now?''

She shook her head.

"I didn't think so....'' Carlos's voice was weary. "He would have known better. You're too smart, you would have figured out there was nothing to it and confronted him.'' Shaking his head, he closed his eyes for just a moment, then opened them again. "I guess I should be glad he didn't say anything before now...God knows what the man might do to you.''

"He wouldn't hurt me. Not that way.''

"You don't know that for sure. If he's capable of killing two women...''

"He isn't!'' she screamed. "Rick is not a killer!''

His dark gaze pinned her with a burning intensity. "Then explain it to me. Explain everything that's happened, and make me believe differently. Make me believe he's an innocent man.''

Silvia stared bleakly at her brother, a thousand

thoughts running through her head at once, a million reasons chasing them. She'd always known Rick wasn't a killer. He just wasn't. But explain it? Make sense out of it? She didn't think she could—all she had were her feelings.

But feelings weren't good enough, were they? She'd told Rick the day she'd arrived that guesses didn't count. Only logic and evidence were important, only facts and the truth counted.

She turned away from her brother's probing eyes, the sting of tears burning in her throat, her heart breaking in two.

The kitchen seemed emptier than ever when Carlos left once more. Silvia wondered briefly where Yolanda was, then she remembered. It was parent-teacher night. She'd be at the school all evening. Silvia wanted to do nothing but lay her head down on the kitchen table and let the tears flow freely, but she couldn't. Not now. She had a job to do.

Her throat burning with the effort of holding back tears, she picked up her briefcase and purse and headed out the door to go to the office. She'd call Don from there. Somehow that would make things less personal, she thought, climbing into her car, less painful.

But would it? She started the car and headed down the street, wheeling the car to the left as she reached Main. Was there anything that would make this decision less personal? She had to call Don and tell him everything. Rick's life would be destroyed, and even if the investigation revealed nothing, his career would be over. She shouldn't care, she told herself, after everything that had happened between them. He'd lied to her and used her just to get to her brother. She shouldn't even care.

But she did.

Dammit to hell, she did care.

Turning into the parking lot at the city buildings, Silvia angled the car between two others then climbed out. It didn't matter how she felt. She had a job to do. That was the only thing that mattered right now. She repeated the words over and over as she crossed the parking lot. She had a job to do.

Walking quickly through the darkened building, she came to her office and unlocked it. Turning on the lights, she immediately reached for the telephone but stopped. She was too upset, too rattled to even make sense. If she called Don right now, he'd think she was hysterical. She had to slow down, make some notes, take stock…then she'd call him and lay it all out in a logical way. In a professional way.

Doing what she always did when she wanted to make sense out of something senseless, Silvia reached inside her desk drawer and pulled out a yellow pad. With fingers that shook, she started making notes remembering what Carlos had said.

Rick had killed Linda Willington during a rape gone bad.

This was the first thing Carlos had said. She thought back to Rick's explanation. He'd never denied being there that night, hadn't even denied having sex with Linda so that part of Carlos's accusation was accurate to a degree. Even if Rick had tried to lie about it, the medal would have proven him wrong. Silvia herself had seen it in the evidence box, and Carlos had mentioned that fact as well. Evidence proved Rick had been there that night, and evidence proved he and Linda had had sex.

Silvia looked at the words she'd just written, and her breath caught in her throat. Her fingers were frozen on the pencil, but she slowly and deliberately unclenched her hand and carefully laid the yellow pencil down on her desk.

Evidence. Not guesses. Not feelings. Evidence.

Her mind shot back eighteen years. She'd saved her money and bought the piece of gold jewelry, Rick's Saint Christopher medal, in a neighboring town. She'd wanted the purchase to be a secret. Carlos would have had a fit had he known she was spending money on Rick.

Rick had worn the chain and medal only one day, then it'd been lost. No one had known she'd given it to Rick, and absolutely no one had known it had been found at the scene of Linda's murder, except Rick. Not even Silvia had known what had happened to it until she'd seen the gleam of gold in the evidence box. She swallowed hard, past the knot suddenly growing larger inside her throat.

So how had Carlos known?

How had he known Rick had owned a Saint Christopher medal, much less known he'd lost it at the scene of Linda's murder?

How had he known?

Silvia slowly turned in her chair, her emotions a confused jumble, her mind too rattled to be working straight. *Think,* she told herself. *Think this through. Remember that night.*

Closing her eyes, she put herself back on the porch, eighteen years before. It was painful, but the images came quickly, came forcefully, almost as if they'd been waiting for this moment to be freed from her subconsciousness.

Her white batiste nightgown, Rick with his shirt torn, his eyes wild. Her heart started to race just remembering. They'd talked, been scared, emotions running high, then Tully had arrived. Within minutes, Carlos had come outside along with her mother and Consuelo. He'd come outside *after* she and Rick had talked, *after* she'd asked him about the Saint Christopher medal. There had been no mention of the jewelry in front of Carlos, or she would have remembered—he would have started yelling and screaming at her about it.

Silvia's mind skipped forward. She remembered the stricken look on her mother's face as Carlos had explained what had happened before he'd sent her back inside. They'd spoken in Spanish, of course. The words sounded in Silvia's head as plainly as if he were standing beside her right now and repeating them.

Linda Willington's been raped and killed.

Her mind spun crazily then clicked to a sudden stop. Carlos had definitely said ''raped.'' The word in Spanish stuck in her mind. *Violación.*

But again...how had Carlos known? Tully had told her and Rick that Linda had been raped, but he'd told them *before* Carlos had come out. Silvia squeezed her eyes harder, tried to remember the scene more carefully.

She'd been so scared when Rick had shown up, so scared that Carlos would hear them and come out. She'd tiptoed past his room after she'd waited for Rick, and it'd been dark, dark as if he'd already gone to bed. But Carlos had been dressed when he came out to the porch, dressed in a spotless white shirt and perfectly pressed slacks. His hair had been wet, as if he'd just stepped from the shower. Why hadn't he been in his nightclothes like the rest of them? Had he showered and dressed *then* come outside? That didn't make sense.

But none of it made sense, did it? She slowly opened her eyes and shook her head against the mounting pile of facts.

Rick had one story…and Carlos had another. Who had the truth?

Silvia's mind skipped forward to Bonnie Kelman's death. Carlos had said Rick killed her because she knew of his kickback scheme. If he was that interested in money, where was it? Silvia recalled Rick's house, her chest tightening at the memory of being there. It had certainly showed no signs of wealth. He lived plainly, simply, drove a pickup when he wasn't in his cruiser. Carlos, on the other hand… She shifted her thoughts to the BMW, the trophy house, the perfectly tailored suits.

She hated the process going on in her head, but she seemed incapable of stopping it. Her mind jumped forward, almost on its own accord, to the only obvious conclusion. She rejected the startling thought, then forced herself to step backward and look at it again.

Carlos guilty of murder? Why?

Why on earth would he have killed Linda Willington all those years ago? And Bonnie Kelman? Did he even have any connection to the woman, other than being her attorney? More importantly, did he fit the profile Silvia had labored over so long?

She stared out into the darkness and went over the case point by point, her heart closing against itself as the evidence mounted piece by piece to build a wall of truth too obvious to ignore.

Carlos fit the profile. Rick didn't.

Pushing back her chair so abruptly it hit the window behind her, Silvia stood. "No." She said the word out loud and shook her head. "No way. Carlos can explain this—every bit of it."

She stood for a few more moments, then grabbed her car keys and ran outside. There was only one way to find out. She'd find her brother, and he'd tell her the truth. Once and for all. He'd tell her what she needed to know.

He'd tell her he wasn't a killer.

Chapter 13

The tires on the rented car squealed as Silvia turned the wheel and forced the vehicle around the corner at the end of the street. She was speeding, but she didn't really care. One thing was on her mind.

Finding Carlos. No one had answered the telephone at his house or at his office. She had no choice but to go look for him.

The empty streets looked lonely and forlorn, but Silvia hardly noticed as she quickly made her way across town to Carlos's house. Pulling into his driveway, she stared up at the two-story mansion. She'd stopped by once before since she'd returned, and the impression she'd gotten then about the house was even more strong now in the eerie darkness.

The home seemed out of place for this part of the country. The brick was too imposing, and the columns lining the porch looked inappropriate. There were no other houses in dusty little San Laredo that even remotely resembled the scale of this one. She shook her head and told herself she was acting silly. What did it matter?

One thing was obvious immediately, though. No one was home, or if they were, they were all in bed and asleep. The house was settled in for the night, quiet and shut down. All the windows were dark as well, their reflective surfaces empty of any light except that coming from the headlights of Silvia's own car.

She got out of her vehicle and made her way up the sidewalk to the front door. Pushing her finger against the brass button to the left of the door, she waited, her pulse pounding against her temples. The house remained dark for a few more minutes, then a dim light came on, somewhere in the back. Peering through the leaded glass that made up the front door, Silvia saw more lights come on, one by one, as they obviously lit the way for someone.

Through the distorted glass, Lydia suddenly appeared, her hair mussed, her expression puzzled. It was only a little past nine, but she was dressed for bed, a robe thrown over what was apparently her nightgown. She held up a finger to Silvia indicating she should wait, then she turned to a keypad beside the door. Punching in a number, she clearly turned off the burglar alarm. A moment later, she threw open the front door and stared at Silvia with concern.

"What's wrong?" she asked. "What are you doing here so late?"

Without preamble, Silvia spoke sharply. "Is Carlos here? I need to see him."

"No...he's not in yet." Lydia raised her hand and pushed her hair off her face. "He...he's working late.

This morning, he told me not to wait up for him. Is something wrong?"

Silvia shook her head impatiently. "Everything's fine. I just need to talk to him, that's all. I tried to call, but you didn't answer."

"We turn off the phones upstairs after we go to bed. The kids…" She shrugged her shoulders apologetically. "They'd be talking all night with their friends if we didn't. Carlos insisted…"

"What about the office? I tried there, too, but no answer."

"There's a switchboard. It closes at six." Her eyebrows knit together in an expression of worry. "Is there anything I can do, Silvia? You seem…upset."

Silvia was already shaking her head and walking backward down the sidewalk. "If you see him, tell him I'm looking for him. Tell him to phone Yolanda's."

Lydia nodded. "I'll do that, but—"

Silvia waved her thanks, then ran the rest of the way to her car. In the rearview mirror, Lydia's robed figure remained on the porch until Silvia could no longer see it.

Within seconds, she was at Carlos's office.

The three-story building, San Laredo's only office site, was as black and empty-looking as Carlos's home had been. Silvia jumped from the car and pounded on the front door anyway. Waiting and pounding for several minutes, she managed to raise no one, her frustration deepening with every moment.

Where was he?

Turning to face the empty street, Silvia leaned against the glass doors to the office, her mind swirling over the possibilities. Where else would he have gone? He'd told Lydia he was working late…working late where?

Suddenly she realized what she hadn't before. The classic excuse for working late—it could only mean one thing. Springing forward, she ran toward her car. Within seconds she was going out of town.

Toward Cemetery Road.

Light from the house poured out the front windows. It stood starkly at the edge of the field, totally alone and isolated from any other houses. Carlos had to be with Barbara Williams, the woman Rick had told her was Carlos's girlfriend. It was the only answer.

Silvia glanced to her right as she eased down Cemetery Road. The proximity of the house to the location where both women had been killed was something she hadn't realized until this very moment. One of the profile points she'd decided on first was that the murderer had to be familiar with the scene. He'd had to be very comfortable with the locale to do his killing along a public road. He'd have to know the traffic patterns, been in the area over time to study them...even to have lived nearby.

Her stomach clenched, but she kept going. A few minutes later, she pulled into the driveway and parked behind the closed garage door. If Carlos was here, there was no sign of his car. Hesitating, her hand on the door release, Silvia thought about turning around. This was crazy—absolutely crazy. Did she really think her brother was capable of killing two women? Brutally shooting them and leaving their bodies on the side of the road like pieces of trash?

And if he hadn't done these horrible things?

If he hadn't, the alternative was just as bad. If Carlos wasn't responsible, then she had to give more weight to his accusations—and that meant Rick might be involved. Shaking her head in denial, she slipped out of the car and headed over the sidewalk toward the front porch.

The two front windows were open. Spilling out of them was light…and angry voices. Silvia immediately recognized Carlos's voice and assumed the higher pitched, female one belonged to Barbara Williams. Paralyzed with sudden indecision, Silvia hovered at the edge of the porch and listened, one hand clutching the railing, the other one poised anxiously at the base of her neck, her pulse thrumming beneath it.

Carlos's angry voice split the evening air, a derisive, belittling tone lashing out. "Are you so stupid you can't understand English? I told you to stay away from him, but you wouldn't listen. He's screwing you, isn't he?"

Her voice was hysterical. "It's not what you think! Rick and I aren't seeing each other, I swear to God—"

Silvia gasped, the breath stopping in her throat. Carlos obviously thought Barbara was sleeping with Rick. If Silvia was right about her brother—if he was a killer—then Barbara was about to be in big trouble. That kind of paranoia would be all he needed to explode completely. Silvia hesitated only a moment longer, then she took a deep breath and went directly to the door, pushing it open and stepping inside.

The tableau was so horrible it took her a moment to even understand it.

Her brother's face was infused with rage and contorted with grim satisfaction. Screaming at Barbara, he had moved closer to her…and lifted his hand. In it, he held an enormous pistol.

They both turned to the door as Silvia entered. A look of shock shuddered over Carlos, then he seemed to recover.

"Wh-what the hell are you doing here?"

Silvia barely heard him above her thundering pulse. Holding out her hands, she moved closer to Barbara. Another two steps, and she'd be between the woman and Carlos. "Carlos, this isn't going to solve anything—"

He waved the gun wildly, looking first at Silvia, then Barbara. "Don't move any closer to her. I don't want you hurt."

"No one's going to get hurt," Silvia answered, her voice calm and soothing. "No one. Because you're going to put down the gun."

Behind Silvia, Barbara sobbed quietly. "I...I wasn't doing anything...."

His eyes flicked to Barbara's face. "Don't lie to me," he thundered. "I know you're sleeping with that bastard again, so don't tell me otherwise. Don't deny it! I know you're lying."

Her heart in her throat, Silvia risked a glance toward Barbara. Her hair in disarray, her beautiful face flushed with fear, the woman cowered to Silvia's left, her only protection a flimsy armchair. She looked terrified, and rightly so.

"I'm not sleeping with Rick, I promise. I'm not. You know I love you, Carlos—"

"You don't love me," he retorted. "You're just like the rest of them—you all love him. I'm going to take care of this here and now. I'm through with it all—"

The roar of the gun was so unexpected, Silvia had little time to react. All she could do was dive to the floor. A moment later, her horrified eyes took in a bloom of red across Barbara's shoulder as she crashed to the polished wood, the room filling with her splitting screams of agony.

Before the sound of the shot had even faded, the back door flew open. Scrambling to her hands and knees, Silvia froze as Rick tumbled inside.

Carlos swirled, his gun now trained on Rick.

Just as Rick's weapon was trained on Carlos.

"Give it up, Hernandez." Rick's heavy breathing filled the room along with Barbara's groans. "Lay down the gun, and let me take you in without anyone else getting hurt."

Carlos's fingers tightened on his gun. A .45 Magnum. "Never," he growled.

"It's not going to end like you want it to. Put the gun down," Rick warned. He moved closer, then stopped as Carlos made a threatening motion with the weapon.

Silvia used every ounce of willpower she had to force herself still. Behind her, Barbara groaned.

"Give it up," Rick repeated.

"No way. I've worked too hard and too long to let you screw up my life anymore, Hunter. I planned it just right, and you aren't going to weasel out of it this time." He waved the gun slowly and smiled.

For the first time, Silvia realized he had on latex gloves. "Recognize this?"

Rick's eyes darted toward the gun then widened.

"I thought you would." Carlos smiled. "I had one of my friends lift it from your house last week. It's registered in your name, and your fingerprints are all over it. You might have managed your way out of Linda's and Bonnie's murders, but this is one you'll never be able to deny. With Barbara gone, you'll go down."

Silvia closed her eyes, a tide of sick disbelief rising in her throat.

"It'll never work, Carlos." Rick edged around him slowly. He was making his way to Silvia's side of the room, to where Barbara lay. "You're a smart man—surely you know it won't work."

"I am a smart man," he answered smugly, "and that's exactly why I know it *will* work. I learn from my lessons. I was too young and too foolish to manage the details with Linda, but that's not the case anymore."

"Oh, God…" Silvia couldn't help herself—the whispered words escaped with an agonized groan. Both men ignored her.

"You killed Linda, then." Rick's voice was matter-of-fact. He was jockeying for time, making his way across the room.

"Of course I killed her. She didn't deserve to live, she'd slept with everyone in town. But I didn't know any better, and I was in love with her. I followed her when she went out Cemetery Road and watched her stop her car to lift the hood. I tried to help her."

His expression twisted. "She didn't want *my* help, though. She said she was waiting for someone else. I drove off, but I stopped and turned my car lights off to watch. Then you came up. I saw what happened." He shook his head, his cheeks flushing as he remembered. "She wanted you instead of me. After you left, though, I went back…and I gave her what she really deserved."

Silvia's gorge rose. She fought the sensation, her entire body starting to shake.

"Then tried to pin it all on me." Rick reached Barbara's side. Two feet from Silvia, he paused and stared at Carlos.

Carlos nodded. "I called the police—told them I'd seen your truck. I made sure they saw that stupid Saint Christopher medal, too—practically put it in Linda's hand after I watched her pull it off you...." Again his expression went dark. "I shouldn't have bothered for all the damned good it did, though."

Keeping his eye on Carlos, Rick slowly lowered himself to kneel beside Barbara. He reached out blindly and touched her neck, searching for a pulse. A moment later, his fingers pressed into her neck, and she groaned. An expression of relief went over his face, then he stood once more, moving slowly, his gaze never leaving Carlos.

Only seconds had passed since Rick had come into the room, but to Silvia it seemed like an eternity. He hadn't looked at her once, and she was glad. She would have fallen apart completely.

"And Bonnie?" Rick's voice was soft.

"She talked too much...and she knew too much."

"About your immigration scheme?"

Carlos nodded.

At Rick's feet, Barbara moaned. The woman needed help. If she didn't get it soon, she'd die. Three women dead by Carlos's hand. Silvia closed her eyes, a sob trapped inside her chest. How could she have been so blind?

Carlos glanced toward Barbara, his face a mask of fury. "I guess my plans are going to have to change again, now." He looked up at Rick, his eyes two slits of rage. "I guess it'll have to be a murder-suicide, huh?"

Silvia couldn't help herself. She spoke softly. "Carlos—please... Don't do this. Think of your family...think of Lydia—"

He turned on her with sudden fury. "You shut up or your lover boy here will die even sooner!"

Rick gave her a warning glance, then took a step

toward Carlos, his eyes trained once more on him. "It won't work."

Carlos lifted the heavy pistol. His hands weren't shaking anymore. "I don't see why not. The insanely jealous sheriff discovers his ex-wife is having an affair. Driven by misguided love, he confronts her then kills her in anger. Afterward, despondent, he kills himself. It sounds perfect to me." He laughed lightly. "Actually I like it even better than the simple plan I'd worked out to implicate you. Killing you is much better than sending you to jail. Like this, I won't have to worry about you anymore." He laughed again, a slight hysterical edge creeping into his voice. "It's perfect." He continued to talk and wave the gun, his attention unfocused and wandering.

He was losing touch with reality, failing to think things through. With absolutely no doubt, Silvia knew his next action would be irreversible. The only way out was a diversion.

In the second that followed, Silvia inched slowly upward, her knees biting into the wood. Rick's eyes flicked to hers, and in that instant, he read her intention. Before he could do anything else, before she could stop to think and realize that she was choosing…finally choosing, she shot to her feet.

A moment later, she leapt forward. Hitting her brother's shoulder with all her might, Silvia spun him around, then they both tumbled to the floor.

Carlos recovered instantly and scrambled to his feet. He stared at her with dazed and disbelieving eyes, then he swirled in Rick's direction and began to fire.

Unprepared for the swiftness of Silvia's actions, all Rick could do was drop to the floor. He hit the wood one second before the gun spit. Turning as soon as he fired, Carlos sprinted toward the back of the house, knocking chairs and tables out of his way as he fled, Rick right behind him.

Both men reached the outer door at almost the same time. Carlos grabbed for the door handle just as Rick launched himself into the air. With a thump and a whoosh, he landed on top of Carlos. Falling heavily, they tumbled to the floor, Rick ending up on top.

The struggle was brief and violent, over within seconds. In a blurring flash of movement, Rick reached for the handcuffs at his side and had them wrapped around Carlos's wrists. Their heavy breathing filled the tiny room, Carlos moaning slightly. Finally, Rick rose.

He took a second, then turned, his eyes meeting Silvia's over the body of her brother. His expression was impossible to read, but for a moment, she was sure she saw regret…regret and dashed hopes for what could have been.

Or did she imagine it?

"That was a stupid thing to do," he said roughly, tilting his head toward the door. "You could have been killed."

"He was about to shoot you." Her voice trembled. "I didn't have a choice."

He held her gaze a second longer, then going quickly to Barbara's side, he pulled a blanket off the sofa. Wrapping it around her, he spoke over his shoulder.

"Call the office and tell them we need an ambulance out here." He looked over at Carlos then back up at Silvia. "And get a squad car, too. Tell them we have a pickup." Without another word, he turned to the woman at his feet.

Her heart pounding, her throat tight, Silvia left to find a phone.

* * *

The rest of the evening was a horrible blur. Bits and pieces of it would haunt her forever, but while it was happening, all Silvia could think about was the havoc Carlos had wreaked. Two women killed, a third injured. Rick almost murdered…

She watched two uniformed deputies drag her brother to his feet and pull him out to a patrol car, the red-and-blue lights of their car slicing through the night in eerie silence. How many times had she watched this same scene played out? Watched dispassionately and felt only satisfaction for a job well done? Now she felt hollow, empty, weak with relief but still disbelieving. Her brother, a killer? Her training made her see what she'd been blind to before, but her heart still didn't want to accept it. Tears filled her eyes, but she brushed them away angrily. He'd lied to her and used her, made her question her trust in Rick when she should have known better. A surge of anger washed over her, mixed with sorrow as well.

She forced herself to walk to the patrol car. He was sitting in the back. Ironically all she could think about was seeing Rick in this same position so many years ago.

She looked into the car and met her brother's eyes. She could only get out one single word. "Why?"

A bruise was darkening his forehead, and blood trickled down from a small cut above his right eye. "You have to ask?"

"I don't understand," she answered. "Rick never did anything to you…yet you carried on this…this vendetta of revenge for years." She shook her head and whispered. "You killed two women just to try to frame him. They didn't deserve that…*he* didn't deserve it."

"He didn't deserve it?" Carlos spit the words out, his Spanish accent suddenly heavier. "What did he ever get he *did* deserve? His whole life he's had everything he wanted—all he ever had to do was snap his fingers, and it was given to him."

She hid her amazement. It was something she'd learned to do a long time ago. "So you decided to teach him a lesson? And these women—their lives were simply incidental to your plan?"

"They didn't matter." Dismissing the victims, he looked over her shoulder, at the swarm of police and lights and confusion. A moment later, his eyes came back to hers. "Anything would have been worth it, if I'd managed to get rid of him...."

She shook her head, grief and dismay flooding her. "That doesn't make sense, Carlos. No sense at all."

"Maybe not to you. It does to me."

"But you had so much yourself. Your practice, your family, your position. Why would you give up all those things to punish Rick?"

"I wasn't going to give them up." His expression darkened. "If you hadn't interrupted, things would have gone like I'd planned."

"And I would never have known about any of this."

"That's right. I would have taken care of things, made them right. Just like I did all those years ago for you." He pursed his lips. "He was no good for you, Silvia. No good at all. If you'd just realized that..."

His words cut directly into her professional persona. She stared at him, dropping all pretense of understanding. "But it's not your place to choose for me! Even if you were right about Rick—which you aren't—it's just not your place."

"I am the head of the family," he said stubbornly. "I know what's best."

"What's best! If you hadn't made me leave here, my life would be completely different now. Rick and I could have been married, had children." She took a deep breath. "Instead I cut myself off from my family and gave up years of being close to the people I love." Turning away from him, she looked out into the night, almost speaking to herself. "And those women...those poor, poor women..."

Before she could say more, one of the deputies approached. "I'm sorry, ma'am. We're going to have to take him now."

She looked up and nodded. Turning back to the car, she leaned down toward the window. "Just one last thing, Carlos...just one last thing, I think you should know.

"I was pregnant when I left here. I was going to have Rick's child."

He blanched in the darkness, her news clearly shocking him. "You...you were pregnant?"

"That's right. But I lost the child. I had a miscarriage right after I left here."

Staring down at him, Silvia's heart turned to stone. "For the longest time I blamed myself for that tragedy. Just like I blamed myself for letting Rick down all those years ago. You know what, though? I wasn't the one to blame. You were." She locked her stare on his. "You—the big keeper of the family, the big leader of us all." Pausing, she shook her head. "You didn't protect anything...you destroyed our family and the happiness we could have had...destroyed it for your own ridiculous reasons. And to think I defended you...."

She held his stare a moment longer, and he started to

speak. Shaking her head, she stepped away from the car and looked toward the deputy waiting behind her. "Take him away," she said. "I have nothing left to say."

A moment later, the car pulled out of the driveway. Right behind it, the ambulance followed, Barbara inside. With dry eyes, Silvia watched it leave. She'd already found out Barbara would be okay. She'd have a nasty scar and a very sore shoulder, but she'd live. Silvia watched the taillights disappear in the darkness, thinking of the difference between Carlos and the woman he'd shot. Barbara had looked at Silvia and thanked her. Thanked her! Feeling like a failure, Silvia had smiled and patted her on the arm.

She turned her gaze back to the house. Rick stood in a corner of the porch, talking to one of his deputies. An overhead light cast harsh shadows on him, and even from a distance she could see his shoulders slumped wearily, his face rough with his beard.

She didn't have to be close to know his eyes were empty and cold. She let herself look at him for as long as she could bear it, then she turned around.

It was time to leave.

"I can't believe you're leaving." A few days after Carlos's arrest, Yolanda sat on the edge of the bed and watched Silvia pack. "I feel like my life has been turned upside down. I don't know what to think."

Silvia nodded, her own heart heavy and old feeling. "I know. I watched them take Carlos away and part of me just couldn't believe it, even after I'd seen it." Her eyebrows knit together and she shook her head. "He had so much going for him.... I understand...but I don't. He was totally unrepentant."

"He never felt good about who he was. He always wanted more." Yolanda spoke simply, her words ringing truthfully. "He was always that way." She pulled herself back into the moment. "And now you're leaving, too. I'm going to miss you so much, and so will the kids."

Silvia looked up from the blouse she was folding and smiled. "I'll miss all of you, but you're coming to visit, remember?"

"I will." Yolanda nodded. "But you shouldn't leave, Silvia. You belong here. In San Laredo." She took a deep breath. "You belong here with Rick."

Without answering, Silvia dropped the blouse into the suitcase then took another from the closet.

"Did you hear me?" Yolanda got up from the bed and came to where Silvia stood. "You love him! Why are you leaving him? It's crazy."

Silvia looked at her sister. "It'd be crazy if I stayed," she said quietly. "There's too much bad history between us. It'd never work."

"You could make it work," Yolanda insisted. "If you wanted it bad enough, you could make it work."

Silvia shook her head. "Not this time." She looked out the window. A blue jay had landed on the picnic table and was pecking at a nail on the top of the wooden slats. "We didn't trust each other, and if I've learned nothing else during all this, I've learned you can't have love if you don't have trust."

"But things are different now." Yolanda's voice forced Silvia's gaze toward her. "You proved your trust in him when you went into Barbara's house."

"It goes deeper than the trouble with Carlos. Our troubles started when I didn't trust Rick all those years ago. I should have told him back then about the baby, and I didn't. It's just too late now.''

"He didn't tell you the truth about everything, either.''

Silvia lifted her eyes to Yolanda's, her gaze filled with tears. "I know, and that was wrong of him, too. But that's exactly what I mean. We kept secrets from each other. I might have had good reasons not to tell him the truth when we were teenagers, but after all this time? Especially after we made love?'' She shook her head. "I was too busy protecting myself to really love him like I should have, and he knows it.''

"These are silly reasons...just excuses.'' Yolanda took Silvia's hands between her own. "Go to him. Tell him how you feel.''

"I can't.''

"Why not?''

"He won't listen.''

"How do you know?''

Silvia dropped her gaze, her tears running down her cheeks. "I wouldn't,'' she whispered, "if I were him.''

Yolanda lifted Silvia's chin with one finger. "But you aren't him, *chiquita.* You'll never forgive yourself if you don't at least try. I'm telling you, the man loves you.''

Silvia immediately dampened the spark of hope that somehow managed to flare inside her. She couldn't hold back the question, though. "How...how do you know?''

"I know because I know you. You love him. You saved his life, you proved your trust, you told him your secrets. Sometimes you have to make the first move in love, you have to expose yourself *first,* and that makes it okay for the other person to do the same.'' She smiled. "Someone has to go first, and it should be you."

"But what if he turns me down?"

"Then he turns you down...and you go home. You haven't lost anything, and you know you did your best. At the very least, you'll know you've put all this behind you, and you'll be free to go on and live the rest of your life."

The words sunk in slowly, Silvia turning them over and over in her mind and examining them. It was good advice, she finally concluded. Advice she'd give to someone herself.

But could she do it?

Chapter 14

Rick was cleaning his pistol at the table outside when Silvia drove up, her rental car pulling into his driveway, the tires crunching the shells and raising small puffs of dust that drifted off in the hot summer sun. Squinting his eyes, he watched her. For several seconds she sat still behind the wheel as if she were gathering her thoughts, then the door creaked open and she emerged.

He'd been expecting her.

He'd known she wouldn't leave town without saying something to him, and he'd been debating for days what he wanted to say in return to her. Actually, he wanted to say nothing. He simply wanted to crush her into his arms and show her exactly how much he loved her, to tell her that nothing else mattered between them. That they'd work everything out and start all over again.

But he knew that was impossible.

They'd hurt each other too much. There was still anger in his heart over her silence, and she held resentment in hers over everything he'd done. They were equally guilty and equally innocent.

Walking up the graveled walk, she held herself with grace, the bright Texas sun glinting diamonds of light in the darkness of her hair, her heels crunching against the crushed granite. She wore a black pantsuit, the slacks trim enough to show off her figure but loose enough to look elegant. A short sleeveless jacket, almost militarylike in style, clung to her breasts and curved beneath them.

He ached just looking at her.

She stopped on the walk, close to where he sat. She spoke without preamble. "I'm leaving."

Staying silent, he nodded, his fingers folding and refolding the soft cotton cloth he'd been using to wipe down the barrel.

"I couldn't go without telling you goodbye."

The words escaped before he could stop them. "You did it before."

Removing her sunglasses, she met his gaze with an unflinching one of her own, immediately making him feel like the jerk he really was.

"And I shouldn't have," she answered quietly. "It was wrong then, and it would be wrong now. That's why I came by. To say goodbye."

He lifted his gaze to her eyes. They were heavy-lidded and full of an emotion he couldn't really read.

Three feet separated them, but her perfume didn't respect the boundary. Chanel No.5 eased across the table and wrapped itself around him.

"When are you going?"

"My flight's in the morning."

"You'll come back for the trial?"

She nodded.

"It won't be easy," he warned. "Can you really testify against your own brother?"

"I don't have a choice, do I?" She stared at him. "I'll be called whether I like it or not...." Pausing for a moment, she dropped her gaze to her feet, then finally lifted it again, to meet his eyes. "I'm sorry I didn't see things the way they really were. I...I've been confused about a lot of things, I guess."

He stood abruptly and walked to the railing surrounding the porch, his fingers digging into the wood, welcoming the splinters of pain. He knew he should say the same, should apologize for everything he'd done. He'd kept things from her, been unfaithful eighteen years ago, used her to spy on Carlos. He'd done wrong, too, but the words of apology just wouldn't come out no matter how hard he tried.

He was mad, dammit.

Mad because she'd taken so long to tell him the truth and mad because they'd lost so much time.

Mad because he still loved her.

Since the day she'd told him about the lost baby, he'd thought of almost nothing else. A baby! The grief had almost overwhelmed him when he'd let himself really think about what could have been.

In the middle of the day, he'd find himself thinking about names he would have chosen. Right after dinner one night, he thought about how old it would have been now. And at 3:00 a.m., when he couldn't sleep, he'd bombarded himself with the most painful questions he'd ever faced in his life.

What if that child, that little lost baby, was his only one? What if he never got another opportunity to hold a child and say it was his? To watch it grow up and mold it into an adult? To teach it what he knew?

The possibility had almost driven him insane, so he'd done the only thing he could—he'd directed his anger toward Silvia, somehow blaming her for the lost chance when it wasn't her fault at all.

He knew all this as surely as he knew the sun was going to rise in the morning and stream through the branches of the pecan tree that faced the east side of his house. He understood it perfectly.

But he was totally incapable of dealing with it.

He gripped the porch and asked the question that had been plaguing him the most. "The baby... What...what was it?" he whispered. "A boy...or a girl?"

She didn't answer right away, and as the seconds passed, he thought she wouldn't. Finally he turned around and looked at her.

Wearing an expression that etched itself into his heart, she spoke quietly, her own voice trembling with emotion. "I didn't want to know. I told them not to tell me." She looked down. "But I overheard two nurses talking. They didn't know I could hear them. The baby was...was a boy."

He stared at her, the empty feeling only growing bigger inside him. They could have had so much, so very much.

He spoke her name softly. "Silvia?"

She looked up.

"Would you have married me? Back then...if nothing had happened that night, and I'd asked you?"

She turned from him then, her profile classic in the morning sun, the delicate turn of her nose, the full roundness of her lips, the soft cleft of her chin—all outlined in the streaming light.

She licked her lips, then spoke. "I...I don't know,

Rick. We were so young, so ignorant—'' She looked at him. "Would you have asked me to?"

"Absolutely." He didn't have to think about his answer, he spoke automatically. "I'd been thinking of nothing else. I didn't want to lose you."

"And you think it would have worked? We were only eighteen."

"It would have worked." Meeting her steady gaze with one of his own, he nodded his head. "We were young, but I had thought it out."

"How?"

"I was going to get a job and put you through college. When you finished, you could have done the same for me. It would have worked."

She stared out into his yard. The silence between them grew, broken only by the call of the mockingbird who lived in the oak tree out front.

She spoke so softly he could barely hear her. "Do you think it would work now? Is there any chance at all for us?"

He'd asked himself that same question a thousand times in the past few days...and every time he'd answered it the very same way.

No. There was no way. They'd never trusted each other. How could they have love without trust?

But he couldn't bring himself to say the words. He loved her too much.

He looked at her instead, his heart pounding. "Do you think there is?"

She studied him for just a moment, then she put on the sunglasses she'd been holding the whole time they'd been speaking. The moment before she slipped them on, he thought he saw the glint of a tear but he couldn't tell for sure. It was there then gone too fast to say.

From behind the dark lenses, she looked up at him and smiled sadly. "I guess if we have to ask…the answer's no."

A band of regret tightened painfully around his chest, but before he could say anything else, Silvia stepped closer. Without a word, she reached up and kissed him. The touch was brief and searing, her lips so warm against his that it took away his breath.

He lifted his arms to wrap them around her, but he wasn't fast enough. She slipped away and ran out to her car. A moment later, she drove off.

Or so he guessed. He could only hear the roar of the engine…he couldn't see through the sudden blur of tears.

Dulles was crowded, hot and noisy. As Silvia made her way through the hordes of vacationers headed to see the White House and the Lincoln Memorial and the Smithsonian and everything else in Washington, she wondered at the wisdom of living in the nation's capital. Every summer, the population seemed to swell by thousands, and the humidity sucked the energy right out of you.

All this had never bothered her before, of course.

Picking up her suitcase from the carousel, Silvia dodged a woman with three children and her frazzled-looking husband as he stared at a map. Stepping outside she hailed a cab, then climbed inside and gave the man directions to her condo. In half an hour, he pulled to a stop just outside her building.

The doorman ran outside and greeted her. Picking up her case, he chattered cheerfully as they made their way upstairs. In seconds, they reached Silvia's floor, and opening her front door, Silvia stepped aside to let him go in first. He put down her bag, then left. Behind him, she closed the door, and suddenly there was nothing but silence.

No voices, no television, no spicy smells coming from the kitchen. No children, no dogs, no family. Along with emptiness, only the musty smell of an un-used home greeted her.

She was all alone.

Trying not to think about what that meant for the rest of her life, Silvia dragged her suitcase to the bedroom and began to unpack. Throwing clothes into the hamper and the closet behind her, in twenty minutes, she had the task done. Mentally she made a list of the errands she needed to run, the stops she had to make. The mail room downstairs to pick up her mail. The grocery store for bread and milk. The office to catch up before Monday morning.

She had a million busy tasks to keep her going, a thousand things to do.

But she simply walked into the living room and collapsed on the sofa. Staring out the window, twelve stories up, she saw nothing but blank sky. If she could clean out her emotions and make them as just as empty, she'd do it in a second.

But she couldn't.

And the feelings and sensations she'd managed to put on hold while she'd been traveling suddenly bombarded her again. Rick's empty expression when she'd told him she was leaving. The cold stony look in his eyes. The way he'd stood so still when she'd kissed him goodbye.

Dropping her face into her hands, she groaned quietly and shook her head. What had she been thinking? Why had she let Yolanda talk her into seeing him one last time? It had been one of the most painful things she'd ever done. She should have known better than to try, but she'd let herself hope. And how wrong she'd been!

The price was always heavy for hope, especially when it didn't work out. Almost as heavy as the price she'd paid for not believing in Rick in the first place. Each time she'd had an opportunity to trust him, she'd failed. The circumstances were always understandable, but then again, trust wasn't something based on logic, was it? You either had it...or you didn't.

You either shared yourself...or you didn't.

And she never had.

Looking around the empty apartment, Silvia sighed. It seemed ironic in a way. She'd never been lonely before—when she'd been pushing away her family and friends, when she'd told herself it didn't matter. But now, now that she'd finally come to realize she needed people, she didn't have anyone.

She didn't know a soul in her building besides the doorman, and Yolanda and the rest of her family were thousands of miles away...and Rick. Rick could have been on the moon for all it mattered. He was lost to her, lost when she wanted him the most, lost when she'd finally realized she loved him. Lost. Everything was lost.

Covering her face with her hands, she finally gave in and wept.

Rick pulled into the driveway of his house, cut off his car's engine, and stared at his front porch. Three weeks had passed since Silvia had returned to Washington. Three weeks.

They'd been the longest three weeks of Rick's life.

He opened the door of the car and pulled himself outside. Ten minutes later he was doing what he'd done every night since Silvia had left. Wearing an old pair of gym shorts and worn sneakers, he went back out the front door and headed toward the dirt road out front to run. To torture his body until the sweat poured off it and it didn't ache to hold Silvia tight. To run until he no longer yearned to tell her he loved her, to beg her to come back.

Six miles later, he stumbled back to the driveway, dripping from the heat, his legs trembling so badly he could hardly stand up. Grabbing the first post of the porch, he gripped it with both hands and dropped his head against it. Every night it was the same thing. Every night he ran until he had no breath left...but he just couldn't outrun his thoughts.

Lifting one arm and wiping his face against his shoulder, Rick stared out into the distance. It was time for him to face the truth. He and Silvia were linked. They had created a life together—and no matter what had happened afterward, that meant something, stood for something. He had no other choice, but to accept that reality. Even if it hadn't lived, the child they'd made would always be in his heart.

And so would Silvia.

No matter what he did, no matter how hard he worked, he would never be able to dislodge either of them from his existence. They were as much a part of him as his arm or his leg. Silvia and the lost child would always be there.

And he would always love them, no matter what.

So what in the hell was he going to do about it?

Silvia was on the phone when Kelly, one of the secretaries from the pool, stuck her head inside her office.

The young woman wore a curious expression as she rolled her eyes to the outer office.

Motioning for the secretary to give her a few minutes, Silvia finished her conversation, then hung up. "What's going on?" she asked.

"You tell me," Kelly answered. "There's a guy here to see you. A really gorgeous guy. He's wearing a sheriff's uniform and a big cowboy hat, and his shoulders are about three feet wide." She put her hands together as if she were praying and rolled her eyes upward. "Please, please tell me he's your cousin, and he needs a place to stay for the weekend."

Without warning, Silvia's heart began to pound furiously. Her mouth went dry. "A sheriff's uniform?"

"Starched and pressed till it squeaks." Kelly nodded. "He's waiting in the hall. Do you want me to send him in, or can I just ravish him out there?"

"I...I think you'd better send him in."

The secretary's face fell in mock disappointment. "I was afraid you'd say that." Turning around, she opened the door and called out, "Dr. Hernandez can see you now." Moving out of the way, she looked back at Silvia and winked.

But Silvia didn't see it. Her eyes were trained on Rick's as he stepped into her office.

He cradled the brim of his hat in his hands, his voice as deep and compelling as it had been in her dreams for the past few weeks. "Am I interrupting anything?"

She shook her head and tried not to stare, but it was impossible. His shoulders *did* look three feet wide inside the perfectly tailored shirt he wore, and his presence filled the tiny office with an energy that seemed to radiate with tension.

She swallowed and finally managed to speak. "This

is…quite a surprise. What…what are you doing here? There's nothing wrong with the case is there?''

He ran his thumb against the edge of his hat and shook his head. ''There's nothing wrong. I'm not here about that.''

''Then what?'' she asked, her pulse racing.

He moved around the chair in front of her desk and came to stand beside her. Very close beside her.

''I've been thinking.''

His eyes were darker than usual, the rims outlining the irises with circles of more intense color. They stared at her unflinchingly.

''You…you've been thinking.'' She repeated his words idiotically. ''About what?''

''About us,'' he answered. ''I think we need to talk.''

Her knees actually went weak. She gripped the edge of the desk. ''I didn't think there was an us to talk about.''

''When you left last month, I didn't, either, but I've been reconsidering that decision,'' he said. ''And I'd like to talk to you about it…if you like.'' He glanced around her office, then tilted his head toward the door. ''Can you leave? Go for a walk with me?''

She started to say no. She didn't want to go out that door with Rick at her side. It could mean disaster if it didn't turn out right.

But if she didn't go, it'd be a disaster, too, wouldn't it?

She nodded weakly. ''All right. Just for a little while.''

Rick slipped on his jacket, then with six pairs of eyes trained on them, they walked through the secretary pool and into the hall. Standing beside the elevator, Silvia could hear nothing but her pulse ringing in her ears.

Five minutes later, they were heading out the door and into the Washington sunlight.

It was a perfect day. Just a hint of coolness in the air, and the barest feeling of crispness creeping in to dispel the usual humidity. Still silent, they crossed the busy street outside her office building and headed into the postage-stamp-size park that covered the block in front of the DCA. The spreading oak trees and lush landscaping insulated them from the noise of passing cars.

Pointing at the first bench they came to, Silvia asked, "Is this okay?"

Rick nodded, and she sat down, watching him closely as he took the seat beside her.

He looked over at her. "I don't know where to start."

Her heart tripping against her chest, Silvia licked her suddenly dry lips. "The beginning always works for me."

His eyes locked on hers. "I don't know where the beginning is," he said quietly. "Was it the first time I saw you in Mr. Dojan's algebra class? Was it the first time I kissed you under that pin oak tree? Was it when you came back to San Laredo a few months ago, and my heart stopped?"

He shook his head slowly. "There doesn't seem to be a place in time I can point to and say 'That's when I started to love you. That's when it happened.'" He looked into the distance then back at Silvia, his stare as dark as ever. "There just isn't a beginning...just like there isn't an end. It's always been there. And I think it always will."

Her heart hammered. "Wh-what are you saying, Rick? I'm not sure I understand."

"I'm saying I love you, Silvia. I've always loved

you…and I always will. We're tied together, have been since we were too young to even understand what that meant…."

"But when I left you said—"

"I know what I said," he interrupted, "but I was wrong. I was wrong because I was mad. I wanted someone to blame for everything we had lost, and like the fool I am, I decided to blame you." He shook his head, a rueful expression on his face. "It's about the most stupid thing I've ever done, and I've managed to do some doozies in my life."

"I've pulled a few of those myself," she said softly. "You're not alone in that department."

He shot her a sideways look. "Maybe not…but that still doesn't make it right." Looking down at his hands, he studied them for a moment, then spoke again. "When you told me about the pregnancy, I just lost it… I couldn't stand to think about the child we could have had, the family we could have made. I…I got furious instead of really thinking about what it meant, especially to you."

His expression shifted. Sadness etched its way across his face bringing furrows to his forehead. His eyes darkened even more than before. "To go through all that alone… It shouldn't happen to anyone, especially an eighteen-year-old girl. I should have been there for you, Silvie, and I wasn't. I'll never forgive myself for that."

"You didn't know," she answered quietly.

"That's true, but I do now. And I've had some time to consider it all, too. I realize you were doing what you thought was best by keeping the baby a secret."

"But I was wrong. I was protecting myself, not you and—"

"It doesn't matter." He stopped her by placing a single finger across her lips. It was the first time he'd touched her, and the intimacy of the moment rippled over her, a wave that spread from his finger outward and down, deep down. "Why you did it isn't important," he said quietly. "The fact is, secrets are no good for any reason. Not between two people who love each other. All this has made me realize that...and I guess I'm here because I hope you've come to the same conclusion, too."

"I do think that you're right," she said, her mouth almost too dry to speak. "But it goes beyond that."

He knit his eyebrows together. "What do you mean?"

"You can't have secrets between each other...but you can't have any with yourself, either. You have to be willing to face the truth in your own heart, as well. I never did that, Rick."

"It would have hurt too much," he stated. "How could you have faced that kind of grief all alone?"

"That's just it," she answered. "I didn't have to do it alone. I had Yolanda...I could have had you. Just because Carlos threw me out, that didn't mean I had to isolate myself as I did." She looked down. "I didn't trust anyone else, though...and I especially didn't trust myself."

Rick moved closer to her in the silence of the park. Slowly, quietly, he put his arm around her shoulder. The weight and warmth of his touch was unlike anything else she'd ever felt in her entire life. Suddenly she felt at home, felt as though she were exactly where she should be.

"You have to feel safe before you can trust, Silvia. And feeling safe isn't just something that happens. The people around you should help...and God knows, I certainly didn't. I gave you absolutely no reason to trust me, or to feel safe around me. All this is more my own fault than it is yours.''

Tears gathered in the back of her throat. She struggled to hold them in, but failed. They poured out, wetting her cheeks and the shoulder of Rick's shirt as well. ''I should have—''

''Take that word out of your vocabulary. *Should* is not the way to describe anything.''

He cradled her face with his hand, his fingers warm against her skin, the expression in his eyes even warmer. ''I love you, Silvia. That's the only *should* that exists for me anymore. There's no other feeling between us but that one because that's the way it's supposed to be. I've fought it for too long to know anything different, and you know that, too.''

She nodded, sudden joy flooding her with the realization of the truth in what he was saying. ''It was meant to be, wasn't it?'' she said from behind her tears. ''Why didn't we see that before now?''

''We weren't supposed to, I guess.'' He pulled her closer to him, into the crook of his arms, into the warmth of his body. ''The timing wasn't right.''

She looked up at him. ''Is it the right time now?''

''It's definitely the right time,'' he answered, warming her with a single look and a touch she'd always remember. ''So I'm going to ask you the question I should have eighteen years ago.'' He paused and took a deep breath. ''Will you marry me, Silvia?''

Her heart swelling with love, Silvia reached up to cradle Rick's face with her hands. ''Nothing would make me happier than being your wife. Now and forever. The time is *definitely* right.''

* * * * *

Return to the Towers!

In March
New York Times bestselling author

NORA ROBERTS

brings us to the Calhouns' fabulous
Maine coast mansion and reveals the
tragic secrets hidden there for generations.

For all his degrees, Professor Max Quartermain has a
lot to learn about love—and luscious Lilah Calhoun is
just the woman to teach him. Ex-cop Holt Bradford is
as prickly as a thornbush—until Suzanna Calhoun's
special touch makes love blossom in his heart.
And all of them are caught in the race to solve
the generations-old mystery of a priceless
lost necklace...and a timeless love.

Lilah and Suzanna
THE
Calhoun Women

**A special 2-in-1 edition containing
FOR THE LOVE OF LILAH and
SUZANNA'S SURRENDER**

Available at your favorite retail outlet.

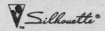

Welcome to *Love Inspired*™

A brand-new series of contemporary inspirational love stories.

Join men and women as they learn valuable lessons about facing the challenges of today's world and about life, love and faith.

**Look for the following March 1998
Love Inspired**™ **titles:**

CHILD OF HER HEART
by Irene Brand

A FATHER'S LOVE
by Cheryl Wolverton

WITH BABY IN MIND
by Arlene James

Available in retail outlets in February 1998.

LIFT YOUR SPIRITS AND GLADDEN YOUR HEART
with *Love Inspired!*™

**Steeple
Hill**™

LI398

ALICIA SCOTT

Continues the twelve-book series— 36 Hours—in March 1998 with Book Nine

PARTNERS IN CRIME

The storm was over, and Detective Jack Stryker finally had a prime suspect in Grand Springs' high-profile murder case. But beautiful Josie Reynolds wasn't about to admit to the crime— nor did Jack want her to. He believed in her innocence, and he teamed up with the alluring suspect to prove it. But was he playing it by the book—or merely blinded by love?

For Jack and Josie and *all* the residents of Grand Springs, Colorado, the storm-induced blackout was just the beginning of 36 Hours that changed *everything!* You won't want to miss a single book.

Available at your favorite retail outlet.

SC36HRS9

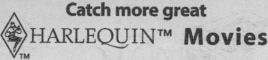

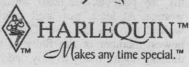

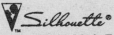

BESTSELLING AUTHORS
IN THE SPOTLIGHT

.WE'RE SHINING THE SPOTLIGHT ON SIX OF OUR STARS!

Harlequin and Silhouette have selected stories from several of their bestselling authors to give you six sensational reads. These star-powered romances are bound to please!

THERE'S A PRICE TO PAY FOR STARDOM... AND IT'S LOW

$1.99 U.S.
$2.50 CAN.
Special Offer

As a special offer, these six outstanding books are available from Harlequin and Silhouette for only $1.99 in the U.S. and $2.50 in Canada. Watch for these titles:

At the Midnight Hour—**Alicia Scott**
Joshua and the Cowgirl—**Sherryl Woods**
Another Whirlwind Courtship—**Barbara Boswell**
Madeleine's Cowboy—**Kristine Rolofson**
Her Sister's Baby—**Janice Kay Johnson**
One and One Makes Three—**Muriel Jensen**

Available in March 1998
at your favorite retail outlet.

PBAIS

DIANA PALMER
ANN MAJOR
SUSAN MALLERY

RETURN TO WHITEHORN

In **April 1998** get ready to catch the bouquet. Join in the excitement as these bestselling authors lead us down the aisle with three heartwarming tales of love and matrimony in Big Sky country.

A very engaged lady is having second thoughts about her intended; a pregnant librarian is wooed by the town bad boy; a cowgirl meets up with her first love. Which Maverick will be the next one to get hitched?

Available in **April 1998**.

Silhouette's beloved **MONTANA MAVERICKS** returns in Special Edition and Harlequin Historicals starting in February 1998, with brand-new stories from your favorite authors.

Round up these great new stories at your favorite retail outlet.

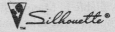